REMEMBRANCE

DAVID LINCOLN

A YELLOW FLOWER PRODUCTION

Previous Books by

DAVID LINCOLN

VOGEL – 2019
ELOISE – 2021
HENRY – 2025

eBooks
VOGEL
ELOISE
HENRY

PROLOGUE

The year was 1209.

In the south of France, in the land called Languedoc, life was rich. Castles stood on the hills. Vineyards stretched across the valleys. Troubadours sang in courts, and merchants filled the markets.

Here lived the Cathars. They taught that the soul was of divine origin, imprisoned in a world of corruption. They sought simplicity. Equality. A life free of greed.

For the Cathars, their faith was light.

The Roman Catholic Church, too, held its vision. It saw itself as the guardian of truth, handed down from Christ through His apostles. To permit other teachings was to invite confusion and division. In its eyes, the path of the Cathar led souls astray.

Pope Innocent III called for a crusade into the heart of Languedoc against fellow Christians. Armies of northern knights, drawn by promises of land and salvation, marched south.

The Albigensian Crusade had begun. The war would last for decades, reshaping Languedoc and with it, the soul of Europe.

Beziers and Minerve: Cathars massacred and the cities burned.

Carcassonne, Toulouse, Termes, and Lavaur: captured, and the Cathars burned at the stake.

Towns and villages that would never be the same. Lives reshaped. Culture altered forever.

In the wake of the crusade, the Cathars were driven to the margins of history, their voices fading, their memory surviving only in whispers.

And yet.

Even in ruins. Even in silence. The memory remains. A whisper carried forward in time.

It is within this crucible of faith and fire that our story unfolds.

A STORY BEST READ SLOWLY

CATHAR GLOSSARY

Credente *(Occitan: "believer")*
A lay follower of Catharism. Believes in the faith but has not taken the *consolamentum*. Lives in the world but aspires to spiritual liberation.

Perfect / Parfaite (f)
A fully initiated Cathar who has received the *consolamentum*. Lives a strict life of asceticism, celibacy, non-violence, fasting, and poverty. Seen as spiritually pure, a "living angel."

Consolamentum
The only true Cathar sacrament — a spiritual baptism by the laying on of hands and prayer. Grants spiritual purification and marks the transition from *credente* to *Perfect*. Ideally given at death, or when one chooses a fully renounced life.

Church of Love *(Cathar self-description)*
The true, invisible church of the soul, opposed to the Roman Church, which they called the **Church of the Wolf**.

Gnosis
Inner spiritual knowledge. Not intellectual belief, but direct memory of the soul's divine origin.

Inquisition
The judicial arm of the Roman Catholic Church was formed in the 1230s to investigate and eliminate heresy. Based on confession, secrecy, and fear.

Montsegur
A Cathar fortress and spiritual stronghold. After a siege in 1244, over 200 Perfects were burned alive rather than recant.

OCCITAN PHONETICS

A few names in the Languedoc / Provençal Occitan sound system, so you can "hear" them more naturally when reading in a sort of "stage whisper phonetics" that might help you speak them aloud with more confidence.

- **Cassien** → *kah–SYEN*
(draw the *kah* low in the chest, then lift *SYEN* like a sigh rising into the nose)

- **Alaïs** → *ah-LAH-ees*
(let the *ah* flow open, *lah* gentle and clear, then separate *EES* like a distinct sparkle at the end)

- **Alain** → *ah–LAN*
(begin with the same open *ah*, then let *LAN* settle forward in the mouth, the *n* soft and almost vanishing into the air)

Try them slowly, almost sung, and you'll notice how the Occitan shapes itself like a chant.

PART 1 – THE FLAME

Brother Cassien

Chapter One

1213

BROTHER CASSIEN COMPLETED his morning prayers, donned his robes, kissed the crucifix, and placed it around his neck. Leaving his chamber, he walked along the stone hallway, making his way to the chapel. Entering, he crossed himself with holy water, genuflected, and knelt at his assigned position in the third row on the right side.

The air was still, thick with the scent of beeswax and centuries. Light filtered through narrow windows, casting gold across the cold flagstones. He did not pray with words—not anymore. Instead, he listened. Not for God above, but for something quieter. A stirring beneath his breastbone. A presence.

His brother monks filtered into the chapel at their customary pace. He took no special notice. The Abbot approached the altar from the adjacent Sacristy to begin the Celebration of the Mass. All rose at once to receive Communion at the appointed time. Holy Communion was Cassien's favorite part of the Mass—the joining of the Christ Spirit with his own. He returned to his seat and listened, feeling the presence within him, unworthy as he knew himself to be.

After the conclusion of the Mass, the monks remained in contemplation for one hour. Cassien tried not to think, but thoughts arose nevertheless. He returned to feeling each time he noticed, and his soul settled within him. Time ceased.

When the bell rang, the brothers rose as one and walked in silence for breakfast. After eating, they proceeded to their daily work—some to the fields, some to care for the animals, some to perform required maintenance of the castle, and some, including Cassien, to the writing room, where he would meticulously copy the sacred texts assigned by the Abbot.

Not long after he had begun, Terce, a novice, entered the scriptorium and murmured his name. Cassien looked up from the manuscript he was illuminating. Terce's voice was hushed, but the tone carried weight.

"The Abbot requests your presence in his study."

A tremor passed through him—not of fear, but of something more ancient, more familiar. He placed his quill in its holder, bowed slightly to the brothers near him, and followed the novice through the winding halls.

The door to the Abbot's study was thick oak, darkened with centuries of polish and prayer. The novice knocked gently, then bowed and withdrew, leaving Cassien alone before it. A pause, then a voice from within: "Enter."

He pushed the door open and stepped inside.

The room was dim, lit only by a single tall candle and the muted daylight filtering through a narrow lancet window. Shelves lined the stone walls, filled with manuscripts, scrolls, and leather-bound tomes—the sacred burden of centuries. A crucifix hung above the hearth, its carved Christ worn smooth by the hands of generations.

The Abbot sat behind a large desk of oak, his robe arranged with careful simplicity. He did not look up at first, but traced the edge of a sealed parchment with a single finger. When his eyes met Cassien's, they held both kindness and gravity.

"Brother Cassien," he said quietly, "please sit."

Cassien obeyed, settling onto the wooden chair opposite him. For a long moment, the Abbot studied him in silence, then reached for a second scroll beside the first.

"A messenger arrived late last night," he said. "From Rome. He is waiting outside."

There was a knock at the door. The Abbot nodded. "Come."

The door creaked open, and a tall, solemn man stepped inside. His cloak, though travel-worn, was of fine wool, and a simple bronze ring bearing the Papal seal adorned his left hand. His face was long, his eyes intelligent and cool, with the detached poise of one long accustomed to authority.

He bowed first to the Abbot, then to Cassien. "I am Brother Matteo," he said. "Envoy of the Holy See."

Cassien's breath caught, though his face remained still. The Field around him stirred. The Abbot invited Brother Matteo to sit on a bench beneath the window to witness.

Once seated, the Abbot turned again to Cassien. His voice remained gentle, but its weight was undeniable.

"Brother Cassien, you are being called to a task of great importance—one that requires both discernment and discretion. Rome wishes to send you to the south of France. You are to travel through Languedoc and report on the rise of a growing sect whose teachings diverge from Church doctrine."

He paused, studying Cassien's reaction.

"These people call themselves 'Good Christians'… but others call them Cathars. You are to assess their beliefs, their practices, and their influence. You will speak with them, live among them if you must, and return with an account—objective, thorough, and faithful."

He let the words settle. "The Holy See trusts your devotion and your clarity of heart. That is why they chose you."

Cassien did not answer. Not yet. He listened—both to the Abbot and to the subtle stirrings beneath his breastbone.

The Vatican messenger raised his hand, seeking permission to speak. The Abbot nodded.

"Brother Cassien," he began, "it is the Holy See's understanding that you speak Occitan, is that correct?"

"That is true, Brother Matteo. I was born not far from that region."

"Do you understand what the Vatican is asking of you?"

"I believe I do, Brother. You are asking for an unbiased assessment of the religious beliefs of the Cathars in relation to the truth of the Holy Catholic Church."

Brother Matteo smiled. "Do you accept this responsibility, Brother Cassien?"

Cassien turned his attention to the Abbot. "Do I have your permission, Father?"

The Abbot inclined his head slowly, folding his hands atop the desk. "You do, Brother Cassien. And my blessing. You will go with the prayers of this house, and with the grace of God upon you."

He paused. "Speak the truth as it reveals itself to you. Be neither eager to condemn nor quick to accept. Let your heart remain still, as it is now. The Lord will guide you."

The Abbot nodded to Brother Matteo, saying, "It is your final decision, Brother."

Brother Matteo rose and approached Cassien, handing him a satchel. "You will carry with you the official documents that will grant you access, Brother Cassien, the official seal of the Holy See. Go with God."

That evening, Cassien remained in the chapel long after Compline, kneeling once more in his assigned pew, though the candles had all been extinguished. The stillness was deeper at night—more vast— and it echoed his own inward silence. He did not pray aloud. He listened. A great hush had opened within him, wide and unending.

What was this stirring he felt? It was not fear. Nor was it ambition. It was the sense that something hidden long ago was rising again—both in the world and within himself—the Cathars. Good Christians. Heretics, they were called. And yet… something in him leaned toward them, though he knew not why, perhaps because of his sister.

Was he being tested? Or led?

He remembered the Abbot's words: Let your heart remain still.

The next morning, Cassien was given permission to delay his usual duties and begin preparations for the journey. Brother Matteo had remained the night in a guest chamber and met him in the courtyard after Prime. He handed Cassien a leather pouch with travel documents, a letter bearing the Papal seal, and a modest purse of coins.

"You are to travel first to Béziers," he said, "stopping briefly in Lyon, Valence, and Avignon for rest and refreshment along the way. From there, follow the trail of communities identified by our contacts. A guide will meet you upon arrival."

Cassien nodded, accepting the pouch. Matteo placed a hand briefly on his shoulder, then turned to speak with the Abbot.

By midday, Cassien had packed his few possessions: a small copy of the Gospels, a change of robes, a flask for holy water, and the crucifix he had worn since his novitiate. He walked the perimeter of the cloister one last time, memorizing the rhythm of each step, each shadow, each breath of the stone walls.

Cluny Abbey stood like a crown above the valley, a masterpiece of Romanesque architecture and spiritual authority. Founded in 910, it had once been the beating heart of a great monastic empire, its abbots wielding influence that rivaled bishops and kings. The Abbey had shaped Christendom through the Cluniac reforms, emphasizing liturgical devotion, ecclesiastical purity, and allegiance to the papacy. Rome held Cluny in the highest esteem—not merely as a monastery, but as a beacon of orthodoxy and sacred tradition. Cassien had been raised in this legacy, steeped in its disciplines and its silences. And now he was being sent from its order into uncertainty, from the stronghold of tradition into the wilds of belief.

Then, just after None, he passed beneath the monastery gate and descended the path toward the valley, alone but not forsaken.

The Field moved with him.

Cassien traveled for nearly two weeks. In Lyon, he stayed at a small monastery perched above the Saône, its library filled with ancient Greek translations and the scent of cedarwood. In Valence, he was given shelter by a humble priest who asked no questions but offered warm bread and quiet companionship. Avignon, bustling and political, unsettled him. He kept to the shadows, resting a single night in a Franciscan dormitory before continuing on.

The roads grew dustier as he neared Béziers, the land flatter and scrubbed with sun. The scent of lavender and olive clung to the wind. As the city walls came into view, memories stirred within him—stories he had heard as a boy.

Béziers had once burned.

He entered the city through the western gate. The streets were narrow and sun-bleached. He walked past market stalls and fountains, his presence drawing little attention. At the designated church, he asked for Armand.

They met in the cool nave, under arches that still bore the scars of an older fire.

Armand was short, lean, with an olive complexion and sharp eyes that missed nothing.

"You are Brother Cassien?" he asked.

"I am."

He bowed slightly. "My name is Armand. I have been instructed to guide you."

They walked outside and sat on a bench in the shade of a fig tree.

Armand gestured toward the surrounding stones. "This city remembers. Four years ago, the crusaders came. They claimed they could not tell the Cathar from the Catholic, so they killed everyone. Women. Children. Priests. All of them."

Cassien said nothing, but the weight of it filled him.

Armand turned to him. "Carcassonne lies ahead. We will leave at dawn. The questions you carry may begin to find their answers there."

Chapter Two

CASSIEN AND ARMAND traveled in silence for much of the morning, following a winding path that led them into the rising hills. The air was cooler there, clearer, as though the land itself had drawn back from the world and settled into a more ancient rhythm.

They paused at the end of the day at a small village named Tourouzelle. The villagers eyed them as they entered, but not with hostility. Some nodded—a few offered cautious smiles.

Armand led him to a modest stone house at the edge of the main path. "You'll find shelter here," he said. "They know why you've come. But they will not speak until they sense you are ready to listen."

He paused, then added, "And they will not speak with the voice of Rome. Only with the voice of the heart."

Cassien remained standing on the threshold before him after Armand left. He felt no fear—only a widening stillness, as though the question he carried was already being heard.

Later that evening, as the sun dropped behind the fortress cliffs, he sat with two villagers by the hearth. Their names were Elias and Maëlys. They spoke slowly, without persuasion. Their words were not doctrine, but something more lived.

"The kingdom of God is not beyond the sky," Elias said, gazing into the fire. "It is the spark that was never created and cannot be destroyed. It is within you, waiting to be known."

"We do not worship a God of wrath," Maëlys added. "We do not fear eternal torment. We fear forgetting. We live to remember."

Cassien did not speak. He only listened. The Field within him stirred —not in contradiction, but in recognition.

Elias leaned forward slightly, his hands resting on his knees. "The Christ we follow did not die to purchase forgiveness from an angry Father. He came to show us what we had forgotten—that we are light clothed in flesh. That the soul need not wait for death to rise."

Maëlys nodded. "We believe in two principles—the god of this world, who rules through fear and illusion, and the True Source, which has no need for dominion. The Church… confuses them. We live simply to keep the memory of the True One alive."

Cassien felt their words ripple through him—not as heresy, but as unfamiliar music. Dissonant to his ear, yet hauntingly beautiful.

"Do you not fear judgment?" he asked quietly.

Elias looked at him gently. "We fear separation. Not punishment. We fear the soul forgetting itself. That is the only exile."

Maëlys added, "And love, true love, cannot send itself into eternal torment. We do not reject Christ. We remember Him differently. As brother. As mirror. As fire within."

Their words lingered long after the fire had faded to embers. That night, sleep came fitfully. He lay on the modest cot, staring into the shadows on the ceiling, unsure whether what stirred within him was revelation or doubt—or both.

He had given his life to the Church. To its structure, its sacraments, its ancient line. In that offering, he had found purpose and peace. And yet… what Elias and Maëlys spoke was not blasphemy. It was not rebellion. It was something quieter, something rooted deeper than argument. A knowing, not imposed but remembered.

Could it be that they were mistaken? That the simplicity of their belief blinded them to error? Or had he, in all his years of cloistered devotion, mistaken tradition for truth?

He rose before dawn, unable to remain still. Kneeling beside the small window, he whispered the only prayer he could find:

"Lord, if this is heresy, guard my soul. But if it is truth—if it is Your voice speaking in another tongue—let me not turn away out of fear."

There was no answer—only stillness.

And yet, that stillness seemed to breathe.

As the first light of morning traced its way across the floor, he slipped quietly from the house. The village was still. Smoke had not yet risen from the chimneys, and the sky above Tourouzelle wore the soft indigo of a world just waking.

He walked without aim, letting his feet find their way along a narrow path that curved upward toward the edge of the village. The mountains loomed above, stone and silence standing like a sentinel over the countryside. Below it, the fields sloped gently into valleys still wrapped in mist.

Each step away from the hearth felt like a step deeper into himself. Doubt and faith moved within him like twin currents—neither dominant, both alive. He loved the Church, truly. Its rhythms were carved into his bones. But now those rhythms were shifting, subtly, as if some deeper song beneath them was rising to be heard.

A part of him longed to dismiss the words of Elias and Maëlys as sweet error, a kindness too soft to carry the weight of salvation. But another part—older, perhaps, or more childlike—recognized something in them. A voice he had not heard since he was very young. Before study. Before vows.

The air carried the scent of thyme and wet earth. The sky brightened slightly. Somewhere in the distance, a cock crowed.

He did not know what he believed.

But he knew he could no longer pretend he had heard nothing.

That evening, he returned to the stone house, finding Elias and Maëlys seated once more by the hearth. The fire was small, but steady, its light dancing against the walls.

He sat across from them, his voice quiet but certain. "May I ask you something?"

Elias inclined his head. "Of course."

"If Christ came to awaken what was forgotten, then why do you not speak His name with the reverence we do? Why do you not take the Eucharist, or venerate the cross?"

Maëlys answered gently, "We do speak His name—with reverence that lives in our breath, not our rituals. The Christ lives not in the bread, but in the being. The cross is not an idol to us—it is the memory of suffering transformed."

He nodded slowly. "And what of the sacraments? Baptism, confession… absolution?"

Elias folded his hands in his lap. "There is no need to wash away what was never stained. We seek not pardon, but remembrance. When the soul awakens to its light, it naturally turns from shadow."

Their words unsettled him—and yet, he could not deny their peace. It was not the peace of certainty, but of presence. They were not trying to convince him. They were simply being what they believed.

And that, somehow, was more powerful than argument.

The next day, Elias invited him to accompany them to a gathering at the edge of the village—a simple meeting held in the shelter of an old barn. As they walked, he explained, "We do not preach. We share. We do not convert. We remember together."

Inside, the barn had been cleared of tools and carts. A circle of benches had been arranged around a low stone basin filled with spring water. Men, women, even children entered quietly, greeting one another with nods or a gentle touch to the shoulder.

There were no icons, no altar, no candles: only stillness and the presence of attentive hearts.

An elder, white-haired and slender, rose and spoke first, not from a pulpit, but from his seat. His voice was steady, almost musical.

"We are not here to escape the world," he said, "but to remember what we are within it. This world is a shadow—but the Light has not abandoned it. We carry that Light. Not as possession, but as birthright."

Others spoke in turn—reflections, dreams, small confessions of doubt or joy. There was no debate, no authority overriding another. Only an invisible current that carried them all.

When it ended, they embraced, wept quietly, or simply sat in silence. It was more communion than Cassien had ever seen, and yet no sacrament had been spoken.

He left that gathering with his heart split open. Not in rebellion. But in recognition of something he had never thought to find outside the Church.

Something alive. Something free.

That night, he could not sleep. He sat by the narrow window, looking out across the starlit hills, the hush of Tourouzelle pressing gently against the edges of his mind. His thoughts circled, not in confusion, but in a kind of reverent awe. He did not know what to do with what he had seen, only that it had entered him like a key turning in a lock he had not known was there.

The Church had given him form. These people had given him space. Could both be true? Could one make room for the other?

He thought of the Abbot's words: Let your heart remain still.

And he knew it was time.

The following morning, after breaking bread in silence with Elias and Maëlys, he opened the letter bearing the Papal seal. He spread a fresh parchment before him, dipped his quill, and began to write.

To His Holiness, through the care of Brother Matteo,

I write to you from a small village near Beziers, having arrived safely and in good health. I have spoken with members of the sect known as Cathars. I have found them not in rebellion, but in remembrance.

Their ways differ from our own—not in defiance, but in essence. They hold Christ in reverence, though not through sacraments or ritual. They live with great humility and clarity of spirit, and I have encountered in them a peace I do not fully understand.

I do not offer conclusions yet—only first impressions. The matter deserves patience and prayer. I will continue to observe, listen, and record. For now, I ask only for your blessing to remain among them a while longer.

Yours in faithful service,

Brother Cassien

He left the sealed message to Rome with Armand, who would carry it to the Convent of Saint Antonin. From there, a messenger would forward it to Rome.

He knew it would be several weeks, perhaps longer, before any reply would reach him—if a reply came at all. The rhythms of Rome
moved slowly, wrapped in layers of protocol and deliberation. In
the meantime, he was under no binding instruction to await further
orders. The letter had been sent. His conscience was clear.

And so he was free.

Free to listen. Free to witness. Free to allow the truth to reveal itself without interruption or judgment.

Whatever came next would come not from the voice of authority,
but from the still, small stirring he had begun to recognize as the
Field itself.

The following day, Elias approached him just after the midday
meal. "There is a healer who lives in the hills beyond the olive
grove," he said. "Her name is Alénya. She is known among us not
only for tending the sick but for the clarity of her sight. Many say
she sees not only illness, but the truth beneath it."

Cassien sensed there was more.

"She once walked among the Church," Maëlys added quietly, joining them. "But she left—not in anger, but in sorrow. She may speak
to you in ways we cannot."

And so he went.

The path was narrow and sun-dappled, winding through groves fragrant with thyme and fig. Cassien walked alone, his feet moving
with purpose, though his thoughts remained unsettled. He did not

know what he hoped to find—only that he was being drawn forward.

When he reached the small stone dwelling, he found her in the garden, bent over a patch of lavender. She stood slowly, wiped her hands, and regarded him without surprise.

"You have questions," she said simply.

He nodded.

"Then come. Let us sit in the shade."

And so began the next phase of his mission—not a debate, not a judgment, but a listening far deeper than words.

Chapter Three

CASSIEN STILL CARRIED a weight he could not name. The more he listened, the more he realized that the transformation rising in him was not seamless. It tugged at the roots of his formation, stretching what he had once held as certain. His soul did not move cleanly from one truth to another—it resisted. It questioned.

He had not abandoned the Church, nor did he intend to. But something within him was loosening. He feared what that meant. He feared what it might cost.

Alénya seemed to see this before he spoke it aloud. As they sat beneath the olive tree, her gaze steady and unhurried, she said, "You are not here to replace one set of answers with another, Brother Cassien. You are here to let go of needing them."

He lowered his eyes.

"Is that not dangerous?" he asked.

"Perhaps," she said. "But the soul was never meant to live in a cage—even a gilded one built from scripture."

Her words struck something deep, something old. A knot of belief tangled with fear. He did not know how to untie it. He only knew it had begun to loosen.

He shifted on the bench, suddenly uncomfortable. "It sounds very poetic," he said, more sharply than he intended, "but if the soul abandons the guidance of scripture, what then anchors it to truth?

If everyone listens only to what stirs inside them, is that not the path to delusion?"

Alénya did not flinch. "And yet, has scripture not also been wielded as a weapon? Interpreted to justify cruelty, to silence the very voice of the heart you now mistrust?"

He frowned. "That may be so. But scripture is not the enemy. It is the sacred record of God's revelation. It has endured."

"Yes," she said softly. "It has endured. But what lives is not the letter. It is the breath behind it. And that breath cannot be caged."

He folded his arms, torn between defensiveness and the strange sense that she was not opposing him, but meeting him at the edge of his fear.

"You speak of breath and presence and light," he said. "But how do you know these things are not simply feelings? Shadows of self-deception dressed in holy words?"

Alénya smiled—not in mockery, but with something like compassion. "Because when I listen to that presence, Brother Cassien, it makes me more whole. It makes me less afraid. It makes me love more deeply—not just those who agree with me, but those who would see me burned."

He said nothing. His chest was tight, and not from anger.

Some part of him, long buried beneath ritual and vow, had stirred.

Her final words echoed darkly within him: *those who would see me burned.* He could not ignore the weight of them. The Inquisition was not a distant rumor. It had begun to creep across the land like a slow fire, kindled by fear and sanctioned by power. He had seen its smoke before—whispers in cloisters. Names spoken and then never spoken again.

"You have been threatened?" he asked.

Alénya turned her face slightly, eyes distant. "Not directly. Not yet. But I have seen the signs. And I know how the Church responds to what it cannot control."

He thought of the Abbot's solemn face, of the scroll bearing Rome's seal. His mission had been to observe—to judge, if necessary. But if judgment had already begun elsewhere, what did that make him now? A witness? A herald? Or something more dangerous?

The tightening in his chest did not release. He realized he was no longer simply discerning truth.

He was walking through a field that might soon burn.

The next morning, news reached Tourouzelle on the lips of a breathless traveler—an apothecary's apprentice whose cousin had escaped from Lavaur.

The city had fallen.

The Church's army, under the banner of orthodoxy, had breached the walls after days of siege. Those who resisted were slaughtered. Over four hundred men, women, and children—Cathars and sympathizers alike—were dragged into the main square and burned. Not interrogated. Not judged. Burned.

"They gave no one a chance to recant," the apprentice whispered. "They said there was no time. That the fire would answer for them."

A silence fell over the village like ash.

Later that day, Cassien found Alénya staring out over the hills from the edge of her garden. Her expression was not surprised—but it was heavy.

"Lavaur is only the beginning," she said. "There will be more. Béziers again. Minerve. Maybe even here."

He turned away, unable to meet her gaze. A sickness churned in his gut. This was no longer a matter of theology. This was not a mission of inquiry.

This was a war of memory against fear.

And he did not yet know which side he was on.

That night, he did not return to Elias or Maëlys. He climbed the path behind the village alone, drawn upward by a restlessness he could neither name nor resist. The stars burned cold above him, distant and dispassionate.

He found a ledge overlooking the dark valley and sat there, legs tucked beneath his robe, his hands folded tight in his lap.

What had he truly come to do?

The official charge was observation. Discernment. But how does one observe without being changed by what one sees? How does one measure spirit with the tools of doctrine? How does one weigh truth when the scales themselves begin to shift?

He thought of the fire in Lavaur. He thought of Alénya's calm defiance, of Elias's quiet certainty. He thought of the cross he still wore around his neck, the feel of its familiar weight against his chest.

Had he been sent here to judge these people—or to find something he had lost?

The wind picked up. It smelled of woodsmoke and distance.

He bowed his head. Not in surrender. Not yet.

But in the ache of not knowing.

And in the prayer that knowing would come—not from Rome, not from rebellion, but from something deeper still.

The Field was not silent.

It waited.

Chapter Four

AT FIRST LIGHT, Cassien descended the hillside and returned to the village. The morning air was thick with mist and the scent of damp stone. He passed silently through Tourouzelle's narrow lanes, uncertain of where his feet would take him, but trusting the gravity of his unease.

Word had spread that a Cathar elder from Minerve, a man named Bernat, had arrived in the village during the night. He had come not only to speak but to warn. Another siege was expected soon. The Inquisition's reach was growing longer by the day.

Elias found him near the well and told him quietly, "There will be a gathering this evening. Bernat will speak, and others will bear witness. You should come."

Cassien nodded. He would go.

But first, he needed to walk.

He left the village behind, following a shepherd's path that wound along the ridge, the land rising and falling beneath his feet like a hymn half-sung. He thought of the stories he had heard, the lives extinguished not for rebellion, but for remembering. And he thought again of Rome—not in anger, but in distance. The center of the Church now felt a world away, slower and less certain than the breath of the people before him.

As he walked, the Field stirred—not as voice, but as presence. And he knew: he was no longer walking toward answers.

He was walking toward truth.

Whatever came next, it would not be safe.

But it would be real.

That evening, as dusk settled over the village like a velvet shroud, he joined the others at the gathering place—a hollow carved by time and reverence beneath the shoulder of the cliffs. Torches glowed gently along the stone walls, and low voices hummed like prayer.

Bernat stood near the center, a tall figure draped in a simple woolen cloak, his face lined by years and sun. His presence was still, but his eyes blazed with a quiet intensity.

When he spoke, it was without force, but every ear leaned in.

"I come not with hope of safety," he said, "but with the clarity of what is. Lavaur has burned. Béziers before it. Minerve may not be far behind. The Inquisition is no longer searching—it is consuming. And yet we are still here. We remember. We do not run."

He paused, letting the words find their mark.

"They fear us not because we defy them. They fear us because we do not. Because we do not need them to see God."

A hush followed, thick as incense. Then another elder stood. Then another. Stories were shared, prayers whispered—not to a distant judge, but to the Light within. One woman spoke of hiding scrolls in the floorboards of her home. Another wept quietly, holding the hand of a child whose father had vanished in the last wave of arrests.

Cassien listened. And as he listened, he began to understand: this was not defiance. It was devotion stripped bare. Faith that had shed its robes and dared to stand naked before the flame.

And still, they did not waver.

The gathering ended in silence. No declarations. No strategy. Only a shared breath.

They were no longer strangers.

The next morning, Cassien awoke before the bell and stepped outside. The sky was pearl-gray, the air tinged with the smoke of early fires and the scent of morning bread. He walked quietly through the village, feeling the weight of the stories he had heard the night before settle into his bones.

Bernat found him near the well.

"There is another place you must see," he said. "A village east of here—Homps. It is not far, but it holds a thread of our memory that may help you understand what we truly are."

Cassien looked at him. Bernat was not asking. He was inviting.

Cassien agreed.

By midday, he had packed again and set off, Elias walking with him partway until the road forked. Elias placed a hand on his shoulder.

"The Field is not limited to Tourouzelle," he said. "It lives wherever truth is remembered."

And so Cassien walked.

The road to Homps was quiet, bordered by trees still green with the
early summer. He passed shepherds, a wandering tinker, and a family carting honey to market. The land was alive—but under the surface, he could feel it: the unease, the waiting, the awareness that
danger moved ever closer.

What he would find in Homps, he did not know. But the Field
moved again—not ahead of him, but within him.

And he followed.

They crossed a small river, and Homps appeared between a rise of
gentle hills and a broader lowland. Its stone cottages and narrow
paths bore the wear of time, but not defeat. There was a hush to the
village—not silence, but reverence.

Near the well, a woman of indeterminate age waited, hands clasped
before her. Her cloak was simple, her face sun-lined, and her eyes
observant rather than knowing.

"You must be tired," she said. "There is food and rest waiting.
Come."

She introduced herself as Noémi. Nothing more.

In her home—a modest room warmed by a hearth—she served bread and broth without ceremony. They ate in silence. Cassien sensed no effort to impress, no probing curiosity—only presence.

After the meal, she said, "I have seen men like you come through these hills. Some searching. Some fleeing. You walk like one who hasn't yet decided which."

Her words startled him. "Is it so plain to see?"

She offered a faint smile. "Only if one is watching closely."

He did not know whether she spoke from spiritual insight or worldly wisdom. But her tone carried neither mysticism nor presumption.

That evening, she led him to a grove behind the chapel, where several villagers had gathered—not in secret, but in simplicity. There were no torches, no altar, no hierarchy—just a circle. A song passed softly from voice to voice—a note sustained, then offered to the next.

He listened. It was not performance. It was invitation.

The Field stirred—not as revelation, but as memory.

Whatever Noémi saw or understood, she kept to herself. There were no proclamations.

Only a quiet recognition that truth, if it comes at all, comes gently.

And it waits to be chosen.

The days that followed were unremarkable to the eye—but they worked on Cassien like water through stone.

Noémi said little, yet her presence seemed to arrange the silence around her like a sacred space. Each morning, he helped gather herbs from her garden, learning their names in Occitan. He watched children chase goats through the dusty lanes and elders sit long hours in sun-warmed doorways, speaking rarely, but always with intention.

There were no sermons. No altars. And yet everything felt... consecrated.

Each evening, a small circle would gather again—sometimes for a shared meal, sometimes to listen as someone recited a passage from memory, or told a dream. Sometimes there were tears. Sometimes only laughter.

He was not asked to speak. But he was invited to listen.

And slowly, without pressure, a rhythm began to unfold—one not dictated by bells or breviaries, but by breath, earth, and trust.

On the fourth evening, as dusk fell and fireflies stirred in the hedges, Noémi turned to him and said, "You have seen our way now. You may still have questions."

He met her gaze, unsure of what to ask.

"I have more than questions," he said. "I have fragments."

She nodded. "Then let us begin there."

Two days later, a rider approached Homps at dusk, his face veiled in dust and urgency. Cassien watched as the man dismounted and handed a folded letter to one of the villagers. It bore his name.

It was from a woman named Clara.

The handwriting was careful, unfamiliar, yet undeniably intimate. Cassien's hands trembled as he unfolded the page. Each word struck him like a bell, echoing memories he had long locked away.

"Brother," it began. "You may not wish to hear from me, but I have heard whispers of a monk walking these hills in the service of Rome. When I learned it was you, I wept. We were not parted by hatred, Cassien—only silence. I had to leave before I could explain. I beg you now to come to Carcassonne. There is much you do not know."

It was signed: *Your sister, Clara.*

Cassien stood unmoving in the fading light, the letter trembling in his hand. Clara. His sister. The one whose name he had not spoken aloud since taking his vows. She had once been his closest companion. They had shared songs, secrets, and summer storms. And then she had vanished—into love, into disgrace, into a path the Church forbade.

He had been told she married a heretic.

He had believed it.

Now she was here, somewhere in these hills, calling to him not with defiance, but with longing.

Noémi found him beneath the fig tree later that night. She said nothing at first, only sat beside him.

"Will you go to her?" she asked at last.

He nodded slowly. "Yes. I must."

But in truth, he did not know what waited for him in Carcassonne —only that it would not be easy, and that something within him, old and aching, had just been called back to life.

Chapter Five

CASSIEN DEPARTED HOMPS before sunrise, the hills still dressed in shadows and dew. His sandals left dark impressions in the damp soil, each step carrying him closer to a past he had never fully understood, and a future he no longer pretended to control.

The path to Carcassonne wound through dense forests and quiet hamlets, where the only witnesses to his passage were crows and the occasional pair of curious eyes behind shuttered windows. He did not travel as a priest this time—not outwardly. He wore no cross, no robes—only the plain tunic of a pilgrim.

Carcassonne, a double-walled fortress, perched like a guardian on the high ground, dominating its surroundings. Its stones glowed in the early light, as if they had held the sun for centuries. Cassien paused at the edge of the city, uncertain of what would meet him.

Would she look older? Hardened? Would she turn away when she saw him?

A child ran past, laughing, and broke the spell. He walked on, crossed the long stone bridge over the river, and entered the immense, fortified city.

Not knowing where to begin his search for Clara, he watched the people milling around. He saw a group of three women quietly working together, ignoring the hustle and bustle that surrounded them in the courtyard.

"Excuse the interruption," he said as he stood near them. "I'm looking for my sister, but I don't know where she lives. Her name is Clara."

All three women looked up at Cassien and then looked knowingly at each other. One of the women asked, "You are her brother, you say?" She looked at the other women, who nodded and resumed their work.

"I know where she lives. Follow me."

She led Cassien back through the city gate and into a hamlet of houses outside the walls of the city. They walked among the houses, turn after turn, before she stopped and pointed, saying, "That's Clara's house." She smiled at Cassien before returning to the city without another word.

Cassien thanked the woman as she walked away and took a deep breath, not knowing what his reception would be. He felt an old stirring in his heart, where hope mingled with fear.

A woman waited at the threshold of the low stone house, her hands wrapped in her apron. She looked up as he approached. Her face—still Clara's, though more lined than he remembered—did not flinch.

"You came," she said.

Cassien could not answer. His throat had closed around a lifetime of silence.

She stepped aside. "Come in, Cassien. We have waited long enough."

Inside, the house was warm and dim, the air scented with thyme and woodsmoke. A kettle murmured on the hearth. She motioned for him to sit at the table, and for a while, they said nothing.

At last, she broke the silence.

"I wasn't sure you'd come," she said. Her voice was lower now, fuller somehow, but unmistakably hers.

"I wasn't sure either," he admitted. "There were reasons I stayed away. Reasons I still don't fully understand."

She nodded. "The silence between us has lasted longer than it should have. But silence does not mean absence, Cassien. It only means something was too painful to speak."

He looked at her then. "You married a Cathar. Father told me you had abandoned the Church."

Clara folded her hands. "I abandoned nothing. I followed what was true for me. You followed what was true for you. It's only now that we've found ourselves in the same place again."

"It's not that simple."

"No," she agreed. "It's not. But neither is it as complicated as we feared."

A quiet passed between them, not awkward this time, but reverent.

"I never stopped loving you," Cassien said quietly. "Even when I wouldn't let myself remember."

Her eyes shimmered. "I know. And I never stopped believing you would come back—not to me, but to yourself."

They sat in the stillness, two lives stretching across a shared wound, and something old began to soften in the quiet between their words.

She rose briefly to fetch the kettle, poured warm broth into a pair of ceramic cups, and set one gently before him.

"Do you remember the summer before I left?" she asked, settling into the seat across from him.

He nodded. "The storms were late that year. You kept watch from the rooftop like a weather prophet."

She laughed softly. "I was foolishly brave. Or bravely foolish. You always warned me not to fall."

"You never did."

Her smile faded into something quieter. "I fell in other ways. For a man the village feared. For a faith I wasn't supposed to know."

Cassien looked at her then, not as a sister lost, but as a woman who had lived deeply. "You loved him."

"With all that I was." Her voice was calm, steady. "He was not perfect, but he was true. He showed me a God I could breathe beside. We lived simply. For a time, we were happy."

"Is he—?"

She nodded once, eyes clouding. "Taken, two winters past. In Minerve. They came in the night."

A silence stretched between them, thick with memory and grief.

"And your children?"

A flicker of light returned to her gaze. "Two. Elian and Maris. Elian is with friends in the hills—safe. Maris is here. You'll meet her. She has your eyes, you know."

Cassien looked down at his hands, suddenly unsure of what he held.

Clara reached across the table and touched his wrist. "You didn't fail me, Cassien. You simply followed a different road. But those roads are no longer separate, not here."

Her touch steadied him more than any scripture ever had.

"Do they know who you are?" he asked softly. "The townspeople, I mean."

"Some," she replied. "Others only know that I heal, that I sing, that I live quietly. I do not hide—but I do not speak of Rome or rebellion. The words matter less than the kindness we give."

Cassien took a long breath. "And Maris?"

Clara's eyes warmed. "She knows enough. She knows her father was brave, and that truth is sometimes dangerous. But I have not filled her with fear. I won't. She deserves to believe the world can be kind."

"And if the world is not?"

Clara looked away for a moment, then back. "Then she will know how to forgive it."

He sat in the silence that followed, knowing he could no longer return to what he had been before.

Outside, the sun had reached the edge of the house. Its light crept across the table, gilding the edges of their hands where they rested —not clasped, but near.

They said no more that morning. There would be time. But in that quiet, something shifted—not only in Cassien, but between them. A beginning, not a return.

A soft knock at the door interrupted the silence. Clara rose with ease and crossed the room. When she opened it, a young girl stepped inside, barefoot and radiant with the careless confidence of childhood.

"Maris," Clara said gently, her voice warm with pride. "This is your uncle, Cassien."

The girl tilted her head, studying him without fear. Her hair was dark like Clara's, but her eyes—wide, thoughtful, unblinking— held something of his own.

"You're the monk from the hills," she said, matter-of-fact.

Cassien smiled, unsure of what to say. "I suppose I am. And you must be Maris."

She nodded. "Mama said you used to climb trees faster than any-one. Is that true?"

Clara laughed softly behind her. He met Maris's gaze. "It was true. A long time ago."

Maris sat beside him without invitation, her small hands folded in her lap. "Do monks eat honey?"

"Sometimes. When we're lucky."

She looked pleased with that answer.

Clara watched them with a softness in her eyes that made Cassien's chest ache. This girl—so bold, so open—was a bridge he had not known he needed.

"Would you like to walk with her later?" Clara asked. "There's a path she loves by the river. It's where she talks to the sky."

Cassien turned to Maris, who was already nodding.

"Yes," he said. "I think I would like that very much."

Clara stood, smoothing her apron. "You'll stay here tonight. We have a room in the loft. It's small, but warm. Maris can show you the way."

"Thank you," Cassien said, suddenly aware of how tired he was. "That would be a kindness."

"Rest," she said. "Tomorrow you can walk. Tonight, you are simply home."

Later, after a humble supper of lentils and bread, he climbed the narrow ladder to the loft. Maris had placed a folded blanket on the straw bed and a candle near the window.

"The stars are very clear here," she said, peering up beside him. "You can hear them if you listen long enough."

He smiled at her wonder. "Then I'll try."

She left him with a small wave, and he listened—not for answers, but for something gentler.

In the morning, Cassien walked with Maris.

The path wound behind the city walls and followed the slow curve of the river. Maris skipped ahead at first, gathering stones and pointing out bird calls. Cassien followed in silence, letting her joy guide him.

"Mama says this path knows our feet," she said over her shoulder. "That the earth remembers us."

He nodded. "Perhaps it does."

They stopped near a bend in the river where the trees opened to a wide patch of sunlight. Maris sat cross-legged and motioned for him to do the same.

"This is where I talk to Papa," she said.

Cassien felt his breath catch.

"He always listens. Even if he doesn't answer with words."

He sat beside her, humbled.

They spoke no more for a while. The river flowed. A breeze stirred the grass. And in that quiet communion, something long buried within him stirred—not grief, but recognition.

Maris picked up a flat stone and studied it thoughtfully. "He used to teach me how to skip them across the water," she said, then gave it a quick toss. It bounced once, then twice, before sinking. "Not bad," she said proudly.

"He would be proud," Cassien murmured.

She turned to him. "Were you sad when Mama left?"

The question caught him off guard. "Yes. I let her go, instead of finding her," he said slowly. "At the time, I thought I was doing what God asked of me."

"But doesn't God want us to stay with the people we love?" she asked, brushing her hands on her skirt.

Cassien looked at her—so young, yet so clear in her questions. "I believe… I'm still learning what God truly wants."

She seemed to accept that answer. "Mama says truth changes as we grow, but love doesn't."

He smiled faintly. "Your mother is wise."

They sat again in silence. The river made no demands. Birds trilled overhead. And the warmth of the sun found the back of his neck.

"Will you stay?" Maris asked softly.

He didn't answer right away. "I will walk where the path leads. But for now… yes. I will stay."

She leaned against him, just enough to be felt, and together they watched the river carry the morning forward.

Interlude – Béziers

BY MID SUMMER, Béziers had become a city holding its breath.

The Bishop's warnings from the pulpit grew more pointed. "We must cleanse the body of Christ," he declared, his voice echoing through the cathedral. "And fire purifies."

Whispers followed his sermons—neighbors turning on neighbors, each afraid to be seen as sympathetic to heresy. Entire streets emptied after dark. Doors were marked in chalk. Children were told not to speak of the names they heard at home.

In a cellar beneath the merchant quarter, a hidden gathering spoke in hushed voices about the path to Montségur, about messages smuggled in the bindings of books, about the names of those already taken.

One boy, no more than twelve, was found in the fields outside the city—his tongue cut and a parchment nailed to his chest: "Let this be the last lie."

At the bishop's residence, more clerics arrived from Rome, bearing sealed scrolls and speaking Latin too fast for most to follow. Behind heavy doors, maps were studied. Names were inked in red.

And always, at the edge of the city, the torches waited.

The waiting, however, was not idle. Small squads of soldiers began appearing more frequently in the alleys and marketplaces, their boots stirring dust and suspicion. There were more arrests now—

quiet, efficient, and often at dawn. A midwife was taken from her bed. A bookseller gone without notice. No charges were ever posted, but the gaps left behind in the community spoke louder than proclamations.

The bishop ordered the construction of new holding cells beneath the church—larger, darker, closer to the confessional booths. He said it was for safety. Few believed him.

Those who still dared gather whispered of Massacre's Eve, remembering the day Béziers burned years before, when the crusaders shouted, 'Kill them all. God will know His own.' The old terror had returned—but this time in the guise of neighborly righteousness and sacred duty.

Even children sensed it. They played games mimicking inquisitors and accused, with makeshift trials in alleyways. One boy wept after being tied to a fencepost, begging to be 'forgiven.' No adults intervened. Not anymore.

And from the spire of the cathedral, each evening bell seemed to toll heavier than the last—less a call to prayer than a warning: judgment is near.

Chapter Six

SHE ARRIVED AT DUSK.

Alais, they called her—though none knew if that was the name she had been born with. She had traveled from Béziers cloaked in dust and silence, her eyes shadowed from days spent avoiding the main roads. The few who saw her approach the village from the river-bank whispered of a woman both hunted and holy.

Clara found her first. Maris had seen the figure kneeling near the reeds, washing her hands as if in ritual, and ran back to tell her mother. Clara did not hesitate. She brought the stranger inside.

When Cassien entered the house that evening, he felt her presence before he saw her—a quiet stillness, like the air before a storm.

Alais stood slowly from the hearth, where she had been sipping from a wooden cup. Her eyes met his—not with fear, but with something like recognition.

"You're the one she spoke of," she said.

"Who?" Cassien asked, unsettled.

"Your sister," she answered. "And others. In Béziers. Word travels on wind and ink."

Her voice carried the weariness of someone who had seen too much and the clarity of one who still chose truth.

Clara placed a gentle hand on her shoulder. "She brings news."

Alais nodded. "There is fire coming, not just in words or warnings. Real fire. The kind that takes everything."

Cassien looked between them, his heart tightening.

"Why come here?"

"Because not all who flee are lost," Alais replied. "Some are sent —to listen. And some, to awaken others."

She turned back toward the hearth, her presence heavy with both burden and purpose. And in the hush that followed, Cassien felt the path beneath his feet begin to shift once more.

Later that evening, Alais spoke again. Clara had coaxed her into a meal, and though her appetite was small, her voice was steady as she told her story.

"I was born near Narbonne," she said, fingers wrapped around a steaming mug. "My mother was a midwife, my father, a mason. We lived modestly, but there was always music in the house. Hymns. Psalms. And laughter."

She paused. "Until the inquisitors came. I was twelve. They came for a neighbor, a teacher who read the Scriptures in Occitan. My father protested. They took him, too."

Her eyes did not waver. "My mother and I fled to Béziers. We found shelter among families who still remembered kindness. That's where I first heard the Perfects speak. Not from a pulpit, but around a table. They spoke of a God who did not punish, who did not demand blood."

Cassien watched her carefully. "You became one of them."

Alais nodded. "I lived among them. Learned. Served. I do not call myself Perfect, but I try to live by the Light. Even when it burns."

Clara stirred the stew slowly. "She has walked through fire and still sings."

Alais smiled faintly. "No song is free. I lost my mother last year. She died hiding others."

The silence that followed was not awkward. It was reverent.

"I don't come here to sow fear," Alais added. "Only to say that what's happening in Béziers is spreading. The map is inked with our names, even when we are silent."

"And you?" Cassien asked. "Why were you spared?"

"I wasn't," she said softly. "But I ran fast. And I've been listening ever since."

Clara insisted that Alais stay the night, and she did not refuse. A spare mattress was laid in the corner of the main room, and though she lay quietly, Cassien could sense she did not sleep for long. Her body remained still, but he imagined her eyes remained open to the dark.

The next morning, Clara woke him gently. "There is something you should see," she said.

Alais stood at the door, already cloaked for the cool air, her expression unreadable but calm.

"Come," she said simply. "There is a Consolamentum today."

The word stirred something in Cassien—half recognition, half resistance. The Cathar rite of spiritual baptism. The laying on of hands. The quiet crossing into purity.

He followed them through the winding paths behind the village, down to a grove where the sun filtered gently through old trees. A dozen people had gathered, some seated on low stones, others kneeling.

At the center sat an elderly woman, frail but composed, her eyes radiant with peace. Alais knelt beside her and took her hands.

Words were not chanted—they were spoken softly, lovingly. Prayers in Occitan, full of light and simplicity. There was no spectacle, no incense, no assertion of power. Only a transmission of presence.

When it was done, and the woman lifted her gaze to the canopy of trees above, Cassien felt something pass through all of them—like the hush after a bell stops ringing.

Alais did not speak to him as they walked back. She did not need to. What he had witnessed refused to be judged—it only asked to be received.

And though he did not yet understand it, he knew he would carry it with him.

That evening, Clara said, "It's time for you to move on, brother. Your presence attracts eyes with questions in them."

Alais asked, "Do you want to come with me, Clara, or will you be safer here?"

Clara smiled. "Maris and I would be no safer with you, Alais, and traveling together would draw suspicion upon us both. We will remain here for now, but if you would, take Cassien with you. Traveling with a Churchman may offer you some protection if you are caught."

Alais turned to Cassien and asked, "Is that your wish?"

Cassien said, "I cannot stay here longer and must move on also. I would be most blessed with your companionship if you would have me."

"It will be dangerous for you, Cassien. Whatever protection you might afford me is countered by the danger I will bring upon you. You will be safer without me."

"My mission is to listen and learn, Alais, not to be safe."

She nodded. "Then we leave before dawn."

They traveled south, keeping to forest paths and shepherd trails. Alais moved with the ease of someone who had lived between danger and grace for too long. Cassien followed in silence for much of the morning, watching how the trees seemed to part for her without effort.

By midday, they paused beneath a ridge to share bread and water. Cassien finally broke the quiet.

"You said you don't call yourself Perfect. But you speak the words of a Perfect as if they are your own."

Alais chewed slowly before answering. "Because they are. Not in title. In essence."

"What is that essence, exactly?"

She looked out toward the hills, her gaze distant. "That Spirit and flesh are not of the same origin. That the God of Love is not the god of this world, that what we suffer here is not punishment, but forgetting."

Cassien frowned. "So you believe in two gods?"

She met his eyes calmly. "No. One source of Love. One false creator. The world we see is not the world that was meant."

He shook his head. "That's dualism. Heresy."

"It's recognition," she replied. "That suffering does not come from God. That violence, cruelty, domination—they are not divine. They are the sickness of a false order."

Cassien bit into his bread, more to avoid responding than from hunger. "And Christ? Where does he stand in this?"

"He comes to awaken," she said. "To remind us of what we are. Light. Spirit. Not bound to the flesh, but caught in it. He did not die to buy God's forgiveness. He died to reveal the lie that flesh must be conquered."

He stared at her. "That undermines everything I've ever been taught."

"I know," she said gently. "But have you never wondered why love and punishment come from the same mouth in your Church? Why must fear be used to keep truth alive?"

He opened his mouth to argue, but the words caught. Because he had wondered, he had feared those contradictions his entire life.

She watched him with compassion, not triumph. "I don't ask you to agree, Cassien. Only to remember what your heart already knows."

They fell into silence again, not from distance, but from the weight of what had passed between them. The wind shifted slightly. The hills remained still.

The road ahead was uncertain, but so too was the one behind. "God left us a map," Cassien said, stepping lightly around a patch of uneven trail. "A way of living, so that we may become worthy of being with Him in heaven. We are not abandoned in this world—we are placed in it, with meaning. With guidance."

Alais walked beside him, listening.

He continued, more fervently now. "We are God's gift to the world, Alais. Through the Church, through the saints, through the tradition passed down like breath from Christ to Peter and onward, we are offered a way to return to Him."

She nodded slowly, though her expression remained calm. "But must we prove our worth to the One who made us? Is a gift given only if earned?"

"No," he replied, wrestling with her question. "But we have fallen. The world is broken. The Church helps us navigate that brokenness. Without it—without the map—we wander. We fall further."

Alais stopped and turned to him. "Or perhaps we were never abandoned. Perhaps the map is already written in our hearts, and the Church has only tried to make it fit into the shape of its own doctrine."

He opened his mouth to argue, but found he could not dismiss her so easily. The sun dappled the forest path around them. The wind in the trees whispered something neither of them dared translate.

And so they kept walking—bound not by agreement, but by the pull of a question that neither doctrine nor defiance could yet answer.

They crested a rise where the trees gave way to an expansive view of the valley below, the mountains rolling like a stone ocean into the horizon. They paused, breath caught by both the climb and the beauty, and Cassien turned to her.

"But we have the Commandments, the Gospels, many tomes of Sacred Writing that must be interpreted for the masses, Alais. If everyone followed their own interpretation of the Gospel, error would abound. Most people can neither read nor write. How can they be expected to discover the truth of God without guidance?"

Alais looked out across the valley before replying, her voice soft but sure.

"Cassien, you speak as if God's truth is fragile—as if it must be protected from the minds of the poor or the unlettered. But have you ever listened to a child describe love? Or an old woman speak to her garden? Truth is not reserved for the learned. It is revealed in how we live, how we love, how we forgive."

She turned to face him fully. "The Scriptures are sacred, yes—but so too is the soul that reads them, even in silence, even without letters. You say error would abound. I say grace already does."

She let the silence return for a moment, then added, "The danger is not in too many paths to God—but in those who claim theirs is the only one worth walking."

"There can be only one truth," he replied. "Truth's revelation is revealed perfectly only by the Church. That is the only reason we exist—to guard it, to teach it, to embody it. If each soul is left to decide what is true, how do we avoid chaos?"

Alais met his words with silence, not because she lacked a reply, but because she seemed to be weighing the weight of what he'd said.

"Cassien," she said at last, "what if the truth is not something kept, but something lived? What if it does not need guarding, only recognizing?"

He shook his head. "But truth must have form. It cannot survive in endless interpretations."

"No," she said gently, "it cannot survive in cages either. What is true will rise, with or without approval. Even in silence. Even in exile."

Her words landed like seeds—quiet, but already pressing toward the light inside him.

They reached a high pasture by late afternoon, where the wind carried the scent of lavender and dry stone. The landscape felt older here, less touched by time, and it soothed some of the tension Cassien hadn't known he carried.

He glanced at Alais. She had been silent for some time, her eyes scanning the horizon. "You're troubled," he said.

She nodded. "There is a heaviness in the air. A shift."

They descended into a valley where an abandoned shepherd's hut rested beneath the shadow of a pine grove. The door creaked open, revealing a space bare but intact. It would be enough for the night.

Cassien gathered kindling while Alais cleared a space to sit. The fire they lit was small but warm, its flicker softening the lines on their faces.

After eating the last of their bread and dried apples, they sat across from each other. The silence was deep—not awkward, but full of the unspoken.

Alais broke it. "Cassien, what happened between you and Clara? She said you left her?"

He placed a little more wood on the embers, giving off a modicum of light. "I was fourteen, and she was eighteen. Clara was visiting with our mother's family in a nearby town. My father told me that she wanted to marry a Cathar, that she was a heretic, and disowned her.

"My father decided that my older brother, who was much like my father, would remain with him to inherit our modest farm, while I was to be offered to the Church as a novitiate at a nearby Abbey. He didn't ask me, he told me. I never saw Clara again until a few days ago."

"What were your parents like?"

"My father was stern, with a rigid demeanor. He lived by the law as he believed it to be. He was always right and never wrong. My mother was quiet and subdued, smothered in sadness I never understood. She smiled rarely, and I never heard her laugh."

"So you dedicated your life to the Church," she said. It was a statement, not a question.

"Yes. The Abbey was small, but I prospered in letters and scholarship. In time, the brotherhood moved me to Cluny Abbey, where I remain still. I was happy there, I suppose, immersed in writings, doctrines, languages, and held secure in the belief that I knew the Truth of God."

Later, wrapped in silence, she watched him sleep. Her thoughts moved like river mist—slow, rising, impossible to contain.

She did not pray for his safety. She prayed for his remembrance.

When dawn touched the stones outside, Alais rose quietly and placed a hand on his chest, feeling the steady rhythm of a man no longer ruled by obedience, but by becoming.

She whispered, "Go with light."

And then she waited.

Chapter Seven

THAT AFTERNOON, as the path curled into a quiet glade, they came upon a small cottage tucked behind a screen of laurel. Smoke rose from its chimney, and the sound of water being drawn from a well reached them before the voice did.

Alais stopped. Her breath caught. "I know this place."

The woman who stepped out of the cottage was perhaps a few years older than Alais, though her bearing was hardened. She carried a bucket in one hand, but it dropped with a dull thud when she saw us.

"Alais?"

Alais nodded. "Hello, Sabine."

Sabine did not move. "I thought you were dead."

There was no embrace—only silence, thick as smoke.

Cassien stepped forward slightly, unsure whether to speak.

Sabine's gaze flicked to him. "And who is this? Another seeker following your trail of ashes?"

"This is Cassien," Alais said calmly. "A friend."

Sabine laughed bitterly. "You always find friends just before the fire comes."

Alais winced. "I didn't know. About your brother. I never meant—"

"You never mean to, Alais. But meaning doesn't matter when the soldiers come. He sheltered you for one night. One. And we lost everything."

Cassien looked at Alais, then back to Sabine. "We don't mean to bring trouble."

"It's already here," Sabine snapped. "They passed through here last week, asking questions. You shouldn't have come."

Alais stepped closer. "Please. We just need the night. We'll be gone by morning."

Sabine hesitated. Her jaw tightened. "One night. No fire. And if anyone comes, I never saw you."

They entered quietly. Cassien could feel the pain in the walls, the echoes of a broken past.

Later, Alais whispered to him, "I once called her sister. Not by blood, but by bond. And I betrayed that."

Cassien said nothing, but the weight of her confession settled in the space between them.

Even trust, it seemed, had a shadow.

I asked gently, "Sabine said her brother sheltered you. Do you wish to share with me what happened?"

Alais sat near the hearth, her knees drawn up beneath her shawl. She didn't answer right away. Her gaze was fixed on the corner of the room, where a cobweb trembled in the draft.

"It was winter," she said at last. "I had escaped a raid two nights earlier. No food, no dry clothing. I came to Sabine's door because I knew her brother—Étienne—was kind. He had once brought bread to our commune when we had none."

She looked down at her hands. "He didn't hesitate. He let me in, gave me a place to sleep, and dried my cloak by the fire. We didn't speak much. But Sabine saw the torchlight on the ridge the next morning. She told us to flee, but there was no time. They were already at the door."

Cassien listened, heart tightening with each word.

"I escaped through a small rear window. The soldiers beat Étienne when he wouldn't tell them where I'd gone. They burned the house. Took him. Sabine escaped through the orchard. I never saw him again."

Alais's voice cracked, but she didn't cry. "I didn't deserve his mercy. Or hers. But they gave it anyway. And I brought them ruin."

Cassien reached across the narrow space between them and placed his hand lightly over hers. "You didn't bring ruin, Alais. You brought your need. The world brought the fire."

She looked at him, eyes searching. And for the first time, she let someone hold her pain.

They rose before the sun. The air was cold, still heavy with the scent of woodsmoke and dew. As they stepped quietly outside, Sabine stood waiting in the dim light, arms crossed over her chest, her face unreadable.

"I didn't expect you to leave without waking me," she said.

Alais stepped forward. "You've given more than I had any right to ask."

Sabine shook her head. "You gave me a chance to speak what I carried. I didn't know I needed that."

She glanced at Cassien. "You're not what I imagined. I thought anyone from the Church would speak in decrees. But you listen. Keep doing that."

Cassien inclined his head. "Thank you for letting us stay."

Sabine handed Alais a wrapped bundle. "Bread and apples. It's not much. But I know the road ahead isn't kind."

For a long moment, the three stood in silence.

Then Sabine said, more softly, "If you ever see Étienne… if by some miracle he lives… tell him I kept the orchard."

Alais nodded, her voice thick. "I will."

They turned and disappeared into the forest, the day just beginning to bloom behind them.

The morning light filtered softly through the canopy as they moved southward. Neither spoke for some time. The encounter with Sabine lingered like incense after vespers—its bitterness, its grace.

The forest gradually thinned, giving way to rolling meadows and low hills. In the distance, the silver thread of a river wound between ancient trees, its surface catching the sun like scattered coins.

Alais adjusted the satchel on her shoulder. "There's a crossing ahead," she said. "A place where the river narrows. We'll be safer on the far side. Fewer patrols."

They pressed on, quickening their pace. A hawk circled overhead, and somewhere in the valley below, a shepherd's flute drifted faintly through the air. The peace of the moment felt fragile—as if the world were pausing, briefly, before reminding them of its wounds.

By midday, they reached the crossing: a shallow stretch where stones formed a crude bridge just beneath the surface. Cassien offered her his hand, and she took it without hesitation. They stepped from stone to stone, the river tugging gently at their ankles.

On the far side, they paused to breathe.

Alais looked back across the water. "It's strange, isn't it? How something as simple as a river can feel like a border between two selves."

"Strange," he said, "but true."

They turned from the bank, feet squelching slightly in the grass. Whatever lay ahead, they crossed toward it—step by step, heart by heart, silence and all.

Beyond the river, the landscape began to shift. The meadows gave way to craggy outcrops, and the path narrowed again into stony ridges framed by sparse trees and wind-scoured brush. The terrain grew harsher, but there was a raw beauty to it—steep hills and limestone shelves that seemed to rise from the earth like broken teeth.

In the distance, tucked between two jagged slopes, they spotted a cluster of low stone buildings clinging to the hillside. Smoke rose from a chimney, thin and wavering in the high air.

"That's Limoux," Alais said quietly. "A place of pilgrimage, though not all who come seek Rome's blessing. Some here remember the Light in ways that do not fit within the Church's walls."

They made our way slowly toward the village, passing a weathered shrine carved into the cliffside, its paint faded, but the image of the Virgin was still visible beneath moss and lichen. A child watched from a distance, then darted behind a doorway.

As they entered the village, a man in simple robes approached, his eyes sharp with both curiosity and caution.

"Travelers," he said. "And not from here."

Alais offered a nod. "Only for a night, if it's permitted."

He studied her, then looked at Cassien. He lowered his hood, letting him see what he was: not just a traveler, but a man of the Church.

His brow furrowed—but then he stepped aside. "Then come. The wind rises hard at night in these hills."

They followed him through narrow alleys and stone archways toward a low house built partially into the slope. As he opened the door, Cassien felt again that sense of crossing into another circle of lives, another test of trust.

Inside the modest dwelling, they were met by two women tending a large iron pot over a low fire. The scent of rosemary and lentils filled the space. One of the women, older and broad-shouldered, gave them a brief nod but said nothing. The other, younger and sharp-eyed, regarded them with something between suspicion and intrigue.

"Sit, if you're hungry," said the older woman. "The food is shared by all."

They took places near the hearth. Around them, more villagers drifted in—some with baskets of roots or jars of oil, others with tired children or worn cloaks heavy with travel. No one asked why they had come. They simply made room.

One man, his hands calloused and stained with dye, introduced himself as Benoît. "We trade cloth with the Cathars. Not all pilgrims come for God. Some come for news. Some come for safety."

Alais nodded. "We are looking for all three."

There were murmurs of agreement. A woman with bandaged fingers, who had clearly come from the fields, said quietly, "The Church's men were in the valley last week. Asking questions. Measuring silence."

Cassien listened closely. The room, though simple, felt layered—each person carrying their own gravity, their own story just beneath the surface.

That night, by firelight, voices rose in low song—not hymns, not chants, but something older, woven of sorrow and endurance. And though no one spoke of God, it felt like a kind of prayer.

Cassien sat quietly, his gaze drifting from face to face, absorbing their presence. These people were neither rebels nor saints. They were survivors. They were keepers of something unspoken, something precious.

And he was beginning to understand that faith, in this place, did not kneel—it endured.

As the fire settled into embers, more voices joined the quiet murmur around the hearth. An older man named Lucien, who had once served as a notary in Carcassonne, leaned forward, his hands clasped over his knees. "They've started arresting those who speak too freely. Not just Cathars now—merchants, midwives, even a priest who refused to name his parishioners."

A young woman beside him, her hair braided with dried lavender, nodded grimly. "My cousin vanished last month. They said he fled north, but no one believes that."

Another voice, from the shadows near the back, added, "They burned a house in Najac. Claimed it was accidental. But the man who lived there had been healing with herbs the Church forbade."

Cassien absorbed every word. The stories differed in detail, but not in weight. Each was a stone laid upon a growing wall—one that divided not just Church from heretic, but the past from whatever future might still survive.

Then a boy, no more than ten, spoke up with the solemnity of a man twice his age. "My mother says we carry the Light inside us. That if we forget, it goes out. But if we speak it—even softly—it grows stronger."

Silence followed his words, deep and reverent.

Alais turned to Cassien and whispered, "This is how the truth survives. Not in doctrine. In memory. In witness. In stories passed from mouth to mouth, even in fear."

Cassien nodded slowly. He had once believed truth required structure, form, and defense. But here, in this dim room filled with weary travelers and watchful hearts, he saw another way.

Truth, it seemed, could travel by firelight and whisper. And it could survive in silence.

Just then, the door creaked open, and a thin gust of cold air swept through the room. A figure stood in the threshold, cloaked and hooded, dripping from the rain that had begun to fall unnoticed.

The older woman by the fire stiffened. "Étienne?"

The figure pulled back the hood, revealing a gaunt man with sunken cheeks and eyes that darted with the caution of someone long in hiding.

"No," he said, voice low. "But I bring word from him. And from Béziers."

All conversation fell away.

He stepped inside, glancing warily at Cassien, then at Alais. "The bishop's guard has issued new orders. Names. Entire households marked. They raided a farmhouse two nights ago outside Figeac. Burned it before dawn."

Cassien stood slowly. "How close are they now?"

"Too close. If you're headed south, you'll need to leave before sunrise. The paths through the gorge are still open—for now. But they won't be for long."

Alais met the stranger's gaze. "And Étienne?"

The man hesitated. "Alive. For now. Hiding near Perpignan. He sent me to warn those still willing to listen."

"When you see him next, please tell him that Sabine kept the orchard. She misses him."

"I will," he said. "He'll be glad to know you are still alive as well, Alais."

"You know me?"

"I was there the night the soldiers came. I followed the soldiers and helped to rescue Étienne three nights later. He dared not return, lest Sabine be taken, too."

A weight settled over the room. The fire popped, and someone muttered a prayer.

Cassien looked around at the silent faces—faces carved by fear and resolve. He knew what must come next. And he knew the road ahead would demand more than silence and stories.

It would demand a choice.

Before anyone could rise, the older woman who had tended the pot stepped forward. Her name, they said, was Mireille, and her presence seemed to carry the weight of many winters.

She moved to stand near the hearth, the flickering light illuminating the fine lines that traced her face like a map of storms weathered and survived.

"We have a choice, yes," she said, her voice calm and even. "But not every choice is made in haste. And not every path lit by fear leads to truth."

The room quieted further, as if the walls themselves listened.

Mireille looked to Cassien, then to Alais. "When the fire comes, some run. Some hide. Others carry water. You must ask yourselves —what will you carry? And who will you become along the way?"

She reached down and stirred the coals gently with a long iron rod. "We have no armies here. No altars. But we remember. And in re-membering, we endure. So long as you walk with memory, and not just mission, you are not lost."

Cassien felt the words settle inside him like a stone in deep water —unmoving, but resonant. Mireille turned away then, saying nothing more.

But the silence that followed her was not empty. It was filled with something rare and ancient—a kind of permission.

And the fire burned on.

Then, from the edge of the gathered circle, a soft voice rose—tentative at first, but clear. It belonged to a young woman, her belly round with child, a small boy nestled sleepily against her side.

"I was twelve when my mother was taken," she began. Her voice wavered, but she did not stop. "They said she was healing without permission. That she had spoken words not found in Latin. But I remember her hands. How they calmed fevers. How they cradled me during storms."

The boy stirred, but she held him gently.

"I married a weaver. He was quiet. Kind. We never spoke of the Church—not aloud. But when he began to dream aloud, to speak of Light and freedom even in sleep, the neighbors started to look away. Not out of malice. Out of fear."

She looked around the room, eyes shining. "They came for him at dusk. I hid with our son in the root cellar. I can still hear his voice, calling to me from the courtyard. Not in pain. In comfort. Telling me to stay hidden. To protect the child."

The fire crackled. No one interrupted.

"He never returned. I traveled here because someone told me Limoux remembers. And now, here I am. Still with child. Still with hope. And if I must raise these children alone, then I will do it in a place where memory matters more than decrees."

She paused, then added quietly, "And maybe one day, they will speak their truth freely—and not in whispers."

The room seemed to breathe together in that moment, as if one heart beat through many bodies. Even the fire, now low, seemed to lean closer.

Cassien bowed his head—not in pity, nor prayer, but in recognition. The faith that lived here bore no seal, no vestments. But it carried the weight of love. And that, too, was holy.

As the room gradually returned to stillness, Cassien turned to Alais and gave a slight nod. She returned it with understanding. The time had come to move on.

They rose early, before the first grey light slipped over the mountains. Quiet goodbyes were exchanged beneath cloaks and shawls. Mireille handed Alais a small pouch of dried herbs and pressed Cassien's hand with a surprising strength.

"Remember what you've heard," she said. "Let it shape your steps."

The young mother offered them a piece of warm bread and kissed her son's forehead before whispering, "Go with care."

Outside, the path was wet with dew and soft underfoot. Cassien turned back once to look at the sloped rooftops of Limoux, still wrapped in shadow. Then he faced forward.

The road called them onward.

Chapter Eight

BY MIDMORNING, they descended from the wooded ridge into a low plain where the wind carried distant voices—children, perhaps, or travelers ahead on the road. But something else moved in the air too: a sense of being watched.

Cassien slowed. So did Alais. They exchanged a glance and said nothing, but their pace quickened subtly.

As they crested a shallow rise, a man appeared on the path ahead. He was unshaven, cloaked in the dust of travel, with a small dagger at his hip. He did not smile.

"Where do you come from?" he asked.

Cassien replied evenly. "From Limoux."

The man's gaze flicked to Alais. "And her?"

"We travel together," Cassien said.

The man's eyes narrowed. "You were seen with her in the south. Some would pay for such news."

Alais stepped forward, her voice sharp. "And would you sell it?"

He hesitated. Then, with a grunt, he stepped aside. "Go. But take a different road. The one ahead leads to questions you won't want to answer."

They passed without another word. Only once they were well beyond earshot did Cassien exhale.

"What road *does* lead to answers?" he murmured.

Alais didn't respond. But her hand lingered near his as they continued, as if reassurance could be passed through breathless fingers.

That night, they made camp near the banks of a river, hidden beneath an overhang thick with ivy. The stars broke through the clouds in slow procession, like memories returning after long exile.

Cassien stirred the fire with a stick, watching the flames lick the darkness. "Tell me more," he said. "About what you believe. About the Cathars."

Alais leaned back against her pack. "We believe in simplicity. In the divinity of spirit. That matter—this world—was shaped by something lesser, something that binds us to pain. But our true essence is not of this world. It's light. Unborn. Eternal."

Cassien frowned. "So all creation is… false?"

"Not false. Just… incomplete. Like a reflection in broken glass."

He shook his head. "And the sacraments? The saints? The holy orders?"

"Man-made paths," she said gently. "Some lead toward love. Others away. We follow the love, Cassien. That is our compass."

He stared into the fire, wrestling. "But where is God in all this?"

Alais reached toward the flame, palm open. "Here. In the warmth. In your asking. In the silence between your thoughts. He has never been far."

Cassien said nothing. But the weight of her words folded into the night like an ember into ash.

They slept under the open sky, side by side but not touching. And still, something passed between them—a prayer without sound.

At dawn, Cassien awoke with a start. The world was still—but something was different.

He stood, scanning the treeline.

A single bird called out. Then silence.

He turned to Alais, who was already awake, eyes watchful.

A messenger hawk flew overhead, circling, then darted west.

They exchanged a glance.

"It begins," she said.

And they packed in silence, walking toward a world that had not yet named them.

By late morning, the hills ahead began to roll open like pages of a forgotten scripture. The road they followed was narrower now, less traveled, edged by wild thyme and crushed lavender. With each step, the distance between them and Limoux grew, but so too did the quiet bond forming between them—threaded from shared danger, from trust offered in fragments.

Cassien found himself watching Alais as she walked. She was striking in her simplicity—tall, with a long, lean grace that made her movements seem more fluid than deliberate. Her hair, the color of chestnut bark in rain, was braided loosely and often caught the breeze like a banner from another world. Her eyes, when they met his, were a shade between storm and dusk—quiet but charged. There was a strength in her face, in the set of her jaw, that spoke of losses endured and not forgotten. Not just the way she moved—quick, sure-footed—but the way she carried memory, like a second cloak. Her strength was not loud, but it was undeniable.

Cassien felt his chest tighten with something he could not name. Once, his prayers had brought him silence, a disciplined stillness. But in her presence, his thoughts fluttered like pages in the wind. He was drawn not only to what she believed but to the unspoken truth that lived in her gaze—the sense that she saw the world as it truly was, and carried that truth without fear.

He wondered if she saw through him, too—to the ache he hadn't yet confessed, to the certainty that his old certainties were crumbling, and to the strange longing that bloomed whenever her shoulder brushed his.

He did not yet know what he was becoming, only that he could not return unchanged.

At midday, they paused beneath a gnarled walnut tree. Cassien handed her a piece of bread and sat opposite.

"You never asked what I used to believe," he said, almost shyly.

Alais looked at him, the ghost of a smile on her lips. "I assumed you believed it completely."

"I did," he said. "And sometimes, I still want to."

She didn't press him. Instead, she broke her bread and shared it with the birds.

"That's what makes you dangerous to them," she said. "You still wonder."

He met her eyes, and for a breath, the air between them grew still again—weighted, luminous.

Then the moment passed. They rose, slinging their packs once more, and continued onward into the narrowing light.

That evening, the sky bruised into violet and the wind turned cooler. A light rain graced the land, soft splatters warning of more to come. They found shelter beneath a collapsed shepherd's hut, its stone walls broken but offering enough cover to keep them dry.

Cassien gathered wood and struck flint, his hands steady but his mind drifting. When the fire finally caught, its glow painted Alais in flickering amber. She sat cross-legged, eyes closed, humming something barely audible—a melody without words.

He listened.

"What is that song?" he asked.

She opened her eyes, slowly. "Something my mother used to sing. I don't remember the words. Only the feeling."

Cassien sat beside her, closer than before. "Peace?"

"Not quite," she said. "Longing. The kind that doesn't hurt, but never quite leaves."

They sat in silence again, the space between them tender with un-spoken recognition.

Cassien turned toward her. "Do you ever miss… what could have been?"

She looked at him, steady and soft. "Sometimes. But not enough to trade what is."

The fire cracked.

He reached out—hesitantly—and brushed a strand of hair from her cheek. She didn't flinch. Her hand came to rest gently over his.

For a long moment, they simply breathed.

Not as priest and heretic. Not as fugitives.

But as two people—flawed, afraid, awakening.

And though they did not kiss, something in them shifted. The night deepened around that silence, sacred and raw.

By dawn, the storm that had threatened all night never came. Mist hung in the low hollows, wrapping the land in soft breath. Cassien stirred before the fire's last embers died, stretching the stiffness from his limbs. He looked to Alais, still sleeping, her features relaxed in a way he rarely saw—unguarded, at peace.

He turned away to give her privacy and began to gather their things.

When she woke, she found him kneeling by the stream nearby, hands cupped under the water.

"Did you sleep?" she asked.

He nodded. "Enough."

They shared a quiet breakfast—dried fruit, bread, and a bit of cheese from Mireille's pouch. As they ate, the mood remained soft but changed—lighter somehow, as if something once unsaid had now been acknowledged.

As they resumed the trail, Alais spoke quietly. "There's a village two days from here. Safe, if it still stands. We'll find out more there. About Béziers. About the others."

Cassien gave a short nod, thoughtful.

But his mind wandered—not to the dangers ahead, nor even the faith that shaped his every step. It lingered on the way she had looked at him the night before. And how he had felt, seeing her truly.

There was no going back.

That afternoon, as the sun crested overhead and the air thickened with heat, Cassien felt a shadow moving in his chest—a heaviness he had not expected. They stopped briefly beneath a leaning pine, and while Alais scouted ahead for signs of travelers, Cassien knelt in the shade and bowed his head.

The words rose unbidden, fragments of psalms and prayers etched deep in his memory. But they rang hollow now. He whispered them anyway, hoping they might ground him.

Why do You test me, O Lord, with this confusion of heart?

He clenched his fists. *I am not who I was. But what am I becoming?*

When Alais returned, she studied his face. "You prayed," she said quietly.

Cassien didn't deny it. "I had to. I needed to hear if something still answered."

"And did it?"

He looked at her, eyes weary. "No. Or maybe I no longer know how to listen."

She knelt beside him, placing a hand lightly on his shoulder. "Maybe it's not silence. Maybe it's a different voice now."

He didn't respond. But he did not pull away.

By the following evening, they approached the village Alais had spoken of. From a distance, it looked untouched—rooftops intact, smoke rising from a chimney, a few goats grazing the hill.

But as they drew closer, the silence pressed in. The fields were unattended. No children ran in the lanes. A door hung open, swinging faintly in the wind.

They passed the well and entered the square. A single woman stepped into view from the church porch, her face pale, hands clasped.

"You should not linger here," she said. "There was a raid four nights ago. Most fled. Some were taken."

Cassien and Alais exchanged a grim look.

"Did anyone remain?" Alais asked.

"Some elders. A few who were too ill to run. They hide now, in cellars and caves. The ones who carried the books—gone."

Alais lowered her head. "We only came for word. And to see what remains."

The woman nodded. "Then you've seen it."

Cassien's heart tightened. There had been hope in Alais's voice that morning. Now there was only ash.

Before they could turn to leave, a faint rustling echoed from behind the church—hurried, deliberate. Cassien moved instinctively, placing himself slightly in front of Alais. The woman on the porch turned sharply.

Out of the shadows stumbled a boy, no more than nine or ten, clutching a bundle wrapped in cloth. His face was smudged with soot, his eyes wide but alert.

"Don't hurt him," the woman said quickly. "He's been hiding since the night of the raid."

The boy looked from Cassien to Alais, then back to the bundle. He opened it just enough to reveal pages—inked, sacred, delicate.

"From the books," he whispered. "They told me to run. So I did."

Cassien stepped forward slowly, kneeling. "You carried them all this way?"

The boy nodded. "They said someone would come."

Alais knelt beside him. "And we have. You did well."

The woman stepped closer. "He hasn't spoken much. But he remembers everything. Names, symbols, where the others are scattered. He's… more than he appears."

Cassien met Alais's gaze. Something unspoken passed between them.

"Then we cannot leave him behind," Cassien said.

The boy clutched the bundle tighter and stepped forward, unafraid. A new path had revealed itself—not one they had chosen, but one they now must follow.

Cassien reached out to steady the boy's trembling hands as Alais examined the cloth-wrapped bundle. She gently lifted a corner of the fabric, revealing a few pages of vellum—each inked with Cathar script and strange markings Cassien didn't recognize.

"We can't carry it all," she whispered. "But we must protect what we can."

Cassien nodded. "And him."

The woman on the porch gestured toward a back alley. "Stay the night. There's a trail that leads east, through the olive groves. The patrols don't go that way, not yet."

Alais asked, "Are you sure we should stay?"

"The soldiers won't be back this soon. It is safe, at least for another night."

"Then we thank you for your generosity. We will remain until the morning."

Cassien and Alais were offered the use of a small stone hut, its roof charred from the fire that had consumed its contents. The boy remained with them.

When they were settled, Alais asked the boy, "What is your name?"

"They call me Remy." He spoke softly, shyly, but the look in his eyes belied his age.

Shortly before dawn, Cassien helped the boy adjust the bundle across his shoulders, then took one last look around the quiet square. Alais touched the woman's arm in thanks.

They left the village before the sun had fully risen. As they moved into the greying of the night, a dog barked once behind them—then silence returned.

The path narrowed between low walls and brush, the dry leaves crunching beneath their steps. The boy walked between them, glancing up occasionally, but never slowing. He did not ask where they were going. He already understood they could not stop.

And so the three of them moved together toward the rising sun, not as pilgrims or fugitives, but as keepers of something fragile—and fiercely alive.

Chapter Nine

THE TRAIL TWISTED sharply between limestone outcrops as the morning deepened. They moved quickly, the quiet weight of responsibility settling over them.

By mid-afternoon, a flock of startled crows burst from the trees ahead. Cassien stopped short and motioned for the others to stay behind. A rustling—no, scuffling—echoed up the path.

From the brush, two riders emerged, wearing Church insignia. Their faces were hard, eyes scanning, swords at their sides.

Cassien turned and whispered, "Down. Into the ravine."

They slid into the underbrush just as the riders passed overhead. One paused, listening.

Alais held Remy close. The boy didn't tremble—he only gripped her tighter.

"They might have come this way," one rider muttered.

Cassien held his breath.

Then: hoofbeats resumed. Fading. Gone.

They waited another minute, then three.

Only when the birds returned to the branches did Cassien speak. "We can't stay on the open road anymore."

Alais nodded. "We head through the gorge. Less traveled, but harder."

Remy looked up. "Hard is fine."

Cassien gave a grim smile. "Spoken like one who's already endured too much."

And with that, they began to descend—into shadow, into silence, into the cleft of the land where no banners flew.

The gorge closed around them like a waiting mouth—high stone walls, slick with moss, rising steeply on either side. The air grew cool, damp, echoing with the distant trickle of water. Light fractured above through narrow shafts, and their voices came back to them distorted.

They picked their way carefully along a narrow ledge, with a river far below. Alais led, her steps sure despite the loose shale. Cassien followed with Remy between them, holding the boy's hand tightly.

Halfway along a bend, the earth shifted beneath them. A low crack sounded.

"Stop," Cassien called, too late.

The ledge collapsed under his feet.

He fell hard—his shoulder slamming stone, one hand grasping instinctively for purchase. He caught the root of a scrub tree and hung, dangling over a sheer drop. Below, the river rushed, dark and unyielding.

"Cassien!" Alais shouted, dropping to her knees.

Remy knelt beside her, eyes wide. "Hold on!"

Cassien gritted his teeth, feeling the root creak under his weight. "I'm not planning to let go."

Alais reached out, lying flat, arm extended. "Give me your hand!"

The root gave a snap.

Cassien lunged upward, catching her wrist just as the root tore free. For a breathless moment, they hung suspended—his weight dragging her forward—until she braced herself with her other hand and pulled.

He scrambled over the edge and collapsed on the stone, breath ragged.

No one spoke.

Then Remy sat beside him, silent, and took his hand.

Cassien looked at them both. "We go slower from here."

They moved a short distance farther until they found a slight hollow, shaded and still, where a patch of wild mint grew between stones. Alais gathered some and crushed it gently between her palms, releasing a cool scent. She knelt beside Cassien and began to examine his shoulder.

"You're bruised, but not broken," she said, voice low but steady. "We should rest. The body remembers shocks even when the mind pushes forward."

Cassien gave a short nod and sat back against the wall, exhaling slowly. Remy brought him a flask of water and sat cross-legged at his side.

"I've seen worse," the boy said with quiet conviction.

Cassien smiled faintly. "I don't doubt it."

Alais pressed a damp cloth to the forming bruise, her touch gentle but firm. "You're lucky the root held as long as it did."

"Luck," Cassien murmured, "or Providence."

She paused. "Sometimes they're the same thing."

They sat in silence while the pain ebbed and the air cooled. The gorge, once a place of peril, had become—for a moment—a sanctuary. A place to breathe, to feel the pulse of one's own body, to be reminded of what still held.

Cassien closed his eyes. The ache in his shoulder had weight, but not bitterness. It was the kind of pain that whispered, *You are still here.*

Alais watched him in the quiet. In Cassien, she had seen something rare—someone unraveling with grace. His doubt did not make him weak; it made him real. And that made her feel less alone.

She turned her gaze to Remy, who sat calmly, tracing patterns in the dust with a twig. The boy's silence wasn't empty—it was layered with knowing, with grief, with astonishing resilience. In him, Alais saw not only a child but a quiet torchbearer. One who carried memory like breath, and meaning like marrow.

She felt a strange affection stirring—maternal, yes, but more than that. A sense of shared purpose. As if the three of them had been flung together not by accident, but by some thread of will woven deeper than fate.

For a moment, she allowed herself to imagine what might come. Not escape or safety, but truth. Communion. Even love.

Then she shook the thoughts away—not because they frightened her, but because they softened her. And softness, she knew, could be dangerous in a world so sharp.

Still, when she looked at Cassien again, her eyes lingered longer than they needed to.

They resumed walking shortly after, but the terrain soon changed. The gorge began to narrow again, the walls pressing in until the path was little more than a series of stones slick with moss, the river running faster and louder beneath them. Every step required precision.

Alais led, one hand brushing the stone for balance. Cassien followed close behind, guiding Remy with soft words and a steady grip. The boy's face was tight with focus, but he moved like someone who had learned long ago to adapt to uneven ground.

Suddenly, a low roar echoed ahead—distant but unmistakable.

"Waterfall," Cassien said, his voice barely carrying above the rush.

The path curved toward the sound, and they found themselves standing at the top of a narrow chute where the river plunged downward in a white fury. The only way forward was across a fallen tree that spanned the gorge.

Alais stepped onto it first, testing its give. "It'll hold," she said. "But one at a time."

She crossed slowly, balancing with her arms stretched wide. Wind caught her cloak, and for a moment, Cassien feared she might lose footing. But she made it safely to the other side.

Cassien looked to Remy. "You next. I'll follow close—and let me carry the bundle for now. You need both arms free."

Remy hesitated, clutching the cloth-wrapped scrolls.

"I'll give it back once we're across," Cassien added gently.

Reluctantly, Remy slipped the bundle from his back and handed it over. Cassien slung it carefully over one shoulder, adjusting the weight.

"I trust you. Trust yourself. I'll follow close."

The boy hesitated. Cassien knelt. "I trust you. Trust yourself."

Remy stepped onto the log, arms out, eyes fixed ahead. The tree creaked slightly but did not shift. Cassien stayed close, whispering encouragement.

Halfway across, Remy wavered. A gust of wind sent pebbles skittering into the depths below.

"Don't look down," Cassien said firmly. "Just keep going."

Remy nodded, jaw clenched. Step by step, he crossed. At last, Alais reached out, caught his hand, and pulled him the final stretch.

Cassien followed, slower but sure-footed, conscious of the precious bundle he carried. When he reached them, they all stood still for a moment, breathing hard, watching the river vanish below.

The path ahead rose sharply into wooded hills. The gorge was behind them now—but the danger it had delivered lingered in their muscles and memories.

Alais looked back once. "We're not being chased anymore. But we are being followed."

Cassien nodded. "And the path only narrows from here."

They turned and kept walking, the earth damp beneath their feet, the air heavy with pine.

Around the next bend, the path sloped sharply upward and opened into a narrow shelf of stone overlooking the river. There, half-buried in mud and moss, stood the broken remnants of a wooden shrine—its beams splintered, the roof sagging inward.

Cassien said, "Be careful. It looks rotted."

Alais approached the crumbling structure, her hand brushing the faded symbol etched above the lintel—a stylized dove, wings outstretched.

"This is ancient," she murmured. "Older than the Church. Perhaps once a place of refuge."

Remy stepped forward, curiosity bright in his eyes. "What was it for?"

Cassien knelt and examined the moss-covered threshold. "Sanctuary, maybe. Or silence. A place to listen."

As they stood in quiet reverence, a faint sound reached them—a soft clinking of metal, distant but steady, like the rhythm of bridles in motion.

Cassien rose at once. "Riders. Coming fast."

Alais scanned the terrain. "We can't backtrack. Not over the log."

"There," Cassien pointed to a fissure in the rock wall behind the shrine. "It might lead somewhere."

Without hesitation, they scrambled toward it, the opening just wide enough for one person at a time.

As they slipped into the shadows, the sound of hoofbeats grew louder—closer—followed by a man's voice barking a command.

They held their breath.

Then, silence again.

And the dark mouth of the cave swallowed them whole, the air pungent with the metallic tang of unseen blood.

Inside, the dim light revealed what the scent had already warned them of—a fresh carcass, half-hidden behind a rise of stone. A wild goat, throat torn, its body still limp. Flies buzzed lazily in the cool air.

Cassien stepped forward, crouching low. "Recent," he whispered. "No more than a few hours."

Alais knelt beside him, her face taut. "A predator's den. Possibly wolf. Maybe bear."

Remy's voice was small. "Are they still here?"

"Maybe," Cassien said. "Or maybe out hunting again. We won't linger."

But they didn't move—not right away. The cave pressed in, heavy with silence and uncertainty. Cassien glanced at Alais and Remy. "If we leave now, we risk being seen. If we stay, we share this space with something that kills to live."

Alais' voice was quiet but resolute. "There are no safe choices. Only the ones we can live with."

Cassien weighed the scrolls slung over his shoulder. "If we're found, they'll take these. If the bear returns—"

"Then we defend what we carry," Alais interrupted, her eyes meeting his. "Not because we want to fight. But because it's worth it."

Remy stepped forward, surprising them both. "We stay, just for a while. We can watch the entrance. And we listen. Always listen."

Cassien studied the boy, then Alais. He nodded slowly. "We stay. Until the night deepens. Then we move under cover."

They settled into the cave's deeper hollow, where the rock walls muffled sound and the faint scent of moss overpowered the tang of blood. Alais sat near the mouth, keeping vigil, while Cassien unwrapped a bit of bread and cheese for Remy.

The boy accepted it without a word, chewing slowly, eyes fixed on the far wall where shadows danced in the shifting light.

Cassien leaned against the stone, rolling his injured shoulder. The pain had dulled, but not vanished. It reminded him of the edge they now lived on—a space between safety and peril, spirit and survival.

Alais broke the silence. "There's something sacred about this place. Even beneath the fear. Can you feel it?"

Cassien listened, truly listened. The air held more than tension—it held memory. Echoes of prayers long ceased. Murmurs lost in stone.

"I do," he said at last. "As if we're not alone. But not in danger either. Watched, maybe. Witnessed."

Remy looked up. "Maybe the old ones used to come here when they had to hide. Maybe they left something behind."

No one answered, but the thought remained, a thread of warmth in the cold dark.

For a while, they said nothing more. Just the rustle of cloth, the flick of a flame from Cassien's flint, and the breath of three souls holding space.

In that moment, the cave was not a den. It was a sanctuary.

When the darkness thickened outside and the sounds of pursuit faded into memory, they emerged, blinking into the stillness of the night. The moon hung low, casting silver across the wet rocks and turning the gorge into a corridor of ghosts.

They moved carefully, every footstep a whisper, following the faint slope of a goat trail that veered east, away from the river. The boy clutched Alais's hand; Cassien led, ears tuned to the hush of danger, the quiet murmur of nocturnal life.

After nearly an hour, they crested a low rise where the cliff wall opened into a hollow of trees and soft grass. A broken stone wall marked the remnants of a herder's shelter—its frame collapsed, but a portion of the roof remained, enough to give them rest.

Here, they stopped.

Alais gathered kindling and started a low fire. Cassien stripped off his damp cloak and laid it near the embers to dry. Remy curled near the warmth, eyes heavy with exhaustion.

Cassien sat back, breathing the cool, pine-tinged air. "No smoke," he said softly. "No sound. We're safe here for now."

Alais nodded. "And we needed this. Even the hunted must sleep."

As the fire crackled low, they huddled near one another beneath the stars, the hush of the trees like a hymn.

Cassien glanced at Alais, who was tracing shapes in the dirt absently with a stick. Her face was soft in the firelight, her brow furrowed in thought.

"Do you ever wonder how we ended up here?" he asked.

She smiled faintly. "Only every night."

"I thought I knew what my life would be. Every step. Every vow. And now…" He shook his head.

Alais reached over and touched his hand gently, her fingers curling over his.

"We're not lost," she said quietly. "Just becoming."

Their hands remained joined for a long time, warm and still between them. The firelight flickered, casting dancing shadows on their faces.

Cassien exhaled slowly. "This is the first moment I haven't felt hunted."

He looked into the fire. "Poverty. Chastity. Obedience. I swore to serve God and the Church in all things."

Alais looked into the fire for a long moment. Then, softly, she asked, "What vows did you take, Cassien? At the monastery."

He hesitated, surprised by the question. "Obedience. Poverty. Chastity. Devotion to the teachings of the Church. A life of prayer and silence. I gave up my name, my desires, even my questions."

She turned to him, her voice still low. "And do you still carry them?"

He met her gaze. "Some of them. Others… feel like garments I've outgrown. Still folded in my pack, but no longer worn."

"And yet here you are," she said gently.

He gave a faint smile. "Here I am."

She reached across the space between them and took his hand. "Do you regret them?"

He thought for a long moment. "I regret the silence they demanded. The distance. But not the devotion. I truly believed I was doing what was right."

Her fingers tightened around his. "And now?"

"Now I believe I was meant to walk beyond them. To remember something I once knew but buried."

"Then rest," she whispered.

Their fingers stayed entwined until their breaths slowed together, the hush of sleep approaching like a tide.

But before silence claimed them entirely, Alais's voice rose once more, quiet and probing.

"Cassien… do you ever miss it? The way it was—before?"

He opened his eyes. "Sometimes. There was order in the life I left. Certainty. But it came at a cost."

"What cost?"

He turned to her. "My heart. I think I learned to silence it too well. To serve God through absence instead of presence."

She brushed her thumb lightly across his knuckles. "Then maybe… this is where presence begins."

He watched her, the softness in her face lit by the fading glow of the fire. "With you, it already has."

Sleep came slowly—but when it came, it came deep.

Chapter Ten

THEY ROSE BEFORE THE SUN, the first light of dawn catching the tips of the trees like whispered promises. The fire had burned low, its embers faintly warm, and the grass around their shelter was still damp with dew. Cassien stirred quietly, careful not to wake Remy, who slept curled beneath Alais's cloak.

Alais sat nearby, already awake, her face calm, as if listening to something beyond sound.

"Today feels different," she murmured, not turning.

Cassien joined her, nodding. "As if something waits ahead. Or someone."

They broke camp in silence and resumed the trail that climbed slowly eastward into higher terrain. The trees grew older here, taller and more twisted, their roots exposed and reaching like veins across the path.

Near midday, they came upon a narrow pass cut into the side of a hill. The air was cooler, and a faint trail of smoke rose ahead.

Cassien paused. "Someone's nearby."

They approached cautiously, Remy clutching his bundle close. As they turned a corner, they came upon a small stone outpost tucked between two boulders—barely more than a hut. Outside sat an old man with a long silver beard and weathered skin the color of smoke. He wore no insignia, no robe—only a simple tunic and a beaded necklace.

He looked up without alarm. "Travelers. From the west?"

Cassien nodded. "And you?"

"I am called Irenus," the man said. "I keep the fire here, for those who still walk with questions."

Alais stepped forward. "Do you know what's become of the towns below?"

The man nodded. "Some still breathe. Others only remember. Béziers burns slowly, but the fire is spreading."

Cassien's jaw tightened. "And here?"

Irenus smiled faintly. "They haven't found me. Or perhaps they've forgotten I exist. Either way, the fire stays lit."

Remy stepped forward, eyes wide. "Do you know the old language?"

Irenus's gaze settled on him. "Some of it. Enough to know what was once sacred. And what still is."

The old man invited them to sit and share bread and a bitter herb tea. They spoke little at first, listening to the wind move through the rocks.

Finally, Irenus asked, "What is it you carry?"

Cassien looked to Alais. She unwrapped a corner of the cloth to reveal the vellum pages. Irenus's eyes softened.

"So, it has reached even you. Then this place is needed more than ever."

They stayed until dusk, gathering fragments of forgotten wisdom from the old man's quiet words. He spoke not of salvation or punishment, but of balance—of the living field between silence and song.

Before they departed, Irenus took Cassien aside. "The path forward is not marked. It must be felt. But you are no longer walking as a man divided. Let that guide you."

Cassien bowed his head. "And the boy?"

"Teach him to listen," Irenus said. "Not to you, but to what moves through him."

That night, as they camped beneath a low-hanging crescent moon, Remy asked if he could read aloud from the pages he carried.

"I don't know what it means," he admitted shyly, "but I know how it sounds." Alais and Cassien listened as his voice filled the clearing with the rhythm of another time.

The fire flickered, the stars leaned close, and for a while, the world forgot how to hate.

They were no longer running.

They were remembering.

And the remembering was enough.

The next morning, the wind carried a faint scent of wild lavender and ash. They left the hillside clearing early, following a thread of path that narrowed into switchbacks through the high forest. The terrain grew rougher. Trees gave way to jagged stone and thickets of thorn.

By midday, they reached a ridge where the valley unfolded like a painted tapestry—small farms, scattered woods, the shimmering thread of a river. Smoke rose from a cluster of dwellings in the far distance, too little to signal danger, yet enough to warrant caution.

Alais shaded her eyes. "We could stop there for food. But only if we approach with care."

Cassien nodded. "We can't afford a wrong step now."

They descended slowly, skirting the edge of the trail when it widened into open stretches. In the mid-afternoon sun, every movement felt exposed.

As they neared the hamlet, the faint sounds of tools and laughter reached their ears—an ordinary life, still intact.

A woman working in a garden spotted them first. She stood, brushing earth from her hands, and watched them with a measured gaze.

"Travelers?" she called. "Or trouble?"

"Only hungry," Cassien replied, raising a hand in peace.

The woman hesitated, then gave a single nod. "Then come with honesty, and you'll leave with bread."

She led them through the garden and toward a small cottage shaded by a walnut tree. Inside, the air was warm and smelled of herbs and woodsmoke. A few children peeked out from behind a curtain, wide-eyed.

"We don't get many visitors," the woman said. "Not since the roads grew dangerous."

Alais offered a smile. "We don't mean to linger. Just a meal and a bit of quiet, if you've room."

"In there," the woman nodded toward a side room. "You should meet him."

Cassien frowned. "Meet who?"

"A soldier," she said, her voice hushed now. "He's wounded. Took a blade to the leg weeks ago and nearly died on our doorstep."

Cassien and Alais exchanged a glance.

"He speaks little," the woman continued. "But last night he talked in his sleep. Said he saw the fires. Béziers. Years ago."

They stepped into the small room where a man lay on a cot, his leg bound in linen. His beard was streaked with gray, and his face held the tight stillness of pain long endured.

When he opened his eyes and saw them, he struggled to sit upright.

"I remember you," he whispered to no one in particular. "All of you. Screaming. Smoke. I carried out a child—dead already. And still, I carried him."

Cassien knelt beside the bed. "You were there? At Béziers?"

The man nodded slowly. "A younger man then. They told us it was God's will. I believed them."

"And now?" Alais asked.

The soldier looked at her with hollow eyes. "Now I believe in mercy. And regret. That's all I have left."

The woman who had welcomed them stepped into the doorway, carrying a fresh poultice wrapped in linen. She moved gently to the soldier's side, her expression neither pitying nor fearful.

"We do not turn away the wounded here," she said softly. "Not even those who once brought pain. Healing must begin somewhere."

Another villager, a broad-shouldered man with soot on his hands, entered behind her and added, "He's done more with silence than most have with words. We tend his wounds. He tends our understanding."

Cassien watched their kindness with quiet awe. There was no hatred here. No retribution. Only a calm, stubborn act of love.

Alais met his eyes. "This too is a form of resistance."

That evening, they accepted the villagers' offer of shelter. A loft above the stable was cleared for them—simple, dry, and warm. Alais helped the woman prepare lentils and root vegetables, while Cassien carried buckets of water from the well and mended a broken latch on the gate.

Remy laughed with the children by the hearth, shy at first but soon animated, his voice carrying through the house like a song remembered.

As night fell, they gathered for a quiet meal. The wounded soldier remained in his cot, eyes closed, but when the villagers sang a low hymn to close the day, he wept without shame.

Later, as they lay in the straw-strewn loft beneath the creaking rafters, Cassien whispered to Alais, "Maybe this is what we're meant to carry forward—not just words, but a way of being."

She reached for his hand. "Then let's carry it while we can."

They lay in silence for a while, their hands still joined, the murmur of wind outside slipping through the cracks in the old boards. Cassien turned his head toward her.

"I didn't expect this," he said. "You. Him. Any of it."

Alais smiled faintly. "Neither did I. But maybe that's what makes it real."

He hesitated, searching her face. "When we first met, I thought you were sent to test me. To tempt me from my path."

"And now?"

"Now I wonder if I was never on the right one."

She brushed a strand of hair from her cheek. "You were on the only one you could be. Until you weren't."

He exhaled softly, the weight of her words settling around him like a balm.

"Do you ever miss it?" he asked. "The certainty?"

"Sometimes. But not as much as I cherish the freedom to feel what's true."

They said no more, but the silence between them was full—of trust, of change, of the quiet gravity of two souls drawing near without needing to name it.

After a few moments, Cassien turned toward her again, voice low.

"Alais… were you ever married?"

She was quiet, eyes searching the darkness above. Then: "Once. Long ago. Before all this."

"What happened?"

"He died in the winter fever, three years after we wed."

Cassien studied her face. "Were you happy?"

She nodded slowly. "In the way young love can be. But I was still becoming who I am. And so was he. I don't think we ever truly knew one another."

He absorbed this in silence, then asked, "Do you miss him?"

"I miss the kindness," she said softly. "And the quiet moments. But not the life we left behind."

Cassien let the silence stretch again, then spoke with a gentleness that surprised even him. "What was it like? Being with someone… before all of this?"

Alais turned to him, her eyes dark and quiet in the moonlight. "It was simple. Shared bread, shared silence. He was kind. We had plans, like all young people do. But they were dreams built on sand. The world shifted, and the dreams crumbled."

She looked down at their hands. "I don't mourn the life we planned. I mourn that we didn't get the time to find who we might have become together. Still, I carry what was good. And I let the rest drift away."

Cassien was quiet for a time, then asked, "And your family? Do you still have any living?"

Alais's face shifted in the dim light, a flicker of memory passing like shadow. "I had a brother. Younger. He left before the wars, went east—I don't know what became of him. My parents are gone. Disease took my father long before the Church ever noticed our village. My mother was taken last year and burned."

"I'm sorry," Cassien said.

She looked at him gently. "Don't be. Loss shapes us, but it doesn't own us. I carry them too, in quieter ways. In how I walk. In what I choose not to fear."

She shifted slightly on the straw, then asked, "And you, Cassien? Did you leave anyone behind?"

Cassien hesitated, the question catching in a place he thought long closed. "You know my sister, Clara. Older by four years. We were close once—shared everything. Games in the vineyard behind our home, secret names for constellations, dreams we promised never to forget."

He paused. "When she fell in love with a Cather, and moved away, she violated everything I thought we shared. She was the only one in my family who truly loved me. I entered the monastery not long after. "

Alais watched him with quiet understanding.

"When I saw her again near Carcassonne, she took me in without hesitation. Still strong, still sharp-tongued. But there was something in her eyes—like a question that had waited years for an answer."

"Did you find one?" Alais asked.

"I don't know," Cassien said. "But I think we both remembered who we were, even if only for a moment."

Alais traced a small knot in the wooden beam above them. "You speak of her with love. Even through the pain."

Cassien nodded. "She never stopped being my sister. I just stopped knowing how to be her brother."

"You still can be," Alais said. "If the door is open even a little, you can walk through."

He considered that, eyes softening. "Maybe this journey is part of it. Part of becoming someone she can know again."

Alais smiled, a touch of light in her expression. "Then let's keep walking."

They rose before the sun, the air cool and carrying the faint scent of woodsmoke from the night's embers.

Quiet farewells passed between them and the villagers who had shown them an unexpected and steady grace. The wounded soldier lifted his head from his cot, eyes clearer than they had been the day before, and offered a slow nod.

Alais pressed a small bundle of wrapped herbs into the hands of the woman who had first opened her door to them, murmuring in-structions in a voice that was both tender and firm. Cassien spoke a blessing in low Latin, the syllables like ripples on still water, and the children wrapped their arms around Remy's waist, reluctant to let go.

At the gate, Remy lingered, the morning light catching the uncertainty in his face. "I want to help more," he admitted. "But I also… I also want to go."

Cassien knelt before him, meeting his eyes. "Then help by staying. You are needed here more than you know. They see you for who you are."

Alais stepped forward, resting her hand on the boy's shoulder. "This isn't goodbye—not truly. We carry each other forward."

Remy's gaze shifted between them. "What about the scrolls? You should take them. They will be safer with you."

"Maybe not, Remy," Alais said gently. "The Church hunts for us."

Her choice of words caught Cassien's attention. Us. Until now, he had believed himself shielded by his Benedictine standing, free to wander and to speak. Was that illusion?

The village matron came forward, her back straight despite her years. "Take them," she said to Cassien, her eyes unwavering. "If they are found here, we will all be put to death. Your robes may yet protect them."

"They may indeed, Matron," Cassien replied gravely. "I will do my best."

Remy placed the bundle into his hands, and Cassien secured it above the pack on his back. Without another word, he and Alais turned eastward, their steps quiet in the pale, rising light. Behind them, the village receded into the folds of the land, but its warmth traveled with them, carried in the heart's keeping.

And somewhere beyond the hills, in the untraveled miles ahead, lay both the shadow of the hunt and the glimmer of what might yet be found.

Chapter Eleven

THEY DID NOT SPEAK for a long time. The silence was not heavy, only full—with memory, and something else unspoken, yet steady as breath.

High on the mountain, hours into their climb, they caught sight of a weathered stone building nestled far from the road, half-hidden by trees and rising rock. It stood like a forgotten watchman, its walls cloaked in moss and time.

Alais pointed. "There. Do you see it?"

Cassien followed her gaze. "Yes. It doesn't look abandoned."

"No. But it also doesn't look watched."

With no better destination and weariness beginning to pull at their limbs, they turned off the trail and made their way across the slope toward it.

The air was cooler here, wind curling through pines like breath through teeth. As they approached, they saw that the building had once been a hermitage—an old place of retreat. The door hung slightly ajar, creaking faintly when Cassien pushed it open.

Inside, it smelled of stone and lichen, but it was dry. A single long bench rested against one wall, and a hearth stood cold but intact.

They stepped inside together, grateful for shelter. There would be time for rest. And questions. And, perhaps, answers that only stillness could give.

They began tidying the space, brushing dust from the bench and sweeping out old leaves that had gathered near the threshold. Alais found a rusted pot near the hearth, and Cassien checked the small alcove behind the building where wild herbs grew tangled with thistle.

As he returned, arms full of what he hoped were edible greens, he asked, "Alais, tell me something… what's the true history of the Cathars? Not the rumors or the charges Rome has cast. But what you've lived, what you know."

She glanced up from where she was arranging dry sticks in the hearth. "That's a long story. And it depends on who you ask. The Church calls us heretics. But we never sought to rival it—only to live in alignment with what we believe Christ taught. Simplicity. Purity. The refusal to kill. The refusal to lie."

"And the rejection of the physical world?" Cassien pressed gently.

She met his gaze. "Not rejection. Discernment. We believe this world is not our true home. That spirit is what's real, and everything else is temporary clothing. But it doesn't mean we don't love. Or feel. It means we remember not to cling."

Cassien settled beside the hearth, setting down the greens. "But where did it come from, Alais? These teachings… did they begin with you?"

She smiled faintly, brushing her hands clean. "No. Not with me. Not even with the ones who taught me. The fire that lit this knowing—this way of seeing—has burned for generations. Longer. It runs like an underground river beneath the Church's stone roads."

She stood, gazing through a crack in the stone wall. "Some say it came from the East before even Rome rose. Others speak of mystics in the desert who spoke with angels, not in thunder but in silence. There were Gnostics and seekers, bearers of memory passed not in books, but breath to breath, life to life."

She turned to face him. "It's not a history you'll find written. It's a memory you awaken in yourself. A remembering of something you never truly forgot."

Cassien listened, eyes steady, as the wind curled beneath the eaves. "And now?"

"Now it lives in us," Alais said. "And in others like us. And maybe… in you, too."

They remained in the hermitage for several days, grateful for its quiet solitude. Each morning brought a rhythm of small labors—gathering herbs, restoring the hearth, walking down to a spring-fed stream to fill their flasks. The air was thin but clean, and the silence carried a kind of sacredness.

During those days, Cassien and Alais grew steadily more intimate—not with haste or expectation, but with the trust that grows in the absence of fear. They cooked together, read from the vellum pages in low voices, and shared dreams as the fire crackled between them. At night, they would lie close beneath the same cloak, their fingers brushing, then lingering, as if they were relearning what it meant to be human with one another.

Sometimes their conversations went long into the night—about God, about truth, about the strange tenderness that had taken root between them. Other times, no words passed at all, and the hush held more meaning than speech ever could.

One night, as the fire dimmed to a glow and the wind outside howled against the stone, Cassien reached for her hand in the dark, his fingers tracing the delicate bones of her wrist. Alais turned toward him, her breath warm against his cheek.

"Is this wrong?" he whispered.

She shook her head slowly. "Not if it's true."

Their lips met—tentative at first, as if testing the silence between them. Then again, longer, fuller, with the quiet desperation of two souls who had spent their lives withholding. It was not hunger that moved them, but recognition. In the dark, they explored each other slowly: a palm cupped to a cheek, fingers woven through hair, breath shared like prayer.

When they finally lay back down, arms entwined and skin warmed from touch, there was no guilt. Only stillness. And in that stillness, peace.

Later that night, as sleep eluded him, Cassien stared at the low ceiling of the hermitage, the soft breath of Alais beside him. The vows he had once spoken came back in fragments—celibacy, obedience, surrender. Words he had clung to like anchors.

But now they felt like distant echoes of a man he no longer was.

He turned toward her, whispering into the hush, "I broke my vows tonight."

Alais opened her eyes, calm and unafraid. "Or you honored something deeper."

He searched her face. "I gave my life to God. Every piece of it. And yet, I feel closer to Him here than I ever did behind monastery walls."

She nodded. "Then maybe you haven't broken your vows, Cassien. Maybe you've rewritten them—with your soul, not someone else's scripture."

Tears stung at the corners of his eyes, not from regret, but from release. He took a breath, and with it, let go of the man he had once been.

"I choose truth," he said. "Wherever it leads. Even if it leads me away from everything I thought sacred."

Alais touched his cheek. "Then you're already on holy ground.

After several days in the quiet shelter of the hermitage, food and kindling grew scarce. Alais and Cassien stood at the edge of the clearing one morning, the silence between them thoughtful rather than tense.

"It's time," Alais said.

Cassien nodded. "We've rested. But we cannot stay hidden forever."

They descended the mountain trail cautiously, following a different path eastward. The air grew warmer, and the brush thickened with signs of wild boar and fox. Before long, they reached a broad valley where the outline of a village wavered in the distance.

As they entered, weary from the climb, they were met with curious stares and guarded greetings. The village elder, a stooped woman with braided gray hair and sharp eyes, offered them bread and a place to sit.

"We have little," she said, "but news travels faster than comfort. You've come from the west?"

Cassien nodded. "From Carcassonne. We knew trouble might follow."

Another villager approached—a younger man with dust-streaked boots and a travel-worn face. He carried a satchel and a grim expression.

"I was there," he said. "I left Carcassonne the day after they came."

Cassien stood, every muscle tense. "What happened?"

"The Inquisition arrived without warning," the man said. "Took six people. Accused them of harboring heresy. One of them… a woman named Clara. She stood up to them. Demanded justice. They bound her anyway."

Cassien's breath caught. "Clara… my sister."

The man lowered his voice. "I'm sorry. I didn't know her, but I remember her name. She fought for others, even then."

Alais touched Cassien's arm. "Then we follow."

The elder nodded. "They took the prisoners south toward a fortress of the Church. But not all roads are closed. Not yet. You'll find help if you know where to ask."

They rose early the next morning, the village still shrouded in mist and the hush of first light. Alais and Cassien stood at the edge of the square, speaking in hushed tones with the village elder, who offered them a small sack of dried lentils, two coarse loaves, and a flask of cool spring water. In return, Cassien left behind a patched cloak and several pages of vellum—carefully chosen—offering wisdom he felt the villagers could preserve.

"I don't want to endanger the scrolls," Cassien said. "Let some remain where they are welcome."

The elder accepted the bundle with reverence. "They'll be read with care," she promised. "And hidden well if need arises."

With that, they made their way southward, the hills rising before them like sleeping beasts. The morning chill clung to their cloaks, but their hearts were aflame with purpose. The silence between them was not void, but thoughtful.

It was Cassien who finally broke it. "We need to be honest with ourselves. If Clara was taken, then we are walking into the fire."

Alais didn't turn. "Yes. And yet, what choice is there?"

"We could hide again. Wait for the fire to pass. But it won't, will it?"

"No," Alais said. "Because we carry embers. And the Church fears those most."

They walked for a while more before Cassien asked, "Do we even know what we hope to accomplish?"

Alais was quiet, then answered, "To witness. To protect what must endure. And to free her, if we can."

Cassien nodded. "And if we can't?"

"Then we still walked the path. Not away from fear, but toward truth."

They paused at a bend in the road where the land opened wide before them—rolling hills and scattered trees, the faint outline of a fortress far to the south.

Cassien exhaled. "Then let's not wait for courage. Let's go while we still believe in what we carry."

And together, they stepped forward into the gathering light, the bundle of memory left safely behind, their burden now made of resolve, not parchment.

By late afternoon, as the sun dipped toward the ridge line, they came upon a small shrine nestled beside a weathered path. There, seated on a low stone wall, was a figure wrapped in a gray wool cloak, sharpening a curved blade with slow, steady strokes.

The figure looked up. A woman—older than Alais, perhaps near fifty, with eyes like river-stone and a voice made rough from wind and time.

"You're heading toward the fortress," she said, not as a question.

Cassien hesitated, then nodded. "You know it?"

"Too well," she replied. "I was inside its walls. Years ago, before they made their trials public. I lived to walk out. Many didn't."

Alais stepped closer. "Do you know where they would keep the prisoners?"

The woman nodded. "The lower vaults. Damp, dark, and cut into the hillside. They keep the condemned separate from the accused. And the accused from each other. It's harder to spread hope when you're alone."

Cassien's jaw tightened. "How do we reach them?"

"Not through the main gates," she said. "But there's a side path the guards use at shift change. It leads toward the kitchens and stables. Less watched. If you want to see someone inside, that's your way. But be warned—it's one thing to walk toward truth. It's another to survive what waits in its shadows."

Alais looked at her closely. "Why tell us this?"

"Because I saw a woman taken from Carcassonne not long ago. Proud. Fierce. Spoke with the voice of a lioness. She reminded me of someone I once was. If she is yours, you'll need more than prayers to find her."

By late afternoon, the winding path curved around a rocky outcrop, and there, in the distance, the fortress appeared—perched like a sentry upon a rise of earth. Thick outer walls rose from the slope in uneven symmetry, their age marked by creeping ivy and the weathered scars of past sieges. A central tower loomed above the compound, square and austere, its bell silent for now, though the metal cross at its peak glinted in the falling light.

Cassien paused at the crest of the trail, eyes narrowed.

That night, they found shelter in the hollow of an abandoned stone hut nestled into a hillside. It offered little more than a roof, a hearth of old ash, and a door that hung loose on its hinges. Still, it was enough.

Cassien gathered dry branches while Alais coaxed a modest flame from a flint stone. They sat close together, sharing the warmth, their bodies still and alert beneath their cloaks.

"It could be our last night," Cassien said softly, not looking at her.

Alais didn't flinch. "Yes. But we've already died a hundred quiet deaths to reach this one. What matters is how we live it."

He turned to her then, seeing not just the resolve in her eyes but the sorrow she carried alongside it. "If we don't make it back…"

"We've already arrived," she interrupted gently. "You're not the man who entered the abbey. I'm not the girl who fled her home. If we walk into the fire, we do it awake. Together."

Silence fell again, filled only by the crackling of the fire and the whisper of wind through stone. Cassien reached for her hand.

"I'm not afraid," he said.

"I know," she replied, squeezing his fingers.

And with that, they rested side by side on a bed of cloaks and dry leaves, the warmth between them more than body heat. It was a vow—not of survival, but of shared truth, no matter the end.

Well before the morning came, still dark and quiet, Cassien rose first. He moved carefully, not to disturb her, then stood at the edge of the crumbling doorway, watching the sky shift from violet to amber.

Alais stirred. "You're already dressed."

Cassien turned, his face unreadable. "I've made a decision."

She sat up, sensing the change. "What decision?"

"I'm going in alone. Through the front gate. As a Benedictine."

Alais's eyes widened. "You'd risk walking straight into their hands? You should not go alone."

"I must," he replied. "If I do not go now, I may never have the chance again. I once belonged to that world. My robes, my bearing —they may still open doors. At least long enough to get inside and see where she is."

"You think they'll believe you're still loyal?"

"I don't know. But I know I can't take you with me. If something happens—if I don't come out—you must carry on."

She stood slowly, anger rising beneath the calm. "You don't get to decide that for me."

Cassien stepped closer. "This isn't about control. It's about strategy. They won't question a monk alone. But a pair—especially with someone like you—will raise every alarm."

She looked away, blinking fast. "You speak as if I'm a burden."

"No. I speak as someone who loves you and wants you to live."

The words hung between them, sharp as flint.

Alais rose and came to him, her small hands clutching his sleeves. "Do not let their chains close on you as well, Cassien. She would not want you lost to them."

He managed a thin smile. "Nor would I see her lost without trying."

She hesitated, then added in a lower voice, "If you reach her, remember the way we used to speak when others listened."

The corner of his mouth lifted — the briefest ghost of a shared memory. "I remember."

Finally, Alais nodded. "Then go, Brother Cassien. But know this: you may still wear their robes, but you no longer speak their language. Not truly."

"My heart is my source of truth now, Alais, but in my head, I can still play the role of devoted and faithful monk. For Clara's sake, I must try."

"We rely on truth, Cassien. You will go in with a lie," Alais said, her voice low, steady—but behind it was the tremor of something deeper. She moved closer, her eyes fierce with clarity. "You say it's strategy. That it's love, and maybe it is. But if you forget who you are in there, even for a moment, they will smell it. Truth clings to the skin like smoke. So if you walk in cloaked in their robes, then you must carry *our* fire beneath them. Promise me that. Promise me you will not let their silence replace your voice."

"There is no other way. If I fail and I am arrested, I will not deny the truth that now lives within me. I will not. My greatest joy, Alais, is to return to you and remain with you as long as you will have me, but I must do this first."

Alais stepped closer, searching his face. For a long moment, she said nothing, then gently touched his chest, where his heart beat beneath the wool. "Then be with me before you leave, Cassien," she whispered. "If this day should take you from me, let me hold and remember what we carry. Not as fear, but as love."

He hesitated, not from doubt but reverence, as if her words had stilled time. Then he took her hand, kissed her palm, and nodded.

They lay down once more beneath the fading stars, not as fugitives or pilgrims, not as priest and heretic, but as man and woman, bound by spirit and flesh. Their lovemaking was not hurried, nor fevered, but tender, deliberate—an act of remembrance and becoming. In each other's arms, they reclaimed their wholeness. And in the stillness afterward, with her head upon his chest, there was no need for words.

Only the breath between them. The sacred pulse of two lives intertwining, as one.

When Cassien finally departed, cloaked in his monastic garb, the road swallowed him in mist and silence. Alais stood for a long time at the edge of the hut's doorway, arms folded against her chest, watching until even the shape of him had dissolved into the gray.

She did not cry. Not yet. Her tears belonged to another time—either his return or the certainty that he never would. For now, she sank to her knees before the cold hearth and closed her eyes.

She breathed in deeply, centering herself in the Field of I AM, the boundless presence that had carried her this far. She felt him there still—not only Cassien the man, but the being he was becoming. She whispered his name into the quiet, not to summon him, but to wrap him in the invisible light she knew could reach even the deepest vaults of the fortress.

Fear stirred like a restless wind in her chest, but she did not yield to it. Instead, she turned it into prayer—not to the distant God of cathedrals, but to the living flame within her. She paced the room slowly, then stood tall, placing one hand over her heart.

"I will not wait in fear," she whispered. "I will wait in power. I will not beg. I will behold."

She lit the last sliver of wax they had carried with them, and held vigil, her eyes fixed on the wavering flame.

Outside, the day brightened. But within her, the night had not ended. She was not just a woman in love. She was the field made flesh—still, radiant, and ready.

Chapter Twelve

THE SHADOW OF THE FORTRESS loomed above him as he approached the outer gate. From within the narrow arch, two mailed sentries stepped forward, their spears crossed to bar the way.

"Hold, brother," said the elder of the two, his Occitan thickened with the burr of the northern hills. "Name your purpose in this place."

Cassien lifted his head just enough for the hood to frame his features. "I am Brother Cassien of Cluny, come by writ of the bishop to speak with a prisoner in your charge."

The man frowned. "We keep no small number of prisoners, monk."

"This one lies in the lower vaults," Cassien answered evenly. "A woman accused of heresy. I am commanded to hear her confession and grant her a final hour to repent ere judgment is passed."

The second guard, a broad-shouldered fellow with a scar across his cheek, let out a short, derisive breath. "Aye… there is such a one below. She has a sharp tongue, that one. Best mind she doesn't turn it on you."

Cassien stilled but did not let his expression change. "My concern is for her soul, not her tongue."

The scarred guard studied him for a moment, then lowered his spear. "Very well. You may pass. But you will be taken first to the captain, for no soul goes below without his leave. He may have questions of his own."

The guard led Cassien across the inner yard, past a well where a pair of soldiers were hauling buckets, the water sloshing dark and cold. Men-at-arms moved among the stables, tending to destriers whose breath steamed in the chill air. Above, narrow windows watched like hooded eyes.

They came at last to a heavy door bound in iron. The escort rapped twice and pushed it open, ushering Cassien into a dim hall smelling of oiled leather and damp wool. At a trestle table sat a man in a black surcoat bearing the lord's device — a red boar rampant. His greying hair was cropped short, and his eyes, sharp as a falcon's, fixed on Cassien the moment he entered.

"This monk just arrived, Captain," the scarred guard said. "Claims the bishop sent him."

The captain rose slowly. "And you are?"

"My name is Brother Cassien of Cluny. I am expected. I carry the seal of the Holy See."

"Tell me, brother, what interest has Cluny in the business of our lower vaults?"

Cassien inclined his head. "The interests of the Church are all matters of the soul, Captain. I come by the bishop's writ to hear the confession of a woman charged with heresy, that she might have a final chance to repent before judgment is rendered."

The captain's mouth tightened. "A final chance." He walked a slow circle around Cassien, the spurs on his boots tapping against the flagstones. "And if she will not repent? Will you speak in her favor before the bishop? Or is your mind already made, as others' are?"

"My mind," Cassien said evenly, "is to hear her speak for herself, as Holy Scripture commands."

The captain stopped before him. "You speak well for a monk. And yet I think you know this woman. Men do not cross leagues of troubled country for a stranger's soul."

Cassien held his gaze. "It is not the monk who travels, Captain, but the calling. I go where I am sent."

The captain studied him for a long moment, then gave a curt nod to the guard. "Take him down. Keep the keys close, and the torches lit. There are rats below who walk on two legs."

The stairs were narrow, the stones worn into shallow curves by countless feet. Cassien's habit brushed the damp walls as they spiraled downward, the only light coming from the torch carried by the guard. The air grew rank — mildew, stagnant water, and the slow rot of despair — until the fortress above felt like another world entirely.

At the base, the stairs opened into a low-ceilinged passage, its arches dripping with condensation. Iron-bound doors studded the walls, each with a small grille that let out the stale breath of the cells within. Shadows moved behind some of the grilles, and soft, disjointed mutters followed them — words in tongues Cassien could not place, the fragments of men broken by time and stone.

The guard stopped before a heavier door, its hinges rusted, the lock thick and black with age. He raised his torch and peered at Cassien. "You'll have little light in there. See to your business quickly — the captain wants you above before the hour changes."

He fitted a key to the lock, the mechanism groaning as it turned. The door swung inward on its protesting hinges, and Cassien stepped into near darkness, a lone flickering candle stub the only illumination.

The cell was little more than a pit, the ceiling low, the floor slick with damp. The torchlight caught the curve of a chain bolted into the wall, and there, crouched at its end, was a figure in a tattered shift. She was thinner than he remembered, her hair matted, but when she turned her face toward the light, her eyes were the same — sharp, searching, alive.

For a heartbeat, neither spoke.

"Cassien?" The name was little more than a rasp, yet it struck him harder than any blade.

"It is I," he said, keeping his voice low.

"You should not have come." Her tone carried no reproach, only warning.

"I could do no other," he murmured. Then, more clearly — for the guard's benefit — "I am sent to hear your confession."

He hesitated, then spoke with deliberate slowness, as if reciting the formula of the sacrament: "Then tell me of the first wrong that brought you here, and the last kindness you remember."

Her eyes flickered — she understood. "The first wrong was at the table of a friend," she said softly, "when I was given bread that was not mine to take." A pause. "The last kindness was from one who risked all to bring me water."

Cassien inclined his head, the meaning clear between them — she had been betrayed by someone close, but there was an ally nearby.

Before the guard stepped back into the passage behind, taking the light with him, his voice cut through. "Make your confession, woman, and be done with it. This monk has far to travel."

Cassien knelt before her, heart breaking, but resolve unabated.

"Why are you here?" she whispered.

"To bring you out," he answered. "If I can."

Her gaze softened. "Then you must be very brave… or very foolish."

"Both," he said, almost smiling.

"They've questioned me already," she whispered. "But they've not yet tortured me. I think they're waiting for the tribunal."

Cassien lowered his voice, leaning in. "Clara, you must know… the man they think I am is not who I've become. I am wearing this robe because it opens doors, not because I still believe everything it represents.”

She blinked, watching him.

“I’ve seen things, learned things. From those I once judged. I’m pretending—for now—because it gives me a chance to reach you. But the Church I served blindly… it is no longer my Church.”

She studied him with a look that was part disbelief, part wonder. “Then there may still be hope.”

Cassien nodded solemnly. “What do you want me to do?”

Clara looked at him—really looked—and something in her expression softened. “You can’t save me by force. Not here. But you can bear witness. You can tell others. And if there is a way to change their minds, it will come through persuasion—not resistance.”

“And if they will not be moved?”

“Then let me go with dignity. I would rather die true than live in silence.”

Cassien’s throat tightened. “I cannot lose you again.”

“You never lost me. You only forgot where to look.”

They sat in silence for a long moment. The candle flashed, then the flame steadied and remained still.

She reached over and touched his hand gently. "You must walk in both worlds now, Cassien. But do not let the old one claim your heart."

Cassien closed his eyes.

"I'll find a way," he whispered.

Clara nodded once. "Then hurry. They mean to make an example of me."

Their eyes met—brother to sister, past to present.

And then he rose and was gone.

Outside the fortress, not far from where she and Cassien had parted, Alais waited.

The sun had risen fully, casting long shadows behind the outcroppings of stone where she kept watch. Wrapped in her cloak, she sat upon a ledge that overlooked the narrow path leading to the fortress. Her hands, folded in her lap, were still. Her eyes, however, flickered constantly—searching for movement, for signs.

A thrush called from a nearby bush. Then, the sound of hooves.

She stood.

Three riders approached along the lower trail, moving with purpose. Their cloaks bore the color of the Church, and one wore a sword at his side.

Alais withdrew quickly behind a curtain of brush, heart pounding. She reached instinctively for the small pouch hidden beneath her sash—dried herbs, a tiny blade, a scrap of parchment she could burn if needed. Nothing that would betray her.

The riders slowed as they neared the fork in the trail, one of them gesturing toward the narrow ridge that led higher. Their voices were too far for her to hear, but one pointed in her direction.

Alais crouched low, weighing her options. If she ran now, she would be seen. If she stayed, she might be discovered.

She closed her eyes and listened.

Moments passed.

Then the horses turned away—taking the lower road that curved eastward, toward the river. Her breath returned.

She remained still a moment longer, then stood slowly, watching them go.

Cassien was still within the fortress. And danger was all around them.

She could not wait here forever.

She turned back toward the grove where they had shared the night, thinking quickly. If something went wrong, she would need to act. But for now, she would wait, not in stillness, but in readiness.

The Field of I AM pulsed faintly within her—a quiet knowing.

She was not alone.

The dungeon door slammed shut behind Cassien with a hollow finality. The corridor's air was cold and sharp, smelling of oil lamps
and damp stone. He had barely drawn a breath before a tall, broad-
shouldered man stepped from the shadows.

"Brother Cassien," the man said, his stride brisk. "I'm Adelric. No
time for questions — you must come with me."

Cassien halted. "Who sent you?"

Adelric's eyes were unwavering. "Friends. And if you want Clara's
words to matter, you'll follow me now. The tribunal is about to begin — they will hear your voice only if you sit with the clergy.

"I was not summoned."

"I have arranged it," Adelric replied, stepping closer. "The hall is
filling. Verdicts will come whether you speak or not — and silence
will serve your enemies."

Without waiting for further protest, he turned sharply toward a
stairwell leading upward. "Walk with me, Brother. Every moment
you hesitate, others speak in your place."

Cassien cast one glance at the barred dungeon door, then fell into
step beside him.

The tribunal chamber was located deep within the fortress—a
vaulted room of stone and silence, where the walls themselves
seemed to lean inward in judgment. Iron sconces lined the perime-

ter, casting a flickering glow upon the flagstone floor. Above, a row of narrow slits admitted thin blades of daylight, illuminating the dust motes that danced like slow-moving spirits.

At the center of the chamber stood a raised dais, upon which sat three robed figures—the appointed clergy and inquisitors—each cloaked in dark wool, faces drawn and impassive. In front of them, a plain wooden table bore a heavy book of canon law, a quill, and a parchment that had not yet been inked.

To the left, a small wooden bench was placed—reserved for the accused. Behind it, two guards stood in polished breastplates, hands resting on the hilts of their swords.

The room smelled of candle wax, old parchment, and something faintly metallic—iron or blood. Its silence was not empty but heavy, as if generations of whispered condemnations still clung to the stones.

Benches lined the far wall for observers, though few had yet arrived. Among them, clergy members moved silently, some avoiding eye contact, others watching everything with sharp, assessing glances.

Cassien entered through the northern passage, his robe still bearing the simple Benedictine cross, his hood lowered. He paused just inside the threshold, letting the chamber impress itself upon him.

He had once believed a room like this to be sacred—a place where truth was revealed.

Now, he saw it differently.

It was a stage. And he would play his part carefully.

Adelric entered quietly behind him and gave a brief nod before moving to the shadows.

The tribunal would begin soon.

Cassien stepped forward and took his place among the clergy.

He was no longer merely a brother.

He was a thread in the weave of something far greater.

And today, it would tighten.

A murmur passed through the chamber as a side door opened. Two guards stepped through, followed by Clara. Her wrists were bound loosely in front of her, and her face bore the marks of sleeplessness and confinement, but she walked with quiet dignity. Her eyes, dark and steady, searched the room—until they found Cassien.

For a brief second, time stilled. She did not smile. She did not weep. But something in her posture softened. She had not been abandoned.

Cassien offered a subtle nod, his hands folded before him. He would not speak to her now—not yet—but his presence was her message: she would not stand alone.

A scribe began to read the formal charges in a monotonous drone, the Latin phrases echoing against the stone. Clara was accused of heresy, of consorting with known Cathar sympathizers, of possessing forbidden texts.

Cassien listened, heart steady. He knew the rhythm of these proceedings, the weight of words meant to crush the spirit. But Clara stood still, her chin raised. No fear. Only fire.

The lead inquisitor—an archdeacon with sunken cheeks and cold eyes—called for testimony.

Cassien waited.

His moment would come.

The first witness spoke — a gaunt man in worn wool, answering the tribunal's questions with clipped, careful phrases. The presiding officials shaped his testimony like artisans with knives, closing off every path that might lead away from their conclusion.

When the man was dismissed, the central official leaned toward his companions, conferred briefly, then straightened.

A priest stepped forward to speak—Father Jourdain, a hard-eyed man who had served in Toulouse during the first Cathar purges. He recounted with certainty how Clara had refused to recant when questioned about her involvement with the sect. He described her as polite, intelligent, and utterly convinced of her beliefs. His words, though measured, carried an undercurrent of warning.

Another voice followed—Brother Lucien, younger, uncertain. He spoke of Clara's kindness in the infirmary, her refusal to condemn even those who whispered doctrines of dualism. He paused more than once, avoiding the archdeacon's gaze.

Cassien could feel the moment tightening.

He rose from his seat and stepped forward slowly.

"May I speak?" he asked, his voice calm but resonant in the still chamber.

The archdeacon's eyes narrowed. "And who are you to speak, Brother?"

Cassien bowed. "Cassien of Fontenay, servant of Saint Benedict, student of Canon Law, most recently stationed at Cluny. I wish to illuminate."

The archdeacon looked to his fellow inquisitors. One nodded, and the other merely shrugged his shoulders. Turning his attention back to Cassien. Enhancing his authority with haughty solemnity, he said, "Then speak, Brother. The tribunal will hear you."

"Thank you, venerable Sir," Cassien said clearly, "but know that I speak not only for myself."

Cassien's eyes swept the hall, and he addressed the assembly.

"You have heard witnesses," he began, "and you will hear more. But there is one voice you have not truly listened to, though she sits before you now."

A murmur ran through the benches. Cassien turned his gaze upon Clara.

"This woman, Clara, whom you call heretic, spoke to me in the depths of your dungeon. She asked for nothing for herself, not mercy, not release, only that truth be known. She spoke of the God we claim to serve. Not in pride. Not in defiance. But in the humility of one who believes enough to speak openly."

He turned to the presiding officials, his tone hardening.

"I have walked the cloisters of Cluny. I have read the law, kept the Rule, and seen faith lived in both humility and dominion. I tell you now, faith that cannot bear honest speech is no faith at all. If her words unsettle you, it is because they call you back to the Christ you have buried beneath your judgments."

Clara remained motionless, but her stillness seemed to hold the chamber in place.

"You may condemn her, as you may condemn any here. But know this — to silence a voice that speaks from conscience is to place your own soul under judgment. And there will come a day when no council, no tribunal, no king nor pope will shield you from the truth you refuse now to hear."

When he fell silent, the hall held its breath.

A low rustle moved through the observers. One of the inquisitors looked to the archdeacon, uncertain.

Cassien bowed again and stepped back, heart pounding beneath his robe.

He had spoken. And now, the silence would answer.

A long, tense silence followed. Then, the archdeacon leaned forward slightly, his voice low and deliberate.

"Truth is not measured by love, Brother Cassien. It is weighed against doctrine."

Cassien did not respond. He knew better than to argue now.

The second inquisitor, a younger man with a narrow face and ink-stained fingers, shifted in his seat. "And yet," he said slowly, "the brother raises a point. We do not condemn for thought alone. There must be evidence of heresy—intentional, persistent defiance."

The archdeacon's eyes flicked toward him but did not interrupt.

"We shall question her directly," he continued. "Bring her forward."

The guards stepped aside. Clara was led to the bench, and the binding on her wrists was removed.

She stood tall, eyes calm.

"Do you renounce the teachings of the Cathars?" the archdeacon asked her.

She took a breath. "I renounce only what feels false in my soul."

A ripple of movement swept through the chamber.

The archdeacon's lips thinned. "You speak in riddles."

"I speak as Christ did," Clara replied. "With truth, and without fear."

Cassien felt his breath catch—not in fear, but in awe.

This moment was no longer his.

It was hers.

The inquisitor leaned back slightly, fingers steepled, as if weighing her soul in his silence. "You claim to follow Christ," he said. "Yet the Church is His body on earth. Why do you place yourself outside of it?"

Clara's voice was steady. "The body is not the truth. The soul is. I do not reject Christ—I seek Him in the quiet fire that speaks within. The Church once taught that fire, but it has grown fearful of its own flame."

The younger inquisitor raised an eyebrow. "You believe yourself wiser than the magisterium?"

"I believe that wisdom speaks to each heart," she said. "And when the heart hears it clearly, it must respond—not with obedience, but with devotion."

A faint murmur passed through the benches. Somewhere, a clerk scratched notes with a shaking hand.

The archdeacon's gaze hardened. "And do you deny the sacraments of the Church? Do you call them false?"

Clara took a breath, then shook her head. "I do not call them false. I call them incomplete. Symbols are not the flame—they are the shadows it casts."

Cassien could feel the words striking the stone walls, leaving cracks where certainty once held. She was not defiant. She was luminous.

And dangerous.

The tribunal was no longer in control. The truth had begun to speak for itself.

A hush fell over the chamber—not empty, but full. The kind of silence that trembles at the edges, too charged to last.

The elder inquisitor shifted slightly, his fingers tapping once against the arm of his chair. Not in rhythm. Not in thought. In instinct.

A clerk had stopped writing.

Even the guards, trained to stillness, glanced at each other uneasily.

The air had changed. The candles flickered with more than a breeze.

Cassien felt it too. Not triumph. Not hope. Something deeper. Something sacred.

Clara's words had not defied them.

They had revealed them.

And for a moment longer, no one dared to speak.

At last, the archdeacon straightened in his seat.

"This tribunal is not swayed by poetry," he said, though his voice lacked its earlier force. "Yet neither shall it move unjustly. The charges stand. But the sentence—"

He paused and glanced toward his fellow inquisitors. A quiet exchange passed between them, a brief, murmured council. The younger man did not look away from Clara.

Finally, the archdeacon spoke again.

"Clara of Carcassonne, you are hereby remanded to ecclesiastical custody. You shall be confined, not as a prisoner, but as one under guidance, for the salvation of your soul. If, in time, your heart returns to the fold, this tribunal will revisit its judgment."

Gasps and murmurs rose across the chamber. It was not absolution. But it was not fire.

Cassien let out a breath he had not realized he was holding.

Clara remained unmoving. Her gaze did not flinch.

But something had shifted.

Not just in the verdict—but in them all.

Chapter Thirteen

CASSIEN STEPPED THROUGH the heavy gate of the fortress just as the late mid-morning sun was casting dark shadows on the worn stones beneath his feet. The air was sharp and cool. A silence followed him like a shadow—part reverence, part exhaustion. He did not look back.

Adelric met him at the outer wall. The older man's expression was unreadable, though a quiet nod passed between them—acknowledgment of what had transpired, and of what it cost.

"You did what you could," Adelric said softly.

The weight of all that had been said, and all that remained unsaid, pressed into his chest.

"She's being moved," Adelric added after a pause. "But you've stirred something. That much is clear."

Cassien turned his gaze to the distant trees. "Thank you, Adelric. I would not have been allowed to enter without your help, but I must go now."

Adelric clasped his forearm briefly, then stepped back. "May the truth guide your steps, Brother. Even when the road darkens."

Cassien walked through the outer gate of the fortress. The path before him was open, the air laced with woodsmoke and the fading breath of winter. He descended the stone road slowly, each step heavy with the echoes of all he had seen and heard within.

Beyond the tree line, just out of view from the fortress walls, Alais waited in the place they had agreed upon. She rose from the grass as he approached, her eyes searching his face before her arms found his shoulders.

"You're safe," she breathed.

He approached her quietly.

They stood facing one another. The silence between them was thick, but not hollow. It was full—of relief, of grief, of something unspoken and growing.

"What did you see?" she asked gently.

"Too much," he said. "And not enough."

She searched his face. "And Clara?"

"She is alive. Stronger than I expected. They will move her soon."

"Did she see you?" Alais asked.

"Yes. And she spoke more clearly than I thought possible."

Alais stepped closer and hugged him. "You are exhausted, Cassien."

He nodded and allowed himself to rest in the embrace.

"Do you believe you helped her?"

"I don't know. I think… I think she helped me more."

Cassien looked away, into the thinning trees. "It was harder than I imagined, pretending to be the man I was. The words came easily. The heart did not follow."

Alais placed a hand lightly on his arm. "You are not that man anymore. And still, you did what you had to do. That is courage."

They stood a moment longer, the weight of decisions pressing in.

"We need to decide," she said at last, her voice careful. "Clara… or the scrolls. The road will not carry us to both."

Cassien's jaw tensed. "She is my sister."

"I know. And these words—" she touched the bundle they still carried, "—are sacred."

"I am torn."

"As you should be."

They were quiet again.

Then Alais lifted her eyes. "Let's walk a while. We don't need to decide here, on this frozen earth, under the shadow of stone. The forest may speak where stone does not."

Cassien met her gaze, something softening. "Then we walk."

They turned, side by side, and stepped into the misted trail beneath the canopy. Each carried a weight the other understood. And together, they began again.

As the sun warmed the land with light and heat, they followed the misted path southeast, uncertain of their next destination until, near midday, they met a traveler on the road.

He was thin and bent, with wind-tanned skin and sharp, gray eyes. He wore the patched robe of a healer and carried a satchel heavy with herbs and bandages. His name was Émeric. He had once been imprisoned in the very fortress Cassien had just departed—and had survived.

Over a fire, he shared what he knew of the fortress's design: the placement of cells, the timing of guard shifts, the secret tunnels used by desperate souls. His voice was low, steady.

"There are still others held within," he said. "And not all are as fortunate as your Clara."

Cassien listened, heart tightening. Alais touched his arm. The scrolls remained hidden, but their purpose was growing clearer.

Alais looked toward the fire, then to Cassien. "Perhaps it's time we accept the truth of why we carry these."

Cassien nodded. "We must deliver them—to someone who can protect them, or share their light."

Émeric stirred. "There are a few sanctuaries left," he said. "But you'll have to go far. Toward the coast. Toward Narbonne or beyond."

Before they could speak further, another figure approached the fire —this one younger, dirt-streaked, out of breath. A boy from a nearby village. He brought news: a Cathar community just west of Montaillou had been attacked the day past. Homes burned. People taken. Some killed.

"And a woman named Clara," he added, "was said to have spoken to them before they were dragged away."

Cassien's breath caught.

"She's been moved already?"

The boy shrugged. "That's what they said. That she's to be tried again, somewhere else. A message to others."

Silence fell.

Alais met Cassien's eyes. "We can't go back. But we can go forward. There's still time to act."

He nodded. "Then we do not rest. Not yet."

That night, as the fire dwindled and stars deepened above them, Cassien and Alais sat apart from the others, speaking in hushed tones.

"We must decide," Alais said, her voice edged with urgency. "The scrolls cannot wait forever, but neither can Clara."

Cassien looked down at his hands. "I know. If we go to her, we risk losing the scrolls to fire or betrayal. If we go to the coast, we may never see her again."

"The scrolls are sacred," Alais whispered, "but she is your blood. And she spoke truth even in chains. That counts for much."

Cassien met her gaze. "I cannot lose her again. But I fear that if we fail to deliver these, her suffering—and the suffering of so many— will be for nothing."

Alais nodded slowly. "Then we must find a way to do both. Perhaps… we find someone we trust to take the scrolls. Someone who will reach the coast in our stead."

Cassien exhaled. "It's a risk. But it may be the only path that honors both callings."

She touched his arm. "Then we make the choice together. And we do it soon."

The following morning, before the fire had fully faded, Émeric returned with a map he had drawn from memory. As Cassien studied the rough path winding southward, his finger paused near a fortified abbey south of Montaillou.

"That place," Émeric said, "is where the new tribunal is rumored to be held. If the Church has moved her, she'll likely be there."

Cassien and Alais exchanged a look that required no words.

"We don't have to decide just yet," Alais murmured as they packed their few belongings. "That abbey lies on our path; we can carry both possibilities with us—Clara and the scrolls—until the way becomes clear."

Cassien felt a weight lift slightly. "Then we walk together, as we have, and trust the path to speak."

And so they hurried, but did not rush. The road unwound gently beneath their feet, through fields glowing with the promise of an early spring, and hills that opened to distant skies. They shared the silence easily now, often walking close without speaking, hands brushing, breaths in rhythm.

They spent that night in the shelter of a thicket just off the old Roman road, sharing warmth and quiet dreams. Beneath starlight and rustling leaves, they lingered in each other's arms. Their intimacy, peaceful and unhurried, deepened—not only in desire, but in knowing. In these moments, they were neither fugitives nor messengers, but simply man and woman, hearts exposed beneath a fragile peace.

For now, the world allowed it. And they let themselves be held by that grace.

By late afternoon the next day, the winding path curved around a rocky outcrop, and there, in the distance, the abbey appeared—perched like a sentinel upon a rise of earth, its walls steeped in centuries of stone and silence.

The abbey south of Montaillou stood half-shrouded in mist, its silhouette framed by the curling smoke of hearths within. Thick outer walls rose from the slope encircling the ancient edifice it protected. The high tower of the Abbey overlooked the inner courtyard just beyond the gates, its cross clearly visible over the surrounding stone walls.

Cassien paused at the crest of the trail, eyes narrowed.

"It's more fortress than abbey," he said.

Alais stepped beside him, arms folded across her chest. "And yet within those walls, they speak of God."

He made no reply. The juxtaposition of sacred purpose and martial form echoed the questions within him.

A narrow road veered toward the entrance, flanked by cypress trees that swayed in the rising wind. A pair of riders emerged from the main gate and turned northward, their figures shrinking as they disappeared into the hills.

"We'll need to approach carefully," Alais said.

Cassien nodded. "There are too many variables. Too many watching eyes."

They withdrew into the cover of a nearby grove, sheltered among pine and shadow. From there, they could observe the rhythms of the abbey—its comings and goings, its guards and couriers, the changes in light and routine. It would require patience and stillness.

Cassien leaned his back against the bark of an old tree. "We're close now. Whatever happens, this is the last bend before the fire."

Alais didn't answer right away. Her gaze remained fixed on the high stone walls. "Then let's not waste our steps. When we go, we go with full hearts."

Cassien exhaled and turned his gaze back to the abbey. "I've been thinking," he said slowly. "You should go on without me."

Alais turned sharply toward him. "What do you mean?"

"Take the scrolls to the Sanctuary," he said. "To Narbonne or wherever Émeric believes they'll be safe. Let me go after Clara alone."

"No."

"Alais, listen—"

"No," she repeated. "We've come too far together to split the path now."

"But we risk everything if we don't. You know this. If the scrolls fall into the wrong hands…"

She clenched her jaw. "And if you do not return? What then?"

Cassien hesitated, then stepped closer. "Then you will carry forward the truth. And I will have done what I could—for Clara, and for the light we both believe in."

She stared at him, pain flickering across her features. "I won't agree to it yet. Not tonight."

He nodded gently. "Think on it. We'll talk again in the morning."

They sat beneath the trees until the sky turned dark, the abbey still visible in the fading light—solid, silent, waiting.

As the chill crept in, they drew closer, warmth rising from their shared silence. Alais reached for his hand, fingers curling around his with quiet resolve. No more words passed between them for a while—none were needed.

Later, by the dim orange flicker of their fire, their closeness became breath. Then heartbeat. Then touch.

Cassien brushed a strand of hair from her cheek, the backs of his fingers lingering against her skin. She turned into his touch, eyes soft with something between invitation and inevitability. When she kissed him, it was not tentative—it was knowing.

Clothes yielded slowly, reverently, to fingers that had once bound themselves to vows now released. The night around them hushed, listening. They moved as if they had always belonged to each other, not with urgency but with aching gratitude—for one more night, one more breath, one more chance to remember this life by its deepest tenderness.

Their bodies folded into one another beneath the stars, the forest holding its breath around them. Nothing of fear remained in their shared space—only the thrum of life, love, and the aching miracle of this fleeting world.

When dawn touched the edges of the canopy with silver, Cassien was already awake. He sat a few paces from the fire, his cloak draped around his shoulders, face lined with quiet resolve.

Alais stirred and rose, brushing sleep from her eyes. "You've made your decision, haven't you?"

He turned to her. "I have. I must go to the abbey alone."

She stepped closer, her arms folded. "And you still think I should carry the scrolls to the Sanctuary?"

He nodded. "They must reach safety, Alais. If I succeed, I will find you. If I fail, then the scrolls are safe. That's all that matters now."

She watched him for a long moment. "You always speak as if you're ready to vanish."

"No," he said. "Only ready to risk everything."

Tears rimmed her eyes, but she didn't let them fall. "Then let's make a place in our hearts where we already meet again."

Cassien stepped forward and embraced her, their foreheads resting together. "Whatever happens," he whispered, "this is not an end."

She nodded slowly. "Then go with all the love I carry. And take none of it lightly."

He kissed her once, gently, then turned toward the path.

Alais stood still long after he had disappeared into the trees. Only when the wind shifted did she reach for the bundle of scrolls, securing it within the folds of her satchel. She exhaled deeply, steadying herself against the ache in her chest.

She did not know the exact path to the Sanctuary—only that it lay farther south, nestled somewhere along the old trade routes where Cathar sympathizers still whispered and harbored the remnants of their faith. Émeric had spoken of it, and others had given clues along their journey, but its true location remained elusive by design.

Her feet moved instinctively, following the southern slope of the hill, her eyes scanning for signs—a symbol etched into stone, a trail marked with the Cathar cross, anything that might guide her. With every step, she felt the weight of solitude return, pressing on her like a second skin.

It was not the loneliness of absence but of parting—a sacred kind of sorrow.

She thought of Cassien constantly—not with longing or regret, but with a fierce kind of love that refused to wane. Their night together burned behind her eyes, a memory already sacred. She held it close, letting it warm her from within.

"I am not alone," she whispered to the trees. "He walks with me still."

And so she went on, into a world still turning, carrying the wordless prayer that they might meet again where the road and grace entwine.

Chapter Fourteen

CASSIEN APPROACHED THE ABBEY from the eastern ridge, the trees thinning as he descended toward the outer wall. The air was acrid with the scent of smoke. At first, he thought it drifted from a chimney—but then he saw it: black coils rising from the inner courtyard, sharp and fast.

His breath caught. He broke into a run.

The main gate was ajar, no guards in sight. He slipped through the opening, staying low as he crossed the threshold. Shouts echoed between stone walls—some sharp with authority, others ragged with grief. The scent of burning wood thickened.

Then he saw them.

Seven women and four men, bound to upright stakes arranged in a semicircle. Piles of wood stacked high at their feet. Hooded monks moved among them, torches in hand. One of the fires was already lit.

Cassien's eyes scanned the prisoners, heart pounding.

Clara.

She stood at the far end, her face calm, as if she were already elsewhere. Her hair was windblown, her cloak torn, but her gaze was steady—fixed not on the monks or the crowd but toward the sky.

"No!" Cassien surged forward but stopped short as a line of guards blocked the way, swords unsheathed.

The second torch fell.

Flames roared to life beneath the feet of the second man.

Cassien sank to his knees, hidden again in shadow, breath shuddering as his fists clenched. He was too late.

Cassien stood slowly, uncaring now who saw him, searching desperately for any way to stop it.

A guard noticed him and nudged his companion, each drawing their swords halfway.

But then Clara turned.

Her eyes, impossibly, found his through the chaos and smoke. For a moment, everything else faded—the guards, the flames, the cries of the dying. Her gaze locked onto his as if they'd been calling to each other across years rather than meters.

Recognition sparked, and then something deeper: peace.

Tears streamed down his face, his mouth open but voiceless. He pressed his palm to his chest—over his heart—once, firmly.

Clara's lips moved. He couldn't hear her, but he understood.

"Brother."

A single tear traced down her cheek. And then, with the calm of a soul already set free, she closed her eyes and lifted her chin.

The flames reached her feet.

Cassien's scream never left his throat.

His fists trembled at his sides, nails digging into his palms. Every fiber of his being demanded he charge forward, to tear down the posts, to carry her out of the fire. But the wall of armed guards remained, their faces like stone, their swords glinting red in the growing inferno.

Inside him, a storm raged. Guilt and helplessness roared louder than the fire. The vows he had once taken, the doctrine he had once upheld—they meant nothing in this moment of raw devastation. He had traded the safety of silence for the pain of truth, and now he watched as that truth was consumed before his eyes.

He wanted to look away. He begged himself to close his eyes. But he could not. Clara had seen him. Had known he was there. To turn from her now would be to abandon her again.

So he watched.

Smoke curled around his face. The acrid sting of burning flesh filled his lungs. He tasted ash and sorrow and a thousand unshed tears.

In that moment, something in him burned too—not his faith, not his hope, but the last remnants of fear. What remained was a vow, forged in grief and flame: he would not run. Not from this. Not from the world as it was.

He would carry her name, her courage, and her light.

Into whatever darkness remained.

The crowd began to thin, their murmurs and shifting feet a dull backdrop to the crackle of fire. Smoke wreathed the courtyard, and still, Cassien stood rooted, breath shallow, vision blurred.

But one figure remained.

A priest, robed in black, his head bowed not in ritual, but in something like mourning. He had not turned away. He stood with hands clasped, lips moving in prayer—or perhaps in silence.

Cassien wiped the soot from his eyes and stepped forward.

The priest looked up as he approached, his face worn with years and sorrow. Their eyes met, and for a long moment neither spoke.

"You stayed," Cassien said quietly.

The priest nodded. "I have seen many burn. I have turned away before. But not today."

Cassien studied him. "Why this one?"

The priest's eyes darkened. "Because she sang as the flames rose. Not with her voice, but with her stillness. I could not leave such a soul alone."

They stood side by side, the embers casting ghostly light across their faces.

"I thought there was to be a tribunal here today," Cassien said softly.

"No. She was too strong to let live, but too holy to be burned at the fortress." He turned and looked at him. "I noticed you in the crowd. Did you know her?"

"I did."

"Who are you?"

"Brother Cassien. Clara was my sister." Cassien studied him, saw his pain, and asked, "Were you one of them once?"

"Perhaps," the priest said, looking down, then added, "Or perhaps I've only now remembered that I was."

Cassien nodded slowly. "Then you understand."

The priest looked at him closely. "And you—Brother. Do you carry her fire?"

"Yes," Cassien said. "And I will not let it die."

The priest reached beneath his robe and handed him a small object wrapped in cloth. "This was dropped before the bindings. I think it was hers."

Cassien unwrapped it—a wooden pendant, shaped like a lily.

He clutched it tightly and met the priest's eyes. "Thank you. What is your name?"

The priest inclined his head. "Bernard. Go now. The world waits for men who do not forget."

Cassien nodded, turned toward the open gate, the flames left behind him.

He did not look back.

Cassien moved swiftly through the wooded foothills, retracing the path he and Alais had walked together only a day before. The sky was low and brooding, as if mourning alongside him. He carried no satchel, no bundle, only Clara's pendant clenched tightly in his hand, its edges digging into his palm like an anchor to the moment he had vowed never to forget.

His boots found familiar tracks in the damp earth—hers—and he followed them with unerring focus. He called her name once, then again, louder, until at last he crested a ridge and saw her, moving along the narrow trail below, the scrolls secured across her back.

"Alais!" he shouted, his voice raw.

She turned quickly, eyes widening as she recognized him. Relief flooded her face, chased by immediate concern as she saw the pallor in his skin, the shadows under his eyes.

He stumbled down the slope, reaching her in a rush of breath and silence. She caught him in her arms before he could speak, steadying him as his legs faltered.

"What happened?" she whispered. "What did you see?"

He pressed his forehead to hers, unable to speak for a moment. Then, quietly, he said, "I was too late."

Alais closed her eyes, her grip tightening around him. "Clara?"

He nodded.

"I saw her, and she saw me. She didn't flinch, Alais. Not once. She met death with peace."

Tears came freely now, and Alais let them. She held him while he wept—not just for his sister, but for all that had been lost, and all that must still be carried.

When his voice returned, it was quieter. "Clara gave me her strength, Alais. And now I give it to you. To all of us."

They stood in silence for a long time, the wind brushing through the trees like a soft benediction.

Finally, she reached up and touched the pendant still clutched in his hand.

"What is it?" she asked.

"A lily," he replied. "She must have worn it beneath her robe. A symbol of innocence, of rebirth. It's all I have left of her."

"No," Alais said, her voice strong. "You have more. You have her fire. And I have you."

Cassien looked into her eyes, the grief in his heart slowly giving way to clarity.

"We walk forward, then," he said. "Together."

"Always," she replied.

And they did. Southward, through the thinning trees, toward a horizon not yet written.

They descended into the valley as the sun began to dip toward the western ridge, casting long amber shadows across the hills. The air grew dense with an unfamiliar weight, the scent of woodsmoke thickening with each step. Then came another smell—charred fabric, scorched earth, and something fouler still.

Alais was the first to halt. "Cassien—look."

Across a low rise, the village lay in ruin. Smoke curled from the skeletal remains of cottages and barns. The blackened beams of once-sturdy homes jutted upward like broken ribs. Livestock pens had been shattered; the animals either fled or burned. The well in the village center steamed with the remnants of a hastily doused blaze.

They advanced slowly, stepping over ash and splintered wood. A tattered shawl hung from a branch. A child's doll, singed and half-buried, stared upward from the mud.

Then came a cry.

Soft. Weak. Human.

Cassien turned sharply. "That came from behind the granary."

They rushed forward and found a half-collapsed shed where several villagers huddled—faces streaked with ash, clothes torn, eyes hollow. A middle-aged woman stood protectively in front of them, holding a stick like a blade.

When she saw Alais and Cassien, her shoulders sagged with relief.

"We thought they might return," she said. "The soldiers."

"We're not soldiers," Cassien said. "We're sorry we didn't arrive sooner."

An elder man coughed from the back of the shed. "They came at dusk. Accused us of harboring heretics. We tried to tell them—we are only farmers."

Alais stepped forward. "Did someone pass through here? A Cathar messenger, perhaps?"

The woman hesitated. "Two nights ago. A young man, asking after a trail south. We gave him bread and warned him not to linger."

Cassien nodded. "He may have led them here without knowing."

"They killed three men," said a teenage girl, voice trembling. "They dragged Maître Julien to the chapel and set it ablaze with him inside."

"And the others?" Alais asked gently.

The woman's mouth trembled. "Taken. Women mostly. Young ones."

A small boy peeked out from behind her skirt, clutching a strip of singed linen. His face was smudged with soot, but his eyes were bright and watchful.

Cassien crouched beside him. "What's your name?"

The boy whispered, "Luc."

"Is this your mama?"

Luc shook his head. "They took her."

Cassien looked up at Alais.

She crouched beside the boy. "Luc, would you like to come with us? We're going south. Somewhere safer."

He nodded without hesitation and reached for her hand.

Cassien turned to the woman. "We'll take him, if that's alright."

She hesitated, then placed a hand on Luc's head. "He'll be safer with you."

As they prepared to leave, the elder man caught Cassien's sleeve. "You carry something. A weight. Be careful where you walk with it."

"I know," Cassien said. "And thank you."

They left the village behind, Luc nestled between them, holding tightly to Alais's hand. As the sky deepened toward indigo and the wind cooled, the firelight behind them faded, but the pain of it did not.

Only the road remained—and whatever they might yet redeem along it. As twilight deepened into indigo, their footsteps softened, the sound of water accompanying them like breath.

Their path led them steadily southward, through parched hills and narrow glens, their pace quickened by the growing awareness of danger. The presence of soldiers had increased in recent days—not the formal patrols of royal edicts, but armed bands roving with impunity, hunting for heretics like game. Their banners bore no consistent insignia, yet all carried the same zeal in their eyes.

Cassien, Alais, and the boy Luc stayed clear of roads and open trails. They slept hidden in olive groves and abandoned shepherd huts, moving mostly by dawn or twilight. The cold of the night made travel punishing, but they endured it, driven by something more than survival: the conviction that the scrolls must reach the Sanctuary, and that truth must be preserved even as the world sought to silence it.

One early morning, as they crested a shale ridge overlooking a winding dirt road below, Alais crouched suddenly and raised her hand. In the distance, the thud of hooves and the jangle of armor reached their ears. A column of mounted soldiers moved like a dark snake through the valley, their helmets glinting dully in the sun.

Cassien pulled Luc behind a cluster of wind-warped shrubs. "Too many to count."

"They search everything now," Alais whispered. "Every village, every shrine."

They waited in tense silence until the last rider passed, then doubled back into the hills. As they made their descent, they met an old man with skin like parchment and a wide-brimmed hat, leading a mule laden with clay jars. He eyed them carefully but did not flinch.

"You're not from here," he said. "And yet, you look like those they hunt."

Cassien answered cautiously, "We mean no harm. We seek only to pass safely."

The old man nodded, then gestured with his chin. "Soldiers move east and west. You'll not make it far if you stay high. But there's a stream path, hidden, runs below the limestone cliffs. It's overgrown but passable."

Alais stepped forward. "Will it take us to the coast?"

He nodded again. "Eventually. Or to the Sanctuary, if you know the signs."

Cassien studied him closely. "You know of it?"

"I know enough to say no more," the man said, then added, "But I'll lead you to the stream's mouth, if you'll help me carry these jars."

They agreed, and for the next hour, they helped him guide the mule and its burdens along a narrow cut in the hillside, half-hidden by brush. At the edge of a thicket, he stopped and pointed to a stand of reeds and brambles.

"There," he said. "It looks like nothing. But follow the water, and the signs will come."

Cassien offered him a hand. "You've helped more than you know."

The old man smiled faintly. "It's what we do, those of us who still remember."

With that, they slipped into the streambed, where cool water trickled over smooth stone and light filtered in narrow beams. The world above faded behind them, and the hush of the hidden path became their shield.

Now, they walked in shadow.

And carried the light with them.

As twilight deepened into indigo, their footsteps softened, the sound of water accompanying them like breath. Luc broke the silence first.

"My mother used to say the Silence was a place you carried with you," he said softly. "Not something far away in the mountains."

Alais looked at him. "She taught you well."

Luc nodded. "She used to light a candle at night and tell me that we are not meant to worship God with fear, but with stillness. She said that's how we listen. Not with ears, but with something inside."

Cassien felt the words settle in him like ash on stone. "She was a believer, then?"

Luc hesitated. "She was careful. But yes. She told me that love is stronger than law, and that truth is not always what men in robes say it is."

Alais reached out and gently touched his shoulder. "You remember her well."

"I try," Luc whispered. "Sometimes I hear her voice when I wake. For a moment, I think she's just outside the door. But it's only the wind."

They walked on in silence for a while, the boy's words lingering like incense in their wake. Cassien glanced toward Alais, who held Luc's hand as they moved. There was strength in her gentleness, and grief beneath it.

He looked away, the weight of the scrolls on his back, and something heavier still, pressing quietly on his heart.

By the following morning, the streambed had grown narrower and choked with brush. Their feet ached, and Luc's hunger had made him listless.

They climbed from the ravine just past dawn and followed the scent of smoke and thyme on the breeze to a low stone dwelling tucked beneath a slope. Chickens scattered as they approached, and a woman appeared at the doorway, broom in hand.

She did not seem surprised to see them.

"Travelers," she said simply.

Cassien inclined his head. "We ask shelter. Only for a day."

She studied them. "Are you dangerous?"

"We carry nothing but words," Alais answered.

The woman nodded once and stepped aside. "Then come inside."

Within, they found warmth, a stew pot bubbling with lentils, and a matting of herbs over the door. The woman's children peered at them with wide eyes. She fed them without questions and gave them blankets to rest in the shaded corner of the room.

That evening, after the children had eaten and curled near the hearth, the woman sat with Alais and Cassien while Luc gently brushed one of the goats tethered near the wall.

"He's a quiet boy," the woman said, her eyes softening. "Carries too much for one so small."

Alais nodded. "He's lost more than most will ever understand."

"Is he yours?"

Cassien answered, "No. We came upon him in the mountains. The soldiers had killed and taken many, but he escaped."

"I see the way he watches the little ones," the woman added. "And they watch him back. If you have to keep going… there is room here. If he wished to stay."

Cassien looked toward Luc, who sat cross-legged now, one of the toddlers in his lap. The boy whispered something to the child, who giggled in return.

"I think he might feel at home," Cassien murmured.

They spoke with Luc later, gently, offering the choice. He was quiet for a long time before answering.

"If it's safe here… maybe I could stay. Just for a while. And remember my mother's voice."

Alais held his hand. "This place will hold you kindly."

That night, beneath a moonless sky, they lay close, bellies full and limbs heavy. They spoke little, except in glances and gestures. Overcome with his grief for Clara still, Alais held Cassien close. She understood both grief and comfort, allowing the one and offering the other.

Chapter Fifteen

THEY LEFT THE SHELTER behind at first light, bidding quiet farewells. Luc stood at the doorway, the toddler clinging to his leg, the woman watching from the shadows. Alais kissed the boy's forehead, and Cassien held him briefly, whispering something only Luc could hear. Then they were gone, walking southward beneath a sky already tinged with heat.

The stream that had protected them grew shallow and then vanished altogether, swallowed by dry brush and lowland sedges. The trees thinned. The air grew sharp with salt.

By midday, they crested a low ridge, and the coastal plain opened before them—wide, exposed, dotted with scrub and the suggestion of fields long abandoned. In the far distance, faint as memory, was a shimmer that might have been the sea.

"We'll have no cover here," Cassien said.

"We don't need to be invisible," Alais replied, though her voice held uncertainty. "Just ordinary."

They followed a path worn more by animals than men, and by late afternoon came upon a crumbling stone waystation—half shelter, half ruin. A man stood outside, stirring something over a fire. He looked up as they approached.

"You look hungry," he called out, voice even, friendly. "And lost."

Cassien and Alais slowed. The man had a weathered face, sun-darkened, and no visible weapon. His clothes were travel-stained, his beard streaked with gray.

"We are travelers," Cassien said carefully. "Southbound."

"Then you're not far off the pilgrim's trail," the man said. "I'm Bertran. I can show you a safer way. Soldiers still ride these roads."

"Why would you help us?" Alais asked.

Bertran smiled, not unkindly. "Because someone once helped me."

He tossed another stick into the fire. "Eat with me, if you like. You can judge my honesty then."

Cassien looked to Alais. She nodded, slow but firm.

They stepped into the firelight.

Bertran ladled stew from the iron pot into chipped wooden bowls and handed one to each of them. The scent of lentils and wild garlic rose in the dusk, rich and earthy. They sat on overturned crates, the fire casting flickering shadows across their faces.

"Foraged most of it myself," Bertran said, blowing on his spoon. "These lands don't yield much these days, but you'd be surprised what grows between the stones."

Alais nodded, but ate slowly, watching him.

Bertran's eyes drifted to the bundle slung across Cassien's back. "That's a heavy pack for such a small road. You carry trade goods?"

"Only what we need," Cassien replied evenly.

Bertran chuckled. "Ah, always the careful ones, the quiet travelers. My father was like that. Said words were like gold—best spent rarely and wisely."

He took a long sip from a flask at his belt and passed it to Cassien. "I travel often. East, mostly. The wars are worse there, but sometimes they spare the messengers."

Cassien accepted the flask but didn't drink. "You deliver messages?"

"Not anymore," Bertran said with a shrug. "Too many tongues cut these days. But I hear things. And I know people who still listen."

Alais looked up, sharp. "What kind of people?"

Bertran smiled faintly. "The kind who ask questions when strangers appear on roads not meant for pilgrims. The kind who trade silence for coin."

The fire cracked. A log fell.

Cassien didn't move. "Are you one of them?"

Bertran's smile faded. He leaned forward slightly, elbows on knees. "I'm the kind who eats with strangers and lets the night decide."

Alais placed her bowl on the ground, unfinished. "And what has the night told you about us?"

He studied her for a beat too long. "That you are not what you seem. That you've come far and carry more than what's on your backs."

The silence was taut.

Then Bertran leaned back and laughed softly. "But maybe I'm wrong. Maybe you're just hungry travelers with secrets of no worth at all."

Cassien met his gaze. "Maybe."

They sat with the fire crackling between them. The stew cooled. The air smelled faintly of salt and something else—metallic and old.

Alais did not eat another bite. And Cassien kept his hand near the strap that held the scrolls.

Something in Bertran's tone had shifted. And whatever kindness he had offered, it no longer tasted the same.

That night, they slept uneasily, weariness outweighing caution. The long days of walking, the burden of the scrolls, and the press of constant alertness had hollowed them to the bone. The small shelter's roof did not leak, and the wind was still. Despite everything, exhaustion won.

But by morning, the fire was cold, and Bertran was gone.

Cassien woke first. He rose slowly, scanning the sparse clearing beyond the crumbling doorway. The stranger's blanket was folded neatly, his bowl rinsed and overturned beside the ashes. There were no tracks in the hard earth—none Cassien could follow.

Alais emerged from the shadows a moment later, rubbing sleep from her eyes. "He's gone?"

Cassien nodded.

She sighed, glancing toward the firepit. "He left too quietly."

"He learned what he wanted," Cassien said. "Or thinks he did."

"We should leave before he returns with others," Alais said, already pulling her cloak around her shoulders. "He knows too much. And if he guessed what we carry…"

Cassien reached for the pack. "We need to find higher ground. And decide how much further we can risk."

They gathered their things quickly. No words passed between them for several minutes, only the sound of boots crunching through dry grass and the morning wind picking up from the sea.

The betrayal hadn't come yet—but its breath was on their necks.

They made their way to a rise just beyond the ruin, climbing to where they could see the land unspool before them. The coastline shimmered faintly in the distance, a silver ribbon beyond scrub and scattered vineyards.

Cassien squinted into the wind. "If we stay close to the fields, we can reach the low cliffs by nightfall. But we'll be exposed for hours."

Alais nodded. "Or we could wait until dusk. Travel in shadow."

He looked to her. "We don't know if we have until dusk. If Bertran truly means to betray us, he may already be on his way."

Alais considered this, her eyes scanning the horizon. "Then we need to move quickly. But not recklessly."

Cassien unrolled a scrap of linen and pointed. "There's a fishing cove marked here. If it still exists, it might offer boats—or at least shelter. A place where we can disappear again."

"Then let's try for it," Alais said, securing her cloak. "We've lived too long in shadow to die in the open."

He touched her arm. "We'll make it."

They turned from the ridge and descended once more, slipping between rows of wild fennel and stone-marked terraces. The sun was high now, and each step forward felt like a gamble cast against the wind.

But they walked together.

And every step was a vow not yet broken.

By late afternoon, they reached the edge of a small coastal village tucked between cliffs and wind-carved hills. Weathered cottages with shuttered windows leaned toward the sea. The scent of salt and fish hung thick in the air, mingled with chimney smoke and something faintly floral—lavender or thyme, perhaps, clinging to the earth.

Alais paused at the first path leading into the village. "We'll need to stay the night," she said softly. "There's no way to arrange a boat before dusk."

Cassien nodded. "Agreed. But we must keep our purpose hidden."

They passed through the narrow lanes as inconspicuously as they could, drawing a few curious glances but no overt suspicion. At the inn near the quay—a low building with a thatched roof and warped shutters—they secured a small upstairs room in exchange for two coins and a claim of traveling to visit family in Narbonne.

The innkeeper was a wiry man with ink-stained fingers who barely looked at them twice.

"Boat leaves at dawn," he muttered, sliding the key across the wooden counter. "You'll want to be on the shore before the bell. Tide doesn't wait for pilgrims or ghosts."

They thanked him and climbed the narrow stairs, the floorboards groaning beneath their weight. Their room held a narrow bed, a bench beneath the window, and a chipped basin of cool water. The shutters rattled in the sea wind.

Once inside, Cassien placed the scroll bundle gently beneath the bench and sat beside it, elbows on his knees, staring at nothing.

"We're close," Alais said, standing by the window. "Narbonne is within reach."

He looked up at her, his expression unreadable. "Yes. But so is whatever comes next."

In the early hush before dawn, Cassien and Alais made their way through the quiet village, their cloaks drawn tightly against the sea wind. The sky was a pale slate, the stars fading as morning crept in from the east.

At the shoreline, a lean man stood beside a small boat pulled up onto the sand, his arms crossed over his chest and a woolen cap low over his brow. He looked up as they approached, eyes sharp beneath heavy lids.

"You're the ones for Narbonne?" he asked.

Cassien nodded. "We were told you'd be here."

The boatman jerked his head toward the water. "Tide's with us, but it won't be long. Payment?"

Cassien reached into his cloak and withdrew the agreed-upon sum, placing it in the man's outstretched hand.

The boatman counted quickly, then tucked the coins into his belt. "Good. Get in. Keep your heads low once we pass the headland."

Alais stepped into the boat first, steadying herself as it rocked with the shifting current. Cassien followed, settling beside her as the boatman pushed them off with practiced ease.

"How long will it take to reach Narbonne?" Alais asked.

The boatman shrugged as he took up the oars. "If the wind stays fair and the sea quiet, three hours. Maybe four. If it doesn't…" He let the silence finish the sentence.

Cassien and Alais exchanged a glance but said nothing more. The shore began to slip away behind them, and the open sea yawned ahead.

The boatman rowed for two hours, glancing at the foggy shore from time to time.

Suddenly, he changed course, heading for the shore.

Alais looked toward the land with sudden alarm and began to rise. "Soldiers."

Cassien rose slightly, his voice low and seething. "You have betrayed us," he said, staring hard at the boatman.

The man didn't look back. His jaw tightened, hands still firm on the oars. "I did what I had to."

Alais turned sharply, her eyes blazing. "You sold us for coin?"

The boatman glanced at them then, only briefly. "For safety. For my family."

Cassien's fists clenched. "And what of ours?" His voice cracked with restrained fury. "What of those we've already lost?"

The boatman said nothing more. The boat drifted closer to the shore, where spears gleamed faintly in the fog.

Cassien did not hesitate.

With a sudden surge of movement, he lunged forward and knocked the boatman's hands from the oars. The man shouted, twisting to grab hold again, but Cassien drove his shoulder into the boatman's chest, sending him backward off balance. With a sharp cry and a splash, the man tumbled overboard into the cold water.

"Row!" Cassien barked, grabbing the oars.

Alais was already moving, dragging herself across the small vessel, reaching for the opposite oar. Together, they pulled hard, backs straining, arms burning. The boat groaned beneath them as it shifted direction, veering sharply away from the approaching soldiers. Shouts rose from the shore.

An arrow hissed through the fog and struck the boat's prow.

Alais didn't flinch. She kept rowing, her jaw clenched, her intent fixed on the open sea.

Another arrow came—and this one struck home.

Alais gasped, her body lurching. She clutched her shoulder, her hand coming away slick with blood.

"Alais!" Cassien dropped the oar and reached for her, guiding her down into the belly of the boat as another arrow clattered against the side.

"I can still row," she whispered, grimacing. "Just a scratch."

"No," he said, voice sharp. "Stay low. Let me."

He took both oars, his muscles screaming, breath coming in gasps. Each pull of the oars put more distance between them and the shore, between them and the betrayal.

Behind them, the boatman floundered in the water, shouting curses and prayers that vanished in the fog.

Alais groaned, one hand pressed tightly to the wound, her eyes fluttering. "We can't stop now."

"We won't," Cassien said, not looking back. "We'll reach Narbonne. And from there—whatever comes."

The sea surged around them, dark and endless. The shoreline grew smaller, the figures of the soldiers vanishing into the mist.

They were still alive.

And still together.

But the cost of trust weighed heavy in the boat beside them.

As the day wore on and the sun rose higher, they drifted in silence. Alais rested beneath the coarse blanket while Cassien watched the shoreline, searching for signs of safety.

Suddenly, he stiffened. "There. Look."

Through the lifting mist, they saw a figure on the shore—a lone person standing still, watching them.

"We have no choice," Cassien murmured. "We need help."

Alais nodded slowly, pain dulling her features. "Let's go to them."

Cassien angled the boat toward the shore. As they approached, the figure did not move. It was a man, wrapped in a faded brown cloak, his face shaded by a hood. His posture was neither welcoming nor threatening.

Cassien called out cautiously, "Can you help us?"

The man said nothing at first. Then he lifted his hand and beckoned them in, wordless and patient.

Cassien glanced at Alais. "Stay behind me."

The boat touched shore, and the man stepped forward, his eyes narrowing as he took in the blood on Alais's cloak.

"You're running," he said.

"Yes," Cassien replied. "We need shelter. And a path inland. Can you give us directions?"

The man studied them a moment longer before nodding. "Perhaps I can. But it depends on who you are running from."

Cassien hesitated. "The Inquisition."

A faint flicker of recognition passed through the man's expression. He stepped closer, his voice quieter. "Then you are not just travelers."

"No," Alais said, steadying herself beside Cassien. "We carry something of importance. We seek a sanctuary."

The man looked to the horizon, then back at them. "You should not have come by sea. But I see you had no choice."

Cassien took a step forward. "Who are you?"

The man's hand rose slowly to draw back his hood. His face was worn but kind, his eyes filled with depth and calm. "I am a Perfect. I was told someone would come, though I did not know who."

Alais let out a slow breath, half relief, half awe. "Then we are where we need to be."

"For now," the Perfect said. "Come. There is a place nearby where you can rest. But you must move quickly. The eyes of the Church are not far behind."

The Perfect led them through a narrow path shaded by olive trees and tall grasses until they reached a low stone hut, half-sunk into the hillside and nearly invisible from the sea.

"This is safe for now," he said, lifting the latch. "But you cannot remain long."

Inside, the space was cool and dim. There were pallets of straw and a small hearth.

Cassien helped Alais lie down, gently easing her to one of the pallets. Her face was pale, but she managed a weak smile.

"Thank you," she murmured to the Perfect.

He nodded and turned to Cassien. "What you carry—these scrolls
—have you considered leaving them with someone who can see
them preserved?"

Cassien looked toward the bundle still tightly wrapped and bound
beside his pack. "You?"

"I am one among many. But yes. I know the way to the Sanctuary.
If something happens to you before you reach it, their message
could still endure."

Cassien looked to Alais, whose eyes were open, watching.

"We'll consider it," he said. "We're not ready to let them go. Not
yet."

"Of course," the Perfect said. "Rest now. I will keep watch."

That night, Alais's breathing grew shallow, and the wound in her
shoulder oozed anew. Cassien hovered beside her, whispering to
soothe her, bathing the injury with a damp cloth, trying not to let
fear take hold.

The Perfect returned with herbs and poultices, kneeling beside her
without ceremony.

"She is strong," he said quietly, grinding leaves in a wooden bowl. "But the wound has deepened. Fever may come."

Cassien clasped Alais's hand. "What more can we do?"

The Perfect looked to both of them, his voice grave but steady. "If the worst comes, she should not pass without the Consolamentum."

Alais stirred, eyes fluttering open. "I hear you," she said faintly.

Cassien bent closer. "Do you want it?"

She was silent a long moment, then gave a faint nod. "Yes. If it comes to that."

"What is it, truly?" Cassien asked. "I've read of it… in the words of the Church. But not in yours."

The Perfect met his eyes. "It is not a rite of death. It is a rite of re-membrance. Of awakening. The laying on of hands, not to prepare the soul to depart—but to remind it that it has never been separate."

Alais squeezed Cassien's hand gently. "It's not about sin, Cassien. It's about knowing who we truly are."

He looked from her to the Perfect and back again. "Then I want to understand. Before you do it. Teach me."

The Perfect sat, his hands resting on his knees, his voice like the quiet earth. "The Consolamentum is the return of the soul to itself. There are no sacraments, no intercessors. Just the recognition of the light within. It is given once, and it binds no one—it frees."

Cassien nodded slowly. "Then I will not stop it. But I will pray it is not yet needed."

The Perfect dipped the cloth into the crushed herbs and laid it on Alais's wound. Her eyes closed again.

He stood. "Sleep if you can. We will keep her warm. And I will remain close."

Cassien bowed his head, overcome by a deep, stirring peace—one he could not name, but felt like the turning of something ancient within him.

Cassien sat quietly beside the fire as Alais slept fitfully, her breath shallow but steady. The Perfect remained across from him, eyes half-closed, hands resting on his knees as if listening to something beyond sound.

Cassien broke the silence. "You said the Consolamentum frees the soul. But where does it go? What happens after… death?"

The Perfect opened his eyes slowly, studying Cassien's face. "You ask not from doctrine, but from love."

Cassien nodded. "Yes."

The Perfect stirred the embers gently. "Death, as you have known it, is not an end. Nor a judgment. It is a return. The soul is not cast upward or downward by decree. It is drawn by its own knowing— its resonance. If it remembers its source, it rejoins the field of Light. If not, it may wander. But it is never lost."

Cassien looked toward Alais. "And if she passes with the Consolamentum?"

"Then she passes with remembrance. She will know herself as whole. As untouched by flame or blade or sorrow. And she will know you, too, beyond the veil."

A long silence passed between them.

"And if she lives?" Cassien asked.

The Perfect smiled softly. "Then the light within her remains in the world a while longer. And your journey together is not yet complete."

Cassien bowed his head, and for the first time since they fled the fire, he allowed his tears to fall.

Chapter Sixteen

THE MORNING DAWNED in a hush of gray mist, the coastline blurred by a veil of sea fog. Cassien stood outside the hut, watching the sky slowly lighten, the air still damp and heavy with salt. Alais stirred within, still weak but no longer feverish.

Then, faintly through the fog, the sound of creaking wood and the soft slap of water reached his ears.

He squinted toward the sea and saw a dark silhouette emerge from the mist—a small boat drifting slowly past, not far from the beach. A single figure stood in its bow, scanning the shoreline.

Cassien's breath caught.

He ducked instinctively beneath the overhang of the hut and whispered urgently, "Alais—stay quiet."

Inside, she stirred again but obeyed without a word.

The boat drifted closer, the figure still peering toward the beach. For a long moment, Cassien feared they had been seen. Then, the mist thickened, and the boat passed by without slowing, the figures aboard unaware of the small vessel beached behind a thicket of sea grass.

Cassien didn't move until the boat had vanished into the haze.

Only then did he breathe again.

He turned back toward the hut, a mixture of gratitude and dread pooling in his chest.

"They're still looking," he whispered, mostly to himself.

But for now, the veil had held.

Cassien and the Perfect waited until the fog had thickened again before emerging fully from the hut. The beached boat, though mostly concealed by reeds and overgrowth, could not remain where it was.

"It will draw attention," the Perfect said. "If the soldiers return by land."

Cassien nodded. "Can we sink it?"

"With time. And care."

They gathered stones from the surrounding cove and loaded them into the vessel's hull. Then, with deliberate force, they pushed the boat farther into the shallows. Cassien stepped into the water, guiding it until the current caught the weight and pulled it down.

The boat groaned once, then tipped and slipped beneath the surface, vanishing into the gray-green sea.

Cassien stood still a moment, watching the ripples fade. The fog hung low, veiling them from above.

When he returned to the shore, the Perfect was kneeling again on the pebbles; hands pressed to the earth.

"What are you doing?" Cassien asked quietly.

"Giving thanks. And listening."

Cassien sat beside him, the water dripping from his cloak.

"I was taught to pray by rote," he said. "Words I never questioned. You… you listen."

The Perfect smiled faintly. "Words have their place. But silence remembers what language forgets."

Cassien lowered his gaze, his voice low. "I don't know what I believe anymore."

The Perfect turned to him. "Then you are close to the truth."

Cassien looked up, startled.

"When belief is undone," the Perfect continued, "what remains is being. Belief is of the mind. Being is of the Field, where no separation exists. You have lived in thought. Now you walk in remembrance."

Cassien closed his eyes, letting those words settle in.

"There is so much I would change," he said.

"And yet, you came," said the Perfect. "You chose love over law. That is the turning. That is the path."

Cassien remained silent, watching the sea.

Behind them, in the dim shelter of the hut, Alais stirred again. Their journey was not yet done.

Inside the hut, the air was warm and heavy with the scent of crushed herbs and damp linen. Alais had been asleep for much of the day, her skin slick with sweat, her breathing shallow. When Cassien returned from the shore, he found the Perfect already kneeling beside her once more, his hand resting lightly on her brow.

"She is burning again," the Perfect said softly. "The fever has returned."

Cassien knelt beside her, brushing damp strands of hair from her face. Her eyes fluttered open, glassy with fever, and for a moment she didn't seem to recognize him.

"It's me," he whispered. "You're safe. I'm here."

She blinked slowly, her lips parting. "Cassien…"

He clasped her hand in both of his. "Yes, my love."

She swallowed hard, then closed her eyes again. "It's… getting harder to stay."

"No," he said, fiercely but gently. "You will stay. Rest. Let your body heal."

But the Perfect met his gaze and shook his head slightly.

"She must choose soon," he said. "The fire is deep. If it does not break by tomorrow…"

Cassien's throat tightened. He could feel her slipping, little by little, her hold on the world loosening like fingers from a ledge. He bent forward and kissed her forehead, lingering there, willing strength into her body.

She turned her head slightly, eyes fluttering. "If I don't wake," she whispered, "will you carry me?"

His breath caught. "To the Sanctuary?"

"No," she said faintly. "Through the veil."

Cassien couldn't speak. He only nodded, tears falling freely now.

The Perfect stood quietly and stepped away, leaving them alone together as night fell once again.

The hush of the hut deepened as the Perfect's footsteps faded into the silence beyond the threshold. Only the crackle of the dying fire and Alais's uneven breathing remained.

Cassien sat beside her, motionless, his hand still wrapped around hers, as if his grip alone could anchor her to this side of the veil. Shadows flickered across her face, delicate and still, save for the occasional wince or shiver that passed through her body.

He whispered, not to stir her but to steady himself.

"I wasn't meant for this," he said quietly. "Not for love. Not for loss. I was to keep my vows, walk the cloister's circle, recite the hours, bury my doubts."

He brushed a strand of hair from her temple. "But you… You called me out of silence. Not the silence of prayer, but the silence of forgetting. And now I remember."

Her eyes opened slightly—only a sliver—but they found him.

"Still here," he said softly.

"You stayed," she whispered, her voice a ghost of itself.

"Always," he replied. "Until your breath is mine. And after."

Alais's gaze drifted to the ceiling, as if following something unseen.

"I hear a song," she murmured. "So faint… like the beginning of the world."

Cassien's throat tightened. "Hold to it. Let it hold you."

She gave a small nod, then closed her eyes again, her chest rising and falling with fragile rhythm.

Cassien leaned back, pressing his free hand to his heart. He could not save her. But he could witness her. He could walk with her to the edge. And if she crossed it, he would remember—fully, and without fear.

The wind stirred outside, catching the edge of the thatch roof, as if the world, too, paused in reverence.

Then, at last, the door creaked open.

The Perfect returned, a wooden bowl in his hands, steam rising faintly from its rim. He knelt beside Alais and met Cassien's eyes with quiet gravity.

"The moment is near," he said.

Cassien nodded.

The Perfect dipped his fingers into the warm mixture of herbs and oil and gently touched them to Alais's forehead.

"My sister," he whispered. "Light of the Light. Flame of the Flame. Remember who you are. You were never born, and you do not die."

Alais stirred at the words. A single tear slid from the corner of her eye.

Then she spoke—not with effort, but with clarity.

"I remember."

The hut filled with stillness—not silence, but something deeper. A Presence. A knowing. The air seemed to shimmer.

Cassien held her hand and breathed, letting her lead, wherever she was going.

The Perfect laid his hand gently atop theirs, and for a moment, there was only that:

Three beings in still communion. No past. No fear. Only the truth of what always was.

The stillness stretched long and holy.

Cassien did not move. His fingers wrapped around hers had grown numb, but he held on—not from fear of loss, but from reverence for her crossing. He could feel her presence gathering, luminous and soft, like dawn pressing against the veil of night.

Alais exhaled, slow and steady.

Then again.

And again—each breath more delicate than the last, as though her body were already receding and only her light remained.

The Perfect whispered ancient words in Occitan, not as ritual but as remembering:

"Lutz dins l'ombra. Es pas una fin, es ton retorn."

("Light in the shadow. It is not an end, it is your return.")

Alais's lips parted.

She smiled.

A breath. So light it could have been a breeze.

Then none.

Cassien felt it—not a departure, but a widening as if she had poured out beyond the edges of her form and become everything: the hush, the warmth, the space between heartbeats.

Her hand, still nestled in his, fell slack.

He bowed his head. No sobs. No collapse. Just the slow and sacred undoing of a bond that would never be broken.

"She is free," the Perfect said.

Cassien nodded, lips parted but speechless. He lifted her hand and kissed it, then laid it gently on her chest.

"She remembered," he whispered.

The Perfect placed a linen cloth across her body, his hands steady, his expression radiant with sorrow and peace. "She walks now in the Field beyond all name."

The fire gave a soft crackle, the last flame curling into ash.

Cassien reached for the scrolls beside him and held them to his chest. "Then I will carry the words forward."

The Perfect touched his shoulder. "And she will carry you."

The morning sun broke gently through the veil of mist, casting long, golden shafts across the hillside where the hut lay hidden. Cassien knelt beside Alais's still form, his fingers brushing her hair one final time. Her face was calm, as if she merely slept, held in the hush of something greater than sorrow.

The Perfect brought a length of undyed linen, and together they wrapped her body with reverent hands. No words passed between them—only breath and silence, as though the land itself mourned.

When all was done, they bore her gently from the hut to a place the Perfect had chosen: a grove of cypress trees hidden between two ridges, known only to those who listened deeply.

There, beneath the canopy of green and sky, they laid her down.

Cassien dug the earth with his hands. The Perfect joined him. They labored not as mourners but as those who honored something holy. When the hollow was ready, they placed her within and covered her with soil, layer by layer, until the hill rose again smooth and whole.

Cassien pressed a flat stone at the head, unmarked, but for a single carved spiral he etched with his knife—the symbol Alais had once drawn in the dust.

He sat beside her grave long after the work was done.

"I don't know how to go on without her," he said finally.

The Perfect stood near, his presence a quiet strength. "You will not go on without her," he said. "You will go on with her, within you."

Cassien nodded slowly, tears drying on his cheeks. "You said once that the Consolamentum is not the end, but a beginning. That it frees the soul. But what of those left behind?"

The Perfect looked toward the east. "They begin again, too. Not as they were. But as they are becoming."

A long silence passed between them, warm with meaning.

Cassien turned to him. "What does it mean to become a Perfect? How did you come to it?"

The man sat beside him, drawing his cloak more tightly. "It is not a title, but a path. One begins by renouncing the illusions of power, possession, and separation. We do not marry or bear arms. We do not own. We serve. Not to be above others—but to remember our oneness with them."

Cassien looked down at his hands, still dusted with earth. "Could I walk that path?"

The Perfect met his eyes. "You already are."

"But there is more," Cassien said. "A way to take the vow?"

The Perfect nodded. "When the time is right. When your heart no longer seeks to prove itself, but only to remember what it is. You will know."

Cassien closed his eyes, feeling Alais in the wind, in the trees, in the ache of his chest and the stillness of his spine.

Then he whispered, "Teach me."

And the Perfect placed his hand on Cassien's shoulder.

"So it begins."

They set out at dawn, the scrolls carefully wrapped in linen and strapped across Cassien's back. The Perfect walked beside him, unhurried, as though each step was both destination and pilgrimage. The air was still cool, the mountains quiet save for the soft shuffle of their sandals on the rocky path.

Cassien had not spoken since they left the grove, but his silence was not hollow. Something within him was listening—deeply, as Alais once had.

The Perfect broke the stillness with a question. "Do you feel her with you?"

Cassien hesitated. Then: "Yes. Not as memory. As presence."

The Perfect nodded. "Then the path has already opened."

As they descended the mountain slopes, the Perfect spoke softly of the inner teachings—of the Two Principles, Light and Shadow, and the sacred silence that lives behind all form. He told of the old prophets, of the ones who knew without needing to possess, of those who surrendered all certainty to live in Truth.

Cassien asked questions when moved, but mostly he listened. Sometimes they stopped in small hamlets, where the Perfect would speak with a nod or gesture to a hidden brother or sister. Now and then, bread would be left on a windowsill, or fresh water offered without a word. There was a quiet network of kindness stretching across the land like an invisible web.

One night, under a vast canopy of stars, Cassien dared ask, "Have you known loss like mine?"

The Perfect looked upward. "I have known many names for love. Each time I let go, it became more vast. What you feel is not absence. It is expansion."

Cassien slept that night holding the scrolls beside him, as if guarding not just words, but her spirit.

Their steps, though slow, were steady.

And ahead, beyond the low hills, the Sanctuary waited.

Chapter Seventeen

BY MIDDAY, the hills began to widen into a high valley flanked with crags. A stream twisted through the grasslands below, leading their eyes to a structure nestled against the stone: weathered but standing, built of pale rock that shimmered faintly in the sun. It seemed to rise from the earth itself, as if shaped by wind and time rather than by men. A round tower stood at its heart, partially overgrown with ivy. Slender windows faced the rising sun.

"The Sanctuary," the Perfect said simply.

Cassien slowed, reverent, as though approaching sacred ground. "It's beautiful."

"It was once a monastery," the Perfect explained. "Older than Rome. The Cathars reclaimed it generations ago, not with force, but with silence and light. It has sheltered many through darkness."

As they drew near, a woman stepped from the archway. Her eyes, calm and clear, met Cassien's without surprise. "You've come far," she said.

Cassien unslung the scrolls and held them out as if presenting an offering. "These are for safekeeping."

She acknowledged them with a small bow. "Then come inside. You are among friends."

They crossed the threshold together. And in that moment, something in Cassien—battered and hollowed—began to root itself anew.

Inside the Sanctuary, the air was still and fragrant with beeswax and lavender. The inner cloister opened into a modest hall, where light fell through arched windows and painted the stone floor in shifting bands of gold. There were no icons, no thrones or relics—only a circle of cushions and low wooden stools, arranged as if for prayer or quiet conversation.

Cassien set the scrolls upon a woven mat in the center of the room. Several gathered nearby, faces lined with humility and watchfulness. None questioned. None praised. One by one, they simply bowed—each gesture a silent vow to protect what had been brought forth.

The Perfect placed a hand on Cassien's back, guiding him toward a bench near the hearth.

"You may rest now," he said.

Cassien sat, feeling the warmth seep through his robes. He had not realized how cold he had become.

A woman brought him broth—rich with herbs and root vegetables. She smiled softly but did not speak. Around him, life flowed without fanfare. Someone mended a cloak by the window. Another cleaned a stone basin. Two others—Perfects by their bearing—tended a fire in the inner garden.

"It's as though time moves differently here," Cassien murmured.

The Perfect nodded. "It does. Here, we move with time, not against it."

They remained at the Sanctuary for several days. Cassien slept deeply, more soundly than he had in many months. He walked the gardens in silence, sometimes with the Perfect, sometimes alone. His grief, once sharp and all-consuming, had softened into something deeper—still painful, but wrapped now in meaning.

Each morning, he returned to the scrolls. He would sit before them, unroll one, and read slowly, feeling Alais's breath in each stroke of ink. They began to teach from them, gently, in the evenings—selecting short passages to share and reflect upon. Others came to sit in a circle, contributing what they had lived, witnessed, and known.

It was not dogma. It was living truth.

And Cassien, for the first time in his life, was not merely a keeper of sacred things. He was becoming one.

Each day began with the chiming of a bell, soft and resonant, echoing through the cloister like a breath returning to its source. Cassien would rise early, his body still sore from the journey, and join the others in silent prayer beneath the open sky. There were no words spoken aloud—only presence. The wind carried its own liturgy.

He had expected instruction, perhaps ritual, but instead he found rhythm. The Sanctuary did not teach with sermons or proclamations. It taught with water drawn from the well, with soil turned by hand, with the slow stitching of robes, and the scent of bread as it baked.

The Perfect, whose name was revealed only as Alon, guided Cassien not with answers, but with questions.

"What do you fear most about being nothing?" he asked one morning as they shelled beans together by the garden wall.

Cassien paused. "That I will disappear. That I will have meant nothing."

Alon nodded, fingers still working. "And what is it you hope to become?"

Cassien looked up at the mountains. "A vessel. For what is true. For what she saw in me."

Alon smiled gently. "Then let yourself be emptied. The vessel fills itself only after it has forgotten its shape."

Later that day, Cassien wandered alone beyond the orchard, scrolls in hand. He read from one of the hidden texts Alais had carried, her markings still clear in the margins. The words spoke of the Light not as an external grace, but as an inward remembrance. That which is of God is never apart from God, he read. And what is born of silence carries the voice of creation.

That evening, he shared the passage with the others. A discussion followed, not of interpretation, but of resonance. One woman spoke of dreams she'd had since childhood. Another of how the scroll mirrored the moment she first chose not to betray a fleeing brother, despite the cost.

No one taught. They simply remembered aloud.

In time, Cassien began copying the texts anew, translating where needed, binding the pages with care. He and Alon took turns preserving the scrolls in secret chambers beneath the Sanctuary, where a thin ribbon of light slipped through the stone at midday, illuminating the sacred table.

"Do you believe they will survive us?" Cassien asked once.

Alon answered with a quiet certainty. "The truth does not depend on survival. It depends only on being lived. And that, you are doing."

Cassien sat with that for a long time.

In the quiet hours before dawn, he often walked the gardens and whispered to Alais. Not seeking answers, simply walking with her, as they had once walked in the mountains. The grief no longer pulled him under—it carried him.

One night, as the fire crackled in the inner circle, a young girl who had remained silent for weeks finally spoke. "I remember my mother's hands. How they carried light into every room. Even when she had nothing. I think she was like one of you."

Cassien reached out and took her hand. "Then you carry her still."

The others bowed their heads, and a hush fell over the circle. It was not the silence of absence, but the silence of presence, too full to speak.

And in that stillness, Cassien understood what Alon had meant.

He was no longer seeking the path. He was walking it.

It began not with clamor, but with a flicker.

A figure appeared at the edge of the orchard one morning—a stranger in worn boots and a cloak dusted by many roads. He waited respectfully beyond the trees, saying nothing, until one of the older women tending the figs noticed him. She approached cautiously, and after a brief exchange, she nodded and beckoned toward the garden.

Cassien and Alon were kneeling by the irrigation trench, guiding water through the channels carved from stone. When the woman whispered in Alon's ear, he rose slowly, dusting off his hands, and gestured for Cassien to follow.

The man—tall, pale-eyed, perhaps no older than Cassien—stood with a satchel slung over his shoulder and a stiffness in his bearing that betrayed long travel. He bowed low.

"My name is Marcel," he said. "I come from the mountain holdfast at Rieussec. I carry a message."

He withdrew a sealed scroll, not of the old Cathar parchment but of Church vellum. The wax bore no crest—only a single line drawn vertically through the center—a sign used in secret by those who walked between both worlds.

Cassien accepted it with quiet hands.

Inside were only a few lines:

The Inquisitors have begun again in earnest. A new tribunal gathers in Limoux. Names have been spoken. Among them, yours.

Alon read over his shoulder, his face unreadable. Marcel waited.

Cassien folded the parchment slowly, then looked to the mountains, where the fog had not yet lifted.

"The path has called me back," he said.

Alon nodded once. "Then the Sanctuary will hold what you leave behind."

Cassien turned to Marcel. "Tell me everything."

Marcel stepped back and unhooked his satchel. "I was sent by one who remembers you," he said. He fears what is coming. The Church has widened its net. No longer content with burning heretics, they now root out sympathizers—those who once offered bread, or water, or silence. He helped me get this far. He said you would know what to do."

Cassien's brow tightened. "And the tribunal in Limoux?"

"They seek to make an example," Marcel said. "It is to be a public reckoning. Not only priests and believers, but children, elders, healers. Anyone suspected of harboring the Silence."

Alon's eyes darkened. "When?"

"A fortnight. Less, perhaps. The inquisitors arrived early. They ride with banners now. Not hiding."

Cassien turned to Alon. "Do we know anyone near Limoux?"

"There is a weaving family in Cournanel. They have helped before."

Marcel added quietly, "And one more thing. There are whispers of a betrayal. Someone close to the path who no longer walks it. A name has not been given, but…"

Cassien's voice was steady. "We'll walk with care."

Alon met his gaze. "We always have."

That night, the fire in the sanctuary courtyard burned with a deeper hue, casting amber light across the gathered faces. Those who had traveled far, those who had stayed hidden for years, those who had lost and loved and lived in silence—all sat shoulder to shoulder in the hush of impending departure.

Cassien sat with Marcel and Alon on either side, their presence grounding him. The scrolls—now translated, copied, and hidden in the chambers beneath the stone—were not spoken of tonight. They lived, and that was enough.

He spoke gently, but clearly, his voice no longer needing to rise to be heard.

"We were given a gift here," he said, "not only in what we learned, but in what we became. The scrolls are part of it—but so are we. What we carry is not only parchment, but presence. Silence that remembers itself. I do not know what will come. But I know that it begins here."

The wind shifted, carrying the smell of pine and distant sea salt.

A woman who had long walked barefoot spoke softly. "We will remember you in our tending of the soil."

A man near the far wall said, "And in the light that filters through the cracks at midday."

A young child asked, "Will we see you again?"

Cassien met her gaze. "You will not need to. The path you walk will be enough."

Alon placed a hand on Cassien's shoulder. "All who walk with love leave footprints on the field of Being. Whether seen or not, they remain."

One by one, they offered embraces, tears, laughter, silence—a shared knowing.

And when the embers dimmed, and the moon was high, Cassien and Marcel rose. Cassien turned to face the circle one last time, and bowed—not as a monk, not as a bearer of sacred words, but as a man who had been emptied and filled again.

"Thank you for letting me remember who I am," he said.

Then he stepped into the night.

Chapter Eighteen

AS THEY WALKED down the sloping path away from the Sanctuary, the light of dawn still caught in the tops of the trees, Cassien turned slightly toward Marcel, his voice low and deliberate.

"You knew where to find me. How?"

Marcel glanced at him, then back to the trail. "Word passes quietly, when it must. You were seen near Narbonne before the fires. A boy said he spoke with you. Someone else remembered you asking about a village near the coast. A pattern emerged."

"But no one knew where the Sanctuary was."

"Some guessed. Fewer knew. One of those few knew you would find it. And that you would leave again when it was time."

Cassien was silent for a few steps. Then, "Who sent you?"

Marcel hesitated. "A man named Adelric. A churchman who hides in plain sight. He remembered you from the abbey near Carcassonne. Said you spoke of light the way others speak of gold. Said if you were still alive, you would answer the call."

Cassien exhaled softly. "Adelric."

Marcel continued, "He sent me with more than just a message. There are places along the way he marked for you—people who still remember the Silence. But we must tread lightly. The inquisitors are ahead of us as well as behind."

Cassien nodded, his gaze on the horizon. "And the symbol on the scroll—was that Adelric's mark?"

Marcel shook his head. "Older than him. Used by those who once carried messages for the Beloved. It means: 'I speak between.'"

Cassien absorbed that. "And you? Why do you help us?"

Marcel slowed, eyes thoughtful. "I lost someone. Years ago. She believed in this path long before I understood it. I never followed it with her. Not fully. But now I do. I carry it forward… for her."

Cassien placed a hand briefly on Marcel's shoulder. "Then we walk together."

They pressed on, silence folding over them like a cloak. Ahead, the road forked and vanished into the mist.

After two days of walking, the clouds gave way to long golden light, and a village came into view, nestled at the base of a wooded rise—Cournanel. A scattering of stone cottages gathered around a central square, with thin tendrils of smoke curling from chimneys into the crisp air. Chickens pecked freely in the dust, and a single bell tower rose beside what looked to be a chapel, its stonework aged but lovingly maintained.

Marcel slowed as they approached, eyes scanning for signs of familiarity. "The weaving family Alon spoke of—look for red-dyed thread on the windowsill. That was the signal."

They passed through the village's edge without drawing undue attention. An old man nodded from a bench, and a pair of girls paused their sweeping to glance at the travelers.

"There," Marcel said, pointing.

A narrow house with a blue-painted door. A skein of deep red thread lay coiled on the stone windowsill, sunlight catching its sheen.

Cassien stepped forward and knocked. Moments passed. Then a panel slid aside in the door, revealing a wary set of eyes.

"Alon sent us," Marcel said softly.

The eyes flicked to Cassien, then back to Marcel. The panel closed. A moment later, the door opened.

The woman who stood there was broad-shouldered and sun-browned, her graying hair tied back in a practical knot. "Inside. Quickly."

They entered, and the door closed behind them with a quiet finality.

"I am Mireille," she said, studying them closely. "And if you are not who you say, I will know before dusk." Her tone was not un-kind—only tired.

Cassien inclined his head. "We carry nothing but what's been given. And seek only to listen, and pass through."

Mireille gave a short nod. "Then sit. There is warm broth. You can speak while you eat."

As Marcel moved to the hearth, Cassien felt the comfort of the place settle over him like a well-worn cloak—woven tapestries on the walls, the smell of lavender and flax, and the sound of a spindle turning in the next room.

They had reached safety for now. But the road beyond would demand more than safety.

It would ask everything.

That night, while Marcel and Mireille spoke quietly in the other room, Cassien sat near the hearth, watching the flicker of firelight dance across the walls. His broth untouched, he held the parchment scroll Marcel had delivered, now folded neatly in his lap. The vertical line on the seal seemed to throb faintly in the shadows—like a blade, or a path.

Limoux. The name turned over in his mind like a stone worn smooth in a stream. He had walked away from fire and death once. Was he now walking toward it? And if so—was it choice, or destiny?

He thought of Clara in the flames, of Alais and the sanctuary she would never see. He thought of the scrolls now hidden beneath earth and stone, and the whispered teachings passed down through generations, each voice risking its breath so that the next might inhale light.

What was he now, truly?

A Brother no longer bound by robes.

A seeker no longer bound by seeking.

A bearer of silence, walking into noise.

Cassien closed his eyes and whispered—not a prayer, not even a question, but a statement of being:

"I will not look away."

The fire cracked softly. The silence around him deepened, not empty, but full—of presence, of memory, of what must come next.

He would go to Limoux. But first, he would listen. And in the listening, perhaps, find again the way forward.

The following morning, Marcel and Cassien stood at the village's edge, where the road sloped gently toward the southern hills. The light had just begun to lift over the horizon, pale and cool, casting long shadows over the cobblestones.

Marcel adjusted the strap of his satchel and turned to Cassien. "You'll be safer without me beyond this point. One man in robes can pass unnoticed. Two draw questions."

Cassien nodded, already robed once more in the dark wool of his former order. He looked down at the frayed cuffs, the cloth shaped by years of use. The hood rested lightly across his shoulders, like a remembered name.

"I understand," he said.

Marcel hesitated. "You know what to say if you're stopped?"

Cassien's voice was calm. "I am a Benedictine envoy of Rome, bearing ecclesiastical correspondence for the tribunal in Limoux. I travel alone and under orders of discretion."

"Good," Marcel said, and then added, more softly, "If you're caught, it will be your conviction that keeps you alive. Not the robe."

Cassien extended his hand. Marcel took it in both of his, eyes steady.

"We meet again in light," Marcel said.

"And in silence," Cassien replied.

With that, Marcel turned and disappeared down the wooded path that sloped eastward, vanishing like mist. Cassien remained for a moment, facing the northbound road, the fields beyond it already stirring in the morning wind.

Then he drew up the hood, steadied his breath, and walked on toward Limoux.

The road narrowed as it approached the outskirts of Limoux, bending past vineyards and low stone walls. Cassien kept his head bowed beneath the folds of his hood, letting the shadows cloak him as he passed through the gate. No one questioned his presence. Monks came and went regularly in these regions, and his gait, solemn and measured, betrayed no urgency.

The city stirred with market activity. Vendors shouted beneath canvas stalls, children darted between carts, and the scent of roasting chestnuts mingled with the musk of damp cobblestones. Yet beneath it all was a current—an unspoken awareness. People spoke in hushed tones, eyes flicking toward the hill where the tribunal was said to convene. It had once been a bishop's manor, but now served other functions.

Cassien moved with purpose, but not haste, observing each face. He stopped near a vendor selling loaves of coarse bread and exchanged a few coins. The woman serving him gave a slight nod—almost imperceptible—but her gaze lingered a moment too long.

Another signal. Someone had marked his arrival.

He made his way toward the Church of Sainte-Marie, knowing it was a common place for Benedictines to pause when entering the city. It would lend credence to his story. A priest met him at the doors, narrow-eyed but deferential.

"I've traveled from Cluny," Cassien said evenly, "bearing word from the Holy See for the Inquisitors convening here."

The priest gestured him inside without resistance. The sanctuary was empty, its vaulted arches cradling silence.

"You'll find the tribunal at the old manor. A day's wait at least before your credentials are seen," the priest murmured, not unkindly. "But take rest. You'll be called."

Cassien bowed and moved to the back pew, kneeling as though in prayer.

He was in.

But to what end?

He lowered his head and allowed his breath to still. Whatever awaited him here, he would meet it not as the man he once was, but as the vessel he had become.

Chapter Nineteen

THE SOUND CAME like a nail struck into the coffin of his wait-ing—three heavy raps upon the wooden door. Cassien rose from the bench where he had been sitting since dawn, the cold stone beneath him having long ago stolen all feeling from his legs. The young Dominican guard stepped in, face expressionless, and spoke only the words, "They will see you now."

The corridor beyond was narrow, dim, smelling faintly of lamp oil and damp mortar. The air was chill, but sweat prickled at Cassien's back beneath his woolen habit. The echo of their footsteps seemed to lengthen the hall, each strike of boot on stone a reminder that he was walking toward the judgment of Rome.

The chamber lay ahead, lit by tall windows whose light was diffused by the pale winter sky. In the center stood a long table draped in scarlet, its edge heavy with the folds of cloth. Upon it rested a crucifix of darkened bronze and a parchment roll waiting to receive the record of his words. Behind the table sat three men, a Cardinal in vivid red, the acolytes in black cassocks, their white collars stark in the muted light. At the center, the visiting Cardinal—tall, angular, his thin fingers steepled—regarded Cassien with an expression that was not unkind, yet offered no refuge.

Along the walls, Dominican scribes waited with their quills poised, while two armed sergeants lingered at the door. A smell of beeswax candles and cold stone mingled with the faint odor of ink.

Cassien bowed low, as protocol demanded, but his heart was steady. He felt no tremor in his breath. His thoughts, sharpened over the long days of waiting, were clear: he would speak truth. Not the convenient truth the Inquisition might wish to hear, but the truth as it had unfolded—the truth of his mission, his encounters, and his conviction that the slaughter must end.

He remembered Alais's still face, serene in death after the consolamentum, and he felt a quiet flame of resolve within him. He had no desire for martyrdom, but if his words could avert another fire consuming the villages of the south, then he would bear whatever judgment came.

The Cardinal's voice broke the silence, low and deliberate. "Brother Cassien of Cluny, you are called before this tribunal to answer for your conduct in the lands of Languedoc. Your presence here is by order of His Holiness in Rome. You will speak plainly. You will speak truthfully. And you will understand that the mercy of the Church rests upon your obedience."

Cassien inclined his head. "I am prepared."

The Cardinal's eyes narrowed slightly. "Then let us begin," the Cardinal said, folding his hands upon the table. "You were sent from Cluny two years ago with explicit instructions from Rome. State those instructions now, for the record."

Cassien straightened. "I was to observe the sect called Cathar, report upon their theology and practice, and determine the nature of their threat to the Holy Church."

The Cardinal nodded slightly. "Observe. Report. Not intervene. And yet, we have testimony that you aided them."

"I offered no sword," Cassien replied evenly. "I shed no blood in their defense. I sought only to know them as they were, and to fulfill the spirit of my mission."

The Dominican to the Cardinal's right leaned forward, his quill hovering over the parchment. "You carried messages. You shielded certain persons from discovery."

"I carried words, not arms," Cassien said. "And the persons I accompanied were pilgrims, not enemies."

The Cardinal's gaze sharpened. "Brother Cassien, do you deny your presence at Montségur? Do you deny witnessing the rites they call consolamentum?"

"I do not deny my presence," Cassien answered. "Nor do I deny that I witnessed a dying woman receive the consolamentum. She faced death with peace and without fear. I saw no evil in it."

A murmur stirred among the scribes. The Cardinal raised a hand for silence. "You speak with dangerous sympathy."

"I speak truth," Cassien said, his voice steady. "The Church sent me to learn, and I learned. They do not worship the Devil, as some claim. They seek purity of spirit, and they do not kill. In these lands, I have seen more cruelty from the sword than from their creed."

The Dominican to the left of the table frowned. "So you would have us suffer heresy to thrive?"

"I would have the bloodshed end," Cassien replied. "If heresy is to be corrected, let it be corrected by reason, not fire."

The Cardinal leaned back, studying him. "Brother Cassien, your words tread perilously close to defiance. You stand here because Rome requires an accounting, and yet you defend those condemned by Holy Church."

"I defend only what I have witnessed," Cassien said. "If I am to write my report at Cluny for Rome, I will write as I have seen, not as I am told to see."

The Cardinal's eyes held his for a long moment. The silence stretched, the only sound the faint scratching of the quill recording his words.

Finally, the Cardinal spoke. "Your candor is… noted. But candor alone will not protect you from judgment. The Inquisition does not act in haste, Brother Cassien. You will remain in Limoux until we determine whether your zeal for truth has overstepped obedience to the Church."

Cassien inclined his head, though inwardly he knew his fate was uncertain. He felt the quiet flame still burning in his chest—the conviction that truth was worth the peril. If his words could plant a seed in even one heart here, perhaps that seed might grow in time.

Two guards stepped forward. The Cardinal dismissed him with a slight wave of his hand. "We will call you again."

Cassien turned and walked from the chamber, the sound of the door closing behind him like the fall of a verdict not yet spoken.

The guard led him back through the narrow corridors, their shadows lengthening as the pale light of afternoon dimmed. No word passed between them, only the muffled thud of boots on stone and the faint clink of the guard's sword at his hip. At last, they reached the small chamber that served as Cassien's quarters—bare walls, a narrow bed, a wooden stool, and a single window cut deep into the masonry, its view limited to a sliver of sky and the uppermost branches of a winter-bare tree.

The door closed behind him with a dull thud. Cassien stood still for a moment, breathing in the stillness. The air was cold, but he welcomed it; it sharpened his thoughts. He crossed to the window and rested his hand on the rough stone sill, gazing at the pale wash of clouds drifting in the fading light.

In the silence, he felt the old self—the obedient monk from Cluny—standing beside the man he had become. Somewhere along the road through Lyon, Valence, Avignon, and the hill towns of Languedoc, he had crossed a threshold without knowing. Now, in the marrow of his being, he knew himself a Cathar, though he bore no outward mark.

He thought of Alais, her last breath a prayer without fear. He thought of the scrolls now hidden in the Sanctuary, their words carrying the hope of another way—one that did not demand the pyre. If these truths could endure beyond the wrath of Rome, perhaps some future might be spared the horror he had witnessed.

His mind returned to the Cardinal's gaze—cool, probing, measuring him like a man weighing whether to release a bird or close his fist. Cassien knew he might not leave Limoux. The Inquisition preferred the certainty of silence over the risk of a voice that would not bend.

A faint sound stirred at the door: the scrape of metal, the whisper of hinges. Cassien turned. A boy stood there—thin, no more than twelve—his dark eyes watchful. Without a word, the child stepped inside, closing the door softly behind him. From beneath his tunic, he drew a folded scrap of parchment and held it out.

Cassien took it, his fingers brushing the boy's cold hand. Unfolding the parchment, he saw a few hurried lines, written in a code he knew at once.

The river runs high, but the bridge still stands. The dove waits in the olive grove.

The boy said nothing. He gave a small nod, as if to say *You understand*, and slipped out into the corridor.

Cassien stood with the message in his hand, the faint scent of ink rising from the paper. A slow breath escaped him. The words were a signal—one known only to a few. Somewhere beyond these walls, an ally still moved in the shadows.

The flame in his chest burned brighter.

Cassien let the parchment rest in his palm for a long while, the meaning of the words settling over him like a veil. He understood the offer behind them—a bridge still standing meant there was a way out, a path unseen by the guards and unconsidered by the Inquisition. The dove in the olive grove was a promise of sanctuary, a place to vanish until the storm passed.

His fingers closed slowly around the scrap. For a moment, he allowed himself to imagine it: the narrow streets of Limoux behind him, the rolling hills opening toward the high pastures, the cold clarity of mountain air filling his lungs. The faces of friends not yet lost to the fire. Freedom, at least for a time.

But the image faded as quickly as it came. He had been sent here by Rome, not to run from danger, but to gather truth. That truth—full, unvarnished—must be placed before the Holy See. It could not be whispered in hallways or passed through the hands of strangers.

He moved to the small table, took a candle stub from the shelf, and lit it. The flame's steady glow caught the edges of the parchment. For a moment, he traced the ink with his eyes, committing every letter to memory. Then, without hesitation, he held it to the flame.

The parchment curled, darkened, and crumbled into ash. The faint scent of burning paper drifted through the room before the cold air swallowed it.

Cassien sat on the narrow bed, his hands folded loosely in his lap. He would answer the tribunal's questions as the protocol demanded: fact without interpretation, witness without judgment. The interpretations—his conclusions about the true nature of the Cathar faith— would be reserved for Rome.

Yet the silence between question and answer would hold his deepest resolve: he would not betray the trust of those who had given him their stories, nor would he provide the Inquisition with more than their authority required.

He leaned back against the wall, feeling the rough stone against his shoulders. Outside, the winter wind rose, whistling faintly in the high gaps of the masonry. Somewhere in the distance, a bell marked the hour of Vespers.

Cassien closed his eyes, not in sleep, but in the stillness of prayer —wordless, without petition, only the quiet offering of his will to stand in the truth.

The summons came with the morning light. The same Dominican guard appeared at his door, his breath misting in the chill air. "They will see you now," he said, in the same flat tone as before.

Cassien rose without a word, smoothing the folds of his habit. He had slept little, yet felt no heaviness. The night had been long with silent prayer, the hours measured by the slow turn of thought rather than the tolling of bells. He knew his path; the day would only test his footing upon it.

The judgment room was colder than before, the light from the tall windows falling pale and sharp across the scarlet-draped table. The Cardinal sat as he had the previous day, but this time the two Dominicans at his sides wore expressions of keener interest, as though they had spent the night preparing the angles of their questioning.

Cassien bowed and took his place.

"Brother Cassien," the Cardinal began, "we spoke yesterday of your mission and your actions. Today, I will have you speak of what you found—what you believe—after these two years among the heretics."

Cassien's eyes met his. "My mission was to observe and record for Rome. My conclusions belong in that report."

The Cardinal's fingers drummed once against the tabletop. "And yet, the Inquisition has its own need to know. You may spare Rome certain details and still speak them here."

Cassien kept his voice calm. "I will not preempt my report, Eminence. It is not my place to grant one court what is bound for another."

One of the Dominicans leaned forward. "Do you then deny that the Cathars have led many souls astray?"

"I have seen them live without violence," Cassien replied. "I have seen them seek purity. Whether they are astray is for Rome to judge. My duty is to tell what I saw, not to pass judgment before the proper authority."

The Cardinal's gaze was steady, but his tone grew more deliberate. "Brother Cassien, you walk a narrow path. The Inquisition does not look kindly upon evasions."

"I have spoken truthfully," Cassien said. "If my answers seem narrow, it is because my duty is narrow. I will not invent, nor will I withhold from Rome. But I will not give here what is meant for there."

A long pause followed. The scribes' quills were still. Outside the high windows, a gust rattled against the glass, the sound filling the silence.

At last, the Cardinal leaned back. "Very well. We will see whether Rome values your loyalty as much as you do." He gestured to the guard. "You may go. We will call you again."

Cassien bowed once more. As he turned to leave, he felt the Cardinal's gaze on his back, like a weight pressing between his shoulders. He knew the questioning was not over—the real test was still to come. But for now, he had held the line.

The guard escorted Cassien back through the twisting corridors, but as they neared his quarters, a figure detached itself from the shadows of an archway. It was the younger of the two Dominican scribes—the one who had sat to the Cardinal's right. The guard hesitated, glanced between them, then moved on without a word, leaving the two men alone in the dim passage.

"Brother Cassien," the scribe said softly, his eyes shifting toward the hallway's dark recesses. "Walk with me a moment."

Cassien hesitated, then followed as the man led him down a side passage to a small alcove where a single arrow-slit let in a blade of pale light. The scribe's voice was low, urgent.

"You must understand—the Cardinal's patience is not endless. He believes you are withholding something that may shield the heretics. Others here are already convinced. If you wait for Rome, it may be too late."

Cassien met his gaze. "If you think to save me by persuading me to speak out of turn, you will fail. My duty is clear."

The scribe's expression shifted—less frustration than something almost like curiosity. "You could end this now. One statement, one admission, and they would send you back to Cluny within the week."

"At the cost of truth?" Cassien asked quietly.

"At the cost of survival," the scribe replied. "You think you are safe because you are a Benedictine. But when suspicion hardens into certainty in these halls, there is no shield strong enough to turn it aside."

Cassien felt no anger, only a slow sadness. "Then I will trust that the truth will be shield enough—or that the cost of speaking it here would be greater than the cost of silence."

The scribe studied him for a long moment, then leaned closer. "There are others who think as you do, Brother Cassien. They will not speak in public, but they watch. If you fall, they will remember."

Without waiting for an answer, he stepped back into the corridor, his black cassock melting into the dimness.

Cassien stood alone in the narrow alcove, the cold light brushing his face. There was no promise in the man's words, yet something in them felt like a thread laid quietly in his hand—thin, fragile, but perhaps strong enough to hold when the strain came.

He returned to his quarters with the sense that the ground beneath him had shifted slightly. The tribunal was not a single mind; there were cracks in its stone face. And through such cracks, sometimes, the truth could pass unseen.

The summons came at midday, the winter light falling straight down through a cloudless sky. Cassien followed the guard once more to the tribunal chamber, feeling the echo of each step through the stone beneath him.

The room was as before—scarlet-draped table, bronze crucifix, the three figures seated in judgment. Yet the air felt different, tighter, as though the very walls had drawn closer.

Cassien bowed.

The Cardinal's voice was measured, but it carried a weight that stilled the chamber.

"Brother Cassien of Cluny, you have stood before this tribunal with restraint, offering only what you deem within the limits of your commission. You have refused to preempt your report to Rome, though pressed to do so. This we cannot call defiance in the fullest sense, but neither can we name it obedience without reservation."

One of the Dominicans leaned forward. "There are those who would see you held until your loyalty is proven beyond doubt."

The Cardinal raised a hand. "And there are those who believe that sending you on to Cluny will serve the Church better than keeping you here. We are not of one mind on this matter."

Cassien met his gaze. "Then I ask only that you honor the instruc-tions given to me when I was sent—observe, return, and report. My report is for Rome, not for this hall."

The Cardinal's lips pressed into a thin line. "Your words yesterday and today will be noted and sent ahead to the Holy See. You may yet find that the judgment in Rome is less patient than mine."

Cassien inclined his head. "If that is so, I will answer there as I have answered here."

For a moment, the Cardinal studied him as one might study an unyielding stone in the path of a river. Then he spoke.

"You will leave for Cluny within the week, under escort. Until your departure, you will remain confined to your quarters, save for the hours of worship. You are not to speak with anyone beyond the brothers of this house. Should you attempt to depart or to send messages beyond these walls, you will not leave Limoux alive."

"I understand," Cassien said.

The Cardinal gave a curt nod to the guards. "It is done."

As they led Cassien from the chamber, he felt no triumph, only a quiet, steady certainty. The path ahead was still narrow, but it was open. Rome awaited, and with it, the chance to speak the whole truth—not only for the sake of the Church, but for the lives that might yet be spared.

In his heart, the small flame burned on.

The morning of departure came with a brittle frost over the courtyard stones. Cassien stood between two mounted guards, their cloaks drawn tight against the cold. The saddle beneath him creaked as he mounted, his pack light—he carried no scrolls, no incriminating pages. The truth he bore was in memory alone, bound for Rome's ear.

The Cardinal had not come to see him off. Only the younger Dominican scribe was there, hood drawn low, standing in the shadow of the gatehouse. Cassien caught his eye for the briefest moment and received a small, almost imperceptible nod. Then the gates swung open, and they rode into the winter light.

Chapter Twenty

THE ROAD NORTHWARD wound along the Aude, the river swollen and swift with melted snow from the high country. The guards spoke little, their eyes scanning the hills. Each village they passed was subdued—doors closed, smoke curling from chimneys, children watching from behind their mothers' skirts. Cassien noted the absence of laughter, the wary glances at the sight of the Inquisition's colors.

By the second day, they reached Carcassonne, its walls looming like a great crown of stone. They lodged in the guesthouse of a Dominican priory, the air heavy with the smell of incense and damp plaster. Cassien kept to himself, eating in silence, aware that eyes followed him even in the refectory.

From there, the road bent toward Narbonne, then inland again along the old Roman route through Nîmes. In each town, the guards exchanged brief words with local clergy, as if to mark his passing. No attempt was made to speak with him beyond the formalities of the journey.

On the fifth day, as they approached the Rhône near Valence, Cassien felt the quiet pull of memory—the same river he had followed south two years before, when the mission lay open before him like an unwritten page. Now, the page was written, but unread. His task was to keep it whole until he reached the one who had sent him.

Beyond Lyon, the weather turned colder still. Frost edged the grasses along the roadside, and the breath of men and horses hung in the air like smoke. They passed monasteries whose bells marked the hours, and Cassien felt the rhythm of the Rule returning—though he knew he could never again be the same monk who had left Cluny.

At last, one clear afternoon, the towers of Cluny rose in the distance, their great stones lit by the low winter sun. Cassien's heart tightened, not from fear, but from the knowledge that here, within these walls, he would speak the truth in full.

The guards led him through the gatehouse into the outer court, then dismounted. A young novitiate approached and gestured toward the main cloister. "You are expected in the Abbot's chambers."

Cassien inclined his head, handed the reins to a stable boy, and walked beneath the familiar archways. Each step echoed on the worn stone, carrying him toward the place where his true trial would begin.

The cloister was hushed in the pale winter afternoon, the air heavy with the smell of burning tallow and the faint tang of damp stone. Cassien crossed the garth slowly, his steps echoing under the arcades. The familiar rhythm of chanting from the chapel reached him in muted waves, and for a moment, it was as though the years in Languedoc had been a distant dream.

At the Abbot's chambers, a novice opened the door and ushered him in. The room was warm from a small fire, the light softened by the tall arched windows. Behind a heavy oak desk sat Abbot Guillaume, his hands folded on a vellum folio. His eyes, still sharp despite his years, studied Cassien as though weighing what had returned against what had been sent.

"Brother Cassien," the Abbot said, rising. "Welcome home."

Cassien bowed deeply. "It is good to be within these walls again, Father Abbot."

The Abbot gestured for him to sit. "I have received word from Limoux—brief, but sufficient. The Cardinal speaks of your… measured answers. Rome will expect more. You have carried out your mission under unusual strain, and it is now your task to make a full account."

"I understand," Cassien replied.

"You will write your report here," Guillaume continued. "It will be in Latin, signed and sealed by your hand, and delivered under guard to Rome. You will omit nothing that bears upon the nature of the Cathar heresy or the conduct of the faithful in Languedoc. Rome must hear what you have to say."

Guillaume leaned forward over his desk, watching Cassien carefully.

"However, in all honesty, it is likely that your report may never leave the Vatican Library."

He leaned back in his chair.

"You were correct to withhold from the Inquisition what was not theirs to preempt. I will not read your report before it leaves Cluny; that is not my place, Brother. But I would appreciate a summary of your general conclusions. Does your conscience allow for that?"

Cassien inclined his head. "I will speak only the truth, Father. When I have finished the report, I can share a one-page summary with you of my general conclusions. It will not include details, names, or places. That would be improper. Will that be satisfactory, Father?"

The Abbot's gaze lingered a moment longer, as though he sensed there was more behind those words than the simple promise they seemed. "Very well, Brother Cassien. Then go to the scriptorium. You will have the table by the west wall. Write until the work is finished."

The scriptorium was cold, even in daylight, the high windows letting in a thin stream of winter sun. Rows of desks stood silent, their surfaces marked by years of careful labor. Cassien took his place at the appointed table, the bare wood smooth beneath his fingers. A fresh sheet of vellum lay before him, an inkwell to his right, a sharpened quill resting across it.

For a long moment, he did not move. The enormity of what he carried—names, faces, the stories of the living and the dead—settled upon him like a cloak. In the hall outside, a novice's footsteps faded into stillness.

At last, he dipped the quill into the ink, touched it lightly to the margin, and began.

Mandatum mihi datum est a Sancta Sede, ut observarem et referrem...

The commission was given to me by the Holy See, that I might observe and report...

The words came slowly at first, as though testing their own weight. But soon they found their rhythm—fact upon fact, the slow unfolding of two years in Languedoc, told in the order the journey had carried him. He gave no flourish, no ornament, yet the truth breathed between the lines. The consolamentum of Alais, the fortresses in the hills, the common sharing in shadowed rooms, the weary faces of villagers who had lost more than the Inquisition would ever name— would all pass beneath his hand.

By the time the bell rang for Vespers, a single page lay filled before him. He sanded the ink, set it aside to dry, and reached for another sheet. The report would take days, perhaps a week, but he would not hurry. Each word was a stone in the foundation of the truth, and the structure must stand when it reached Rome.

Cassien set the fresh vellum in place, dipped the quill again, and continued.

The scriptorium became his world. Each morning after Prime, he returned to the west wall table, the same shaft of pale light sliding slowly across the surface as the day advanced. Monks came and went in silence, their quills scratching in steady rhythm, but Cassien scarcely noticed them. His eyes and hand moved as one, ink flowing into lines that carried the weight of witness.

In villae Beziers et Carcassonae, vidi populos pavore oppressos, non solum ob doctrinam haereticorum, sed, magis, ob, timorem, gladii.

In the towns of Béziers and Carcassonne, I saw the people oppressed by fear, not only for the doctrine of the heretics, but more for fear of the sword.

He paused, letting the ink dry, then continued.

Multi erant qui nullam partem in doctrina Catharorum habebant, sed in eodem igne consumpti sunt.

Many there were who had no share in the Cathar doctrine, yet were consumed in the same fire.

Cassien wrote with care, weighing every phrase. He did not accuse Rome directly—such words would find no welcome in the Curia—but neither did he hide the truth. The cruelty of the campaigns, the needless deaths, the confusion sown among the faithful: all were set down without flourish, as facts observed and attested.

Of the scrolls delivered to the Sanctuary, he said nothing. They were not part of his commission, and their revelation would only bring danger to those who now guarded them. Nor did he name the friends who had offered him aid or shelter; instead, he recorded their actions as the work of "certain persons of conscience," leaving their identities hidden beneath the veil of anonymity.

When he wrote of Alais, he paused a long time before the words came.

Feminam vidi, morientem sine metu, in fide quae non est nostra sed quae eam sustentavit usque ad ultimum spiritum.

I saw a woman die without fear, in a faith not our own, yet one that sustained her to her last breath.

By the fifth day, the folios were stacked neatly at his right hand, each page bearing the neat, measured script of a man who understood that history could be shaped by the ink he set to parchment.

On the morning of the seventh day, as he laid down the final page, he dipped the quill one last time to sign his name. The black ink stood stark against the pale vellum:

Cassienus, Monachus Cluniacensis

He set aside the quill, breathed out slowly, and pressed the Abbot's seal into the warm wax at the bottom of the first page. The report was complete.

He took one more sheet of vellum, dipped his quill in the ink again, and wrote his summary for the Abbot.

When he rose from the table, the scriptorium felt different—less a place of confinement, more a place from which something living had been sent into the world. The folios would leave for Rome within the week, carried under guard along the winter roads. Cassien knew that whatever judgment awaited him would now be shaped by these pages.

And in his heart, he prayed that the truth, carried on the steady hand of his witness, might plant a seed even in the stoniest of ground.

The morning was sharp with frost, the air pale and still. In the outer court of Cluny, a single horse stood saddled, its breath pluming into the cold. Beside it waited the Abbot's appointed courier—a broad-shouldered monk in a travel-stained cloak, his gloved hands resting lightly on the reins.

Cassien held the sealed packet in both hands. The red wax bore the impression of the Abbot's seal beside his own smaller mark, each impression deep and unbroken. Within the folded vellum was all he had seen, all he dared to speak: the faces, the flames, the roads through a land torn between two faiths.

The Abbot stood nearby, his expression unreadable. "It will go first to Lyon," he said quietly, "then south again along the Rhône to Avignon, and from there to Rome. It will be delivered into the hands of the Cardinal who sent you to Lanquedoc."

Cassien inclined his head. "Then the work is no longer mine."

Guillaume's eyes held his. "No. But the weight of it will remain with you."

Cassien stepped forward and placed the packet into the courier's hands. The monk tucked it beneath his cloak, securing it with a leather thong, then mounted in a single, practiced motion.

For a moment, Cassien simply watched—watched the way the horse shifted under its rider, watched the brief flare of sunlight on the seal as the courier adjusted his cloak. Then the gates creaked open, and horse and rider passed beneath the arch into the winter road beyond.

The sound of hoofbeats faded, swallowed by the stillness.

Cassien stood a moment longer, breathing the cold air. The report was gone, its path and fate no longer his to guide. Whatever Rome would decide, it would determine without him. He turned to the Abbot, waiting expectantly, and placed the summary in his hand. The Abbot nodded and returned to his office.

Turning back toward the cloister, Cassien felt the strange lightness that comes when a long burden is set down. Yet beneath it ran a steady current of resolve. His mission was complete, but the truth he carried within him—unwritten, unspoken—would remain.

In the silence of the garth, he whispered a prayer that the seed he had planted might one day bear fruit, even in soil turned hard by fear.

And with that, Cassien walked back into the life of the monastery, the winter sun at his back.

It was late spring when the letter from Rome arrived. The Abbot summoned Cassien to his chambers, the sealed parchment resting upon the desk between them. Guillaume's eyes searched his face before he broke the wax and read aloud.

To the venerable Abbot Guillaume of Cluny,

The Holy See has received and examined the report of Brother Cassien, your envoy to the province of Languedoc. His diligence, restraint, and adherence to his commission are commended. No fault in loyalty to the mission or the Church has been found. He is hereby released from any suspicion and restored without censure to the full duties and privileges of his order.

Given in Rome, under our hand and seal, this Feast of Saint Philip and Saint James, in the Year of Our Lord, 1215.

The Abbot lowered the parchment and met Cassien's gaze. "You are free of this shadow, Brother."

Cassien bowed his head. "I am grateful, Father Abbot."

But in the stillness of his heart, gratitude was tempered by the knowledge of what had not changed. Rome had exonerated him, yet had found no cause to temper the fire of the Inquisition. The machinery would grind on—its judgments and punishments untouched by the truths he had labored to set down.

That night, after Compline, Cassien walked alone to the small side chapel where an old icon of the Virgin hung above the altar. Its frame was cracked, the paint faded by centuries of candle smoke. Kneeling before it, he whispered the prayer he had carried since Languedoc—part blessing, part plea for those who still lived under the shadow of the sword.

When the chapel was empty, he rose and gently lifted the icon from the wall. Behind it lay the narrow hollow he had discovered years before, where the plaster had broken away to reveal bare stone.

From his sleeve, he drew a small folded packet: a few pages in his own hand, written not in the careful, formal Latin of his report, but in the plain, unguarded tongue of his own heart. Here he had set down the truest thing he knew—that faith without violence was the only faith worth holding, and that even the smallest mercy was greater in the eyes of God than the fiercest victory.

He placed the packet into the hollow and set the icon back in its place, the Virgin's worn face gazing out into the flickering candlelight.

No one would see those words—not now, perhaps not for generations. But one day, when the time was right, they might be found, and the truth he had carried might speak again.

Cassien turned, the chapel silent behind him, and walked into the cool night air. Above the cloister roof, the stars burned steadily, as they had when he left, as they had when he returned.

And in his heart, though the world remained unchanged, the small flame endured.

EXCERPT FROM THE REPORT OF
BROTHER CASSIEN OF CLUNY

Ad Reverendissimum Abbatem meum, cui obedientia mea in Domino debetur: Ego, frater Cassienus de Cluniaco, humillimus servus Ecclesiae, relationem hanc brevem de haereticis Albigensibus submitto.

Anno Domini MCCXV.

To my Most Reverend Abbot, to whom my obedience in the Lord is owed: I, Brother Cassien of Cluny, most humble servant of the Church, submit this brief report concerning the Albigensian heretics, in the Year of Our Lord 1215.

The people who call themselves Good Men and Good Women profess reverence for Our Lord Jesus Christ, though they do not worship Him in the manner prescribed by the Church. They honor His teachings, particularly the commands to love one another and to seek purity of life.

They live simply, without ornament, and share their goods freely. Their humility is without pretense, and their steadfastness of conscience is remarkable—many labor with their hands, offering the fruits of their toil to sustain both neighbor and stranger.

Yet, they reject the Sacraments as instituted by Christ through His Apostles. Baptism they consider of no effect, regarding it as mere outward washing. The Eucharist they deny, saying that Christ cannot be made present through the consecrated bread and wine. Holy Orders they disdain, and Penance they dismiss as unnecessary, claiming that forgiveness may be sought directly of God without priestly mediation.

They neither build churches nor adorn altars, holding that the body of Christ dwells not in stone but in the living hearts of the faithful. They preach little, yet their manner of life itself becomes a sermon.

Though they err gravely in doctrine, I must testify that they are earnest in charity. They care for the sick, comfort the dying, and lift burdens from the poor. Their words are soft, their temper moderate, and they refrain from violence. In this, they reflect, though imperfectly, the command of Our Lord to love one another.

Nevertheless, their persistence in error and their refusal of correction pose a danger to the faithful. For the unlearned, swayed by kindness more readily than by truth, may easily be led astray. Thus, though they live as lambs, their teaching is a snare.

Such is the substance of my observations, humbly and faithfully submitted according to the mandate entrusted to me.

Humillimus servus vester, Frater Cassienus de Cluniaco, Anno Domini MCCXV.

THE HIDDEN LETTER OF BROTHER
CASSIEN OF CLUNY

Alais, ma soeur de lumière,

I set these words down not for Rome, not for my Abbot, not for the brethren who chant beside me, but for you. For my own heart. For the truth that I cannot allow to be lost.

I was there. I saw you. In that poor hut, with Alon at your side, the air heavy with silence, as you received the Consolamentum. I held the stillness with you as if the walls themselves bowed in reverence. You did not falter. Your eyes lifted to heaven, and in that moment the world grew hushed, as though creation itself bore witness. And when you left this life, it was as gently as a candle extinguished by a soft breath — not consumed in terror, but carried in peace.

That sight has never left me. Nor will it.

The Church has restored me now. They call me faithful again. I obey, outwardly. I rise at the bell, chant the psalms, and bend to the Rule. My brothers see nothing amiss. To them, I am what I was before. But I know otherwise. I am not the man who first set out from Cluny.

The truth has burned too deeply. It cannot be untaught. You, and Clara before you, showed me what I could not learn from parchment or decree: that Christ is not confined to Sacrament, nor caged in doctrine, nor wielded as authority. Christ is love. Pure. Simple. Fierce in its gentleness.

I will not rebel. That is not my calling. I have chosen to remain here in this cloister, not because I believe its stones shelter the truth, but because my heart now seeks simplicity. Silence. Prayer. A quill scratching ink across parchment. They will not suspect me. They need not. My witness lies not in public rebellion, but in memory. And in these words.

If one day these pages are uncovered, let it be known: I saw with my own eyes men and women who lived the Gospel of Love. They sought neither wealth nor war, but only to remember Christ in kindness. For this, they were named heretics. But I knew them. I loved them. And I cannot call darkness what shone with so much light.

Alais — sister of my soul — you live still, within me. Clara by blood, you by spirit. I will walk quietly, obedient in form, free in truth, until God gathers me also into that light where you wait.

Cassien, your brother in the light

PART 2 – THE DOOR

Father Bernard

Chapter Twenty-One

THE AIR IS foul with damp stone and smoke. I descend the steps slowly, robes brushing against the wall, the guard's torch throwing restless shadows ahead of me. I have been here before. Many times. The condemned await, chained and broken, and I am the voice of God to them — their last chance to speak truth before the fire claims them.

I steady myself, whispering the familiar words of the ritual under my breath. They have never failed me.

The guard unlocks the iron door. The stench meets me first: unwashed flesh, mildew, rot. Inside, she sits against the wall, shackles cutting at her wrists, her hair matted, her gown darkened with filth. Clara.

I stand tall, drawing the torchlight between us. "Daughter," I begin, my voice even, practiced, "this is the hour appointed for you. I come not as your enemy but as your confessor. If your soul holds sin, speak it. If your heart strays from the true Church, repent. God is merciful still, if you will only return."

Silence.

Her eyes lift to me through the tangles of her hair, steady, unblinking. No plea. No defiance. Only stillness.

I continue, as I must. "You know the wages of heresy. The fire awaits, yet I tell you this: renounce your error and you may be spared its agony. Many have turned back, even at the final hour. Do not spurn this mercy."

Still, she does not speak. I feel the weight of her gaze, as if she sees through the words, through the armor of office itself.

"Will you confess?" My voice sharpens. "Will you name your sin before God?"

At last, she speaks — her voice low, hoarse, yet clear. "Tell me, Father… do you believe God desires this fire?"

The question startles me, though I do not show it. I answer quickly, reflexively. "The fire purifies. It defends the flock from corruption. It is His justice."

She tilts her head. "And His love?"

My jaw tightens. "His love saves the obedient."

Her chains clink as she shifts, drawing closer to the torchlight. "Or does His love burn brighter than obedience? Even for those who strike, even for those who condemn?"

I feel the words pressing into me. I remind myself — I am the confessor, not the accused. I raise the ritual phrases again, firm, practiced: "Repent, and His mercy will cover you."

But she does not bow. She does not beg. She leans forward, eyes aflame in the torchlight, and whispers:

"Father, I hold no hatred. Not for them. Not for you. Do you hear me? Even for you."

Her words sink into me like a blade. For a moment, the chamber seems to still — no dripping water, no torch crackle, only her gaze, her voice echoing in the hollow of my chest.

I step back, reciting again, too quickly now, too rigid: "God will judge. God alone."

But her voice follows me as the guard pulls the door shut: *Even for you.*

The door slams shut behind me. Iron upon stone. I draw in a long breath, as though the stench of the dungeon might cling to me even now.

The guard avoids my eyes. He has heard nothing, or perhaps he has chosen not to hear. To him, she is only another prisoner, another condemned. To me—

No. I straighten my shoulders. I am the confessor. My role is clear. My duty has not changed.

I walk the narrow passage upward, the torch guttering in my hand. The ritual words still taste on my tongue, but their certainty falters. Her question echoes in the hollow of my chest: *Do you believe God desires this fire?*

At the landing, two friars wait. They rise quickly, bowing their heads.

"Well?" One asks.

"She spoke little," I answer. My voice is firm, controlled. "She remains obstinate. The sentence stands."

The friars nod. They do not look into my eyes. They do not ask more. That is mercy, or cowardice. Perhaps both.

I move past them into the cloister. Night air greets me, cool and sharp, yet I feel no relief. The stars gleam above the courtyard, but her voice follows me still: *Even for you.*

I press the cross at my breast as though it might anchor me. *God's love saves the obedient*, I had told her. That is the truth I have spoken countless times. The truth I have lived. And yet—

Why, then, do I feel as though it is my own soul in chains?

The cloister is quiet, but sleep does not come. I pace the shadows, her words clinging like smoke to my garments.

At last, I make my way to the bishop's chambers. The guard outside nods, admits me without question.

He sits at a desk piled with parchment, quill in hand, his features hard in the lamplight. He looks up, eyes narrowing with impatience until he recognizes me.

"Father Bernard," he says, gesturing for me to enter. "You have heard the prisoner's confession?"

I bow. The name — my own name — sounds strange to me in his mouth, as though it belongs to another man.

"She is unrepentant, my lord."

"As expected." He dips the quill again, scratching a note upon the parchment. "The Cathar poison runs deep. But the fire will cleanse what words cannot."

I nod, but the assent feels heavy in my throat. "She… she spoke little."

The bishop glances up. "Little or much, it matters not. Their silence damns them as surely as their heresy."

I hesitate. "Yet I wondered, my lord, if mercy—"

His hand slams upon the desk. The inkpot trembles. "Mercy? Do you question the justice of Holy Church, Father Bernard? These people drag souls into perdition. To falter in our duty is to betray Christ Himself."

The words strike sharp, rehearsed, as though he has spoken them many times before. Still, he softens his tone as he leans back, folding his hands. "You are weary, I think. You have served long in this work. Remember: obedience is mercy. The flame is mercy. Through us, God's will is done."

I bow again, more deeply this time. "Yes, my lord."

Dismissed, I step back into the night air. The stars are cold above the cloister roofs. His words should strengthen me. They always have before.

But as I walk beneath the arches, my hand strays to my chest where the cross hangs, and I hear again the prisoner's voice: *Even for you.*

The chamber is narrow, bare stone and cold air, but the cross hangs above my cot, carved of dark wood, arms outstretched. I fall before it, knees pressing hard into the floor, hands clenched together.

"My Lord," I whisper, then louder, until my voice fills the room, "my Lord, hear me. I have served You without wavering. I have obeyed every command, spoken every judgment in Your name. I have given myself to the fire of Your justice."

The silence answers me. My breath quickens. I bow lower, pressing my forehead to the stone.

"Yet tonight I am troubled. This woman—Clara—they call her heretic. She refuses repentance. She is chained, condemned, and yet..." My throat tightens. "She spoke of love. Not rebellion, not defiance — love. Even for me."

I raise my eyes to the cross, the shadow of Christ's face flickering in the candlelight. "Tell me, Lord! Is this Your will? Do You desire these fires? Do You delight in the smoke of their flesh? Speak, that I may not falter! I am Your servant. Command me!"

My words echo against the walls and fall back into my ears. Nothing answers. Not thunder, not whisper. Only the creak of timbers, the gutter of flame.

I grip the edge of the cot, my knuckles white. "Have I mistaken zeal for truth? No — no, it cannot be. The Church is Your body, Your voice. To doubt her condemnation is to doubt You."

Still, the silence holds. I tremble, torn between obedience and a terror I cannot name.

At last, I collapse fully, arms outstretched on the stone, my voice breaking: "Show me, Lord… let me know I have not been deceived. Confirm Your will, for I cannot walk in shadows."

The silence presses heavier still, until Clara's voice slips unbidden into my mind: *Even for you.*

I cover my ears, but it remains.

Sleep takes me like a thief. My body sags upon the cot, but my mind does not rest. It burns.

I am standing again in the square. The pyres rise before me, taller than men, the logs stacked with careful hands. The crowd presses in, faces hungry for the spectacle. I lift my hand, give the signal, and the torches plunge.

Flame leaps.

A hundred voices scream at once. They are men, women, even children. Their cries twist together into one long wail that rattles the marrow in my bones. The smoke chokes me, yet I do not move. I stand, rigid, as the flesh melts, as the bones crack, as eyes roll white in their sockets.

I hear the calling — not to God, but to me. "Father! Mercy! End it! Father!"

I try to cover my ears, but my hands are bound at my sides. The flames roar louder. Their faces blur, blackened, skin falling from bone, yet still they scream. Their mouths open wider, until fire pours from within them as if they themselves have become the torches.

One face emerges from the smoke. Clara. Her eyes are unburned, steady, holding me fast. She opens her mouth— not in a cry, but in a whisper. *Even for you.*

I stumble back, but the fire closes around me. My robes catch. I feel the heat, the blistering pain searing my arms, my chest. I am in the pyre now, among them. I am the condemned.

"Father Bernard," the crowd jeers. "Confess! Repent!"

The bishop's voice thunders above them all: "Obedience is mercy! The flame is mercy!"

I scream.

I jolt awake, drenched in sweat, the candle burned low, my breath ragged in my chest. The chamber is silent, but the echoes remain — the cries, the fire, her eyes.

I clutch the cross at my breast, shaking. *Even for you.*

I do not sleep again.

The bells toll before the sun has cleared the rooftops. Harsh, unrelenting, they summon the faithful to judgment.

I rise from the cot as though my body were made of lead. My cassock clings damp with sweat. The nightmare has not left me — the cries still ring in my skull, the smell of burning flesh still curls in my nostrils. I wash my face in the basin, but the water cannot cleanse it.

The courtyard is already stirring. Friars move in silence, their faces grim, their hands busy with preparations. Torches are stacked, ropes coiled, the pyre built high in the square beyond the gates. I walk among them, head bowed, lips murmuring prayers I do not feel. My tongue shapes the words, but my heart is stone.

At the edge of the square, the bishop waits in full vestments, a golden cross raised in his hand. He looks to me as I approach. "Father Bernard," he says with iron calm. "You will stand at my side."

I bow, though my stomach knots. "Yes, my lord."

The crowd thickens, villagers pressing close, faces alight with eagerness and fear. Children are hoisted to shoulders. Merchants abandon their stalls. They come not only for justice, but for spectacle. My mouth dries.

Then the prison doors open.

The guards drive the prisoners forward in chains, one by one, a line of shadows against the rising sun. Clara is among them.

I know their faces. I have stood before each of them in the dim of the dungeon, recited the same ritual, spoken the same offer of mercy. Not one recanted.

The first, a man with hollow cheeks and eyes like embers, had spat blood on the floor and whispered a prayer in the tongue of his people. His silence was more defiance than despair.

Another, a young woman scarcely more than a girl, had trembled as I spoke the words, but when I urged her to repent, she only shook her head. Tears streaked her face, yet her lips formed the name of Christ with quiet stubbornness.

An old man, broken in body, barely able to stand, leaned on his chains like a crutch. His voice cracked as he refused me, but he refused still.

I had expected at least one to falter, to seize the lifeline of absolution. But none did. Not one.

I told myself their obstinacy was proof of the devil's grip, that the pyre alone could cleanse such hardness. Yet in the silence of the night, their faces had returned to me, heavy with something I could not name.

And now, as they shuffle toward the stakes, I see them anew — weary, gaunt, chained — but walking as though they carried something I could not take from them.

The crowd roars. The guards shove. The bishop raises his hand for silence.

My eyes are drawn to Clara, her gown torn, her hair wild from the dungeon's filth. Yet she walks with a calm that unsettles me more than all my dreams. She does not resist. She does not stumble. She looks ahead as though the pyre were no more than a doorway.

The people jeer. Some spit. Some weep. She does not turn to them.

Her eyes search the platform, and for one terrible moment, they find mine.

The nightmare floods back, the screams, the fire, the words: *Even for you.*

I swallow hard, forcing myself into stillness. I am a priest of God. I am the confessor. My face must show no weakness.

But inside, I burn.

The bishop lifts his staff, and the crowd stills. His voice booms across the square, rich with authority, reciting the litany of judgment. "These souls have strayed from the fold. They have denied the sacraments, defied Holy Church, and blasphemed the truth of Christ. By His justice, their bodies shall be given to the flame, that their heresy may be consumed."

The people answer with a roar. Some cheer, some curse, some weep. I stand beside him, my hands folded, my face carved from stone. Inside, I am trembling.

The guards bind them to the stakes. The ropes bite into bone, pulling arms wide. I hear the iron rattle of chains, the muffled prayers, the last deep breaths of those who know the fire is near.

I fix my eyes on the cross above the platform. *Obedience is mercy. The flame is mercy.* The bishop's words repeat in my head, but they do not hold.

Then Clara lifts her face.

The smoke of torches wavers around her, yet her gaze cuts clear. She does not shout. She does not struggle. She looks outward, across the crowd, as though searching for something — or someone.

Then I see him. A monk, standing behind a wall of soldiers, his face a mask of agony, his hand over his heart.

She mouths something to him I cannot hear over the roar of the crowd.

And then her eyes find mine.

The air leaves my chest. Her lips move, silent at first, then I hear it, carried on a voice steady and strong: "I forgive you."

I stagger. My knees nearly give way. Did anyone else hear? The crowd shouts too loud, the bishop thunders his final benediction. But I know the words were for me.

The torches drop into the pyre.

Flame surges, ravenous, devouring the wood, racing up the stakes. The prisoners cry out — some in agony, some in prayer. The sound is unbearable, flesh and faith mingled into one long cry.

Clara does not cry out. Her body writhes, yes, the fire consuming her, but her face holds — calm, unyielding, her lips still shaping words I cannot hear.

Even for you.

The fire reflects in her eyes until the smoke veils her from me.

I cannot breathe. I clutch the cross at my breast, but it feels heavy, foreign, like iron dragged from the fire itself. The bishop raises his hand, proclaiming the cleansing complete, but his voice is distant.

All I hear is her whisper, rising through the roar of flame: *Even for you.*

The fire crackles, devouring what remains. Smoke coils into the sky, black against the morning sun. The screams are gone now, leaving only the hiss of fat on embers, the snap of wood collapsing into ash.

The bishop turns to me, eyes gleaming with grim satisfaction.

"It is done," he says, voice steady. "God's work is accomplished. Souls are spared corruption. You see, Father Bernard, this is mercy."

I bow my head because that is what I must do. But inside, the question gnaws: *Could he be right? Have I been shaken by nothing more than a trick of a heretic's tongue?*

The bishop strides away, his robes stirring the dust, the crowd parting before him. There is no doubt in his step, no hesitation in his voice. He is the rock. I am the reed trembling in the wind.

The people begin to scatter. Their voices fade into the alleys, children chasing one another, merchants reopening stalls. For them, the spectacle is finished.

But I cannot move.

My eyes remain fixed on the stake where Clara had stood, on the place where her gaze held mine, on the ashes that still glow with red embers.

Something gleams near the blackened wood. I step closer.

It is a lily — the small carving she carried in her hand, dropped when the guards dragged her forward. I had seen it then, noted it, dismissed it. But now it lies before me as though waiting.

I bend, lift it from the ashes. The edges are scorched, darkened, but the shape endures — delicate petals, carved with care. I turn it in my hand, the wood warm from the fire, and feel its weight press into my palm.

I hold it tight, unwilling to release it.

I remain there as the last of the crowd drifts away, as the torches burn low, as the smell of smoke lingers heavy in the square. I do not know what I am keeping vigil for — her soul, my own, or something between us. But I cannot leave.

A figure approaches through the haze. A young monk, soot streaking his face, eyes sharp with grief. He steps close.

"You stayed," he says quietly.

I lift my head. "I have seen many burn," I answer, my voice rough. "I have turned away before. But not today."

I have seen many burn, yes. I have turned away before, yes. But not today. Not after her words. Not after her gaze.

He studies me, this young monk. His eyes search mine as if to read what I dare not speak.

"Why this one?"

Because she forgave me. Because her love broke me. Because she sang in silence, and I cannot silence it still. I swallow the words and give him the truth I can bear. "Because she sang as the flames rose. Not with her voice, but with her stillness. I could not leave such a soul alone."

We stand together, two strangers bound by one fire. The smoke curls between us, carrying her memory.

"I thought there was to be a tribunal here today," he says softly.

"No," I tell him, though I hear my own voice distant, hollow. "She was too strong to let live, but too holy to be burned at the fortress."

I turned to him. "I noticed you in the crowd," I say. "Did you know her?"

"I did."

"Who are you?"

"Brother Cassien. Clara was my sister." He studies me again. "Were you one of them once?"

My chest tightens. *I still am.* I cannot say it. I say instead, "Perhaps. Or perhaps I've only now remembered that I was."

He nods slowly, as if he understands more than I wish to reveal.

"And you—Brother," I ask him, unable to stop myself, "do you carry her fire?"

His answer is simple, steady. "Yes. And I will not let it die."

I reach beneath my robe. My fingers find the lily, wrapped in cloth, still warm against my chest. I press it into his hand. "This was dropped before the bindings. I think it was hers."

He unwraps it, clutches it, eyes shining. He thanked me, and asked my name.

I incline my head. My voice is low. "Bernard," I tell him. "Go now. The world waits for men who do not forget."

He turns toward the open gate and does not look back.

I remain, the smoke drifting around me, Clara's gaze still fixed upon my soul.

The pyres are ash now. The square has emptied, but the stench lingers, seared into stone and bone alike. I have not slept.

Before noon the next day, I am summoned. The bishop waits in his chamber, light slanting across parchments stacked like fortifications on his desk. His eyes rest on me as I enter, sharp and steady.

"Father Bernard," he says, voice smooth as polished stone. "You look worn."

I bow. "It has been a heavy season, my lord. Yet I serve still."

He studies me, fingers steepled. "You served well yesterday. Your presence honored the work. But I saw it in your face — the toll. This labor is not for the faint of spirit. Too many flames, too many cries. Even the strongest can grow weary."

I keep my eyes low. My hands twitch against my robe. *He knows. He has seen.*

"You are loyal," he continues, softer now. "I do not question it. But zeal, left untended, may wither. A fire needs rest as much as fuel. Do you understand?"

I nod, though my chest tightens.

He leans back, the chair creaking. "Go home, Bernard. Take leave. A season only. Return to your people, breathe the air of your youth, walk where you first knew God's call. Let the soil of your beginnings refresh you. Then, when you return, you will be strong again. Strong for the work that lies ahead."

I lift my eyes at last. His face is serene, certain, untroubled by doubt. *He believes this will heal me. He believes obedience will root deeper when I rest in familiar ground.*

I bow again, lower this time. "As you command, my lord."

"Good," he says, already turning back to his parchment. "God's mercy is shown in rest as well as in fire. Do not squander it."

Dismissed, I leave the chamber. The stone corridors are cool around me, but Clara's words are still hot in my chest. *Even for you.*

Home. The thought startles me. It has been years since I walked those roads, since I saw the face of the one who first showed me mercy in my troubled youth. My grandmother.

Chapter Twenty-Two

I LEAVE THE fortress on foot. No retinue, no company. The bishop believes solitude will restore me. Perhaps it will.

The road stretches before me, winding through fields just beginning to green with spring. The air is sharp, clean, unlike the stench of smoke that still clings to my robes. Each step carries me further from the pyres, yet I cannot shake the sound of her voice.

Even for you.

I press the cross at my chest, but it offers no comfort. The lily is gone — I gave it to the young monk. He will carry it forward. I have only memory.

By the second day, I reach a parish church, small and rough, its stones weathered, its priest long since dead. The villagers greet me as Father, bowing their heads, eager for blessing. I am welcomed, fed, offered a cot.

At dawn, I stand at the altar. The words of the mass roll from my tongue as they always have, precise and unwavering. *Dominus vobiscum. Et cum spiritu tuo.* Their responses rise like well-worn echoes. For a time, I almost believe I am steady again.

Then the confessions begin.

A farmer, shoulders bent from labor, kneels before me. He confesses envy of his neighbor's land, the theft of a hen. I speak the rite, assign penance. He thanks me, kisses my hand.

Another kneels — a mother confessing impatience with her children, a youth confessing lies told at market. Ordinary sins, ordinary absolutions. Each one looks to me as the voice of God. Each one leaves lighter.

Yet I do not.

The words are right. The forms are true. But as they kneel before me, I hear Clara's question whispering in the silence between us: *Do you believe God desires this fire?*

The farmer rises, absolved, yet I feel nothing. No certainty. No peace. Only the hollow echo of my own voice.

On the road again, I walk alone. The fields are wide, the sky immense. The quiet should soothe me, but her face rises with every step. Not her suffering — not the flames — but her stillness. Her eyes. Her words.

I tell myself I am only weary. The bishop is right. Rest will restore me.

But as I walk, I feel instead that something long buried is pressing upward, like a root breaking through stone.

It is the fifth night of my journey when I come to a village nestled against the hills. The church is small, its walls rough stone, its bell cracked. Yet the people welcome me with reverence, as though a bishop himself had come among them.

That evening, I hear their confessions, one by one. A woman frets over harsh words to her husband, a boy admits to stealing fruit. I

listen, absolve, bless. The words come easily, though my heart remains heavy.

Then the old man enters.

He kneels slowly, joints stiff, his hands trembling. His voice is low,
almost broken.

"Father… I have carried a heavy weight three years. I could bear it
no longer, knowing you were here."

I lean close, steadying him with my gaze. "Speak, my son. The
mercy of God is wide."

He draws a breath, shuddering. "There was a man — a good man,
kind to my family. But he was a Cathar. When the Inquisition
came, they took my wife. Said they would burn her unless I told
them where he hid. I… I told them. I betrayed him."

His voice breaks. Tears spill down his cheeks. "They burned him.
My wife was spared, but I see his face every night. I hear his
screams. I damned him to save her. And I have hated myself ever
since."

His sobs fill the silence. I feel my own breath catch, my chest tight
with an ache I cannot name.

"Father… can God forgive such a thing? Can He forgive me?"

My mouth opens, but no words come. I have spoken absolution a
thousand times, to a thousand sins. But here, the ritual feels like
ash upon my tongue.

I see Clara in the flames, her stillness, her eyes upon me. I see the man's tears, his trembling hands. *Even for you.*

At last, I manage a whisper: "God's mercy is deeper than any fire. His love… reaches even here."

The man weeps harder, clutching the edge of the grille. I raise my hand, bless him, speak the words of forgiveness — words I scarcely believe, yet words he clings to like a drowning man to driftwood.

When he departs, he looks lighter, as though a burden has been lifted. But the burden has not left the room. It has settled upon me.

I kneel where he had knelt, the wood still warm from his touch, and for the first time I confess in silence what I dare not speak: *Lord, I too have betrayed. I, too, have stood and watched as souls burned. And I do not know if You forgive me.*

Two more days I walk, the road winding through forests and streams, until I come upon another village. Smaller still, its cottages huddled together as though clinging for warmth.

They welcome me with joy, as if Christ Himself had entered their square. They kiss my hands, press bread into them, bow as I bless their children. I feel their hunger — not of the body, but of the soul.

That evening, the church is crowded. Every bench filled, men and women kneeling in the aisles, eager for the sacrament. Their voices rise with mine, rough but earnest, the Latin words strange upon their tongues but fervent nonetheless. *Credo in unum Deum.* I lift the chalice, and their eyes shine as though heaven itself were pouring into their hands.

Later, I hear their confessions. A man burdened by anger toward his son. A widow tormented by bitterness. A child who admits to lying, trembling as though it were mortal sin. I absolve them all. I bless them all. I see their shoulders straighten, their eyes grow calm.

And I feel, for a time, whole. This is what I was ordained for — to bring God's mercy to the people. Out here, far from the fortress, the smoke, the fire, I can almost believe again.

Almost.

But when the night grows quiet and I lie upon the cot they've offered, Clara's voice returns. Her eyes in the torchlight, her whisper: *Even for you.*

I gave the villagers words. She gave me something greater — love that asked nothing, love that forgave all. I spoke to them of mercy. She was mercy.

And so the road continues. Each village greets me the same: with reverence, with need, with gratitude. I serve them gladly. I am their priest. I do not regret it.

But in the silence between their voices, in the pauses of my prayers, she is there. Her stillness is stronger than my sermons. Her love greater than my absolutions.

And though I walk as Father Bernard, priest of the Church, part of me walks with her still, chained in the dungeon, singing in silence as the flames rose.

The road narrows as I draw nearer to the village of my birth. Hills roll gently, fields patched with stone walls I remember from boyhood, though I have not walked them in twenty years.

The air is different here — sharper, carrying the scent of tilled earth and wild thyme. My steps slow of their own accord.

I pass a grove of oaks, their branches twisted with age. As a child, I used to sit beneath them, tracing shapes in the bark, whispering prayers I did not yet know by rote. Back then, I believed God's ear bent close to me, as close as the wind that stirred the leaves.

A memory rises unbidden: my grandmother's hand on my shoulder, her voice low as she guided me in prayer. Not in Latin, not in the words of priests, but in the tongue of our people, plain and warm. *God is love, Bernard. He hears you because you are His child, not because of the words you say.*

I shake the memory off, yet it clings. It feels truer than the liturgy I carry on my lips.

At the crest of a hill, I see it at last — the village, small and weathered, huddled around its single church. Smoke rises from hearths, children chase one another across the square, dogs bark at my approach. Nothing has changed, and yet everything has.

I pause at the edge of the road, staring down at the place I once called home. My chest tightens. For years, I told myself I left willingly, chosen by God for higher service. But now I wonder if I fled — from grief, from wounds I dared not face, from the boy I once was.

I draw the cross from my breast and kiss it. I am still a priest. I am still Father Bernard. Yet as I take the first step down into the village, I feel less certain of what that means than ever before.

The lane is narrower than I remember, the cottages leaning close as though whispering to one another. Faces appear in doorways as I pass. Some nod, some cross themselves, some only stare.

I come at last to the house where I was born. Its timbers sag, the shutters hang loose, the yard overgrown. The door is shut, but not barred. I push it open.

The air inside is stale. Dust lies thick upon the table, the hearth cold, cobwebs stretching between the beams.

A neighbor appears in the doorway behind me, cap in hand. He bows, then hesitates. "Father Bernard. You have returned."

I turn. "This house—my father?"

The man clears his throat. "He died two winters past. Fever, they said. No one tended him."

I nod slowly. My mother, I lost long ago, taken in childbirth with a second child who did not survive. My father raised me alone, though I cannot call it raising. His temper was sharp, his hand heavy. He drank, he stole, he took what he pleased. None dared oppose him, though all despised him.

"No one mourned him," the neighbor adds softly, as though reading my thoughts. "We buried him quickly. It was… enough."

I look around the ruin of the house, the silence thick with memories I would rather forget. My father's voice, harsh and bitter. The nights I hid from his rage. The shame that clung to me like smoke.

The neighbor clears his throat again. "But your grandmother lives still. Your mother's mother. Old now, but strong. She dwells near the edge of the village, in the cottage by the stream."

My chest tightens. I had not dared hope she still lived. In her arms, I once knew gentleness. In her voice, I once heard truth. She alone had shielded me from my father's storms.

I leave the house without looking back. The past lies in ashes. Ahead, perhaps, a flame still burns.

The path narrows as I leave the village, winding toward the stream that glitters in the fading light. I know this way. My feet remember it even if my mind does not. I walked it as a boy, clutching her hand, listening to her stories.

The cottage stands as it always did — small, weathered, its thatch patched with straw, smoke curling from the chimney. The sound of the stream mingles with birdsong in the trees. For a moment, I am ten years old again, carrying a bundle of wood to her door, eager for her smile.

I raise my hand to knock. My knuckles pause above the wood. My heart pounds like a boy's.

The door creaks open before I touch it. She stands there.

Bent, thin, her hair white as wool, her hands knotted with age. Yet her eyes — her eyes are the same: clear, steady, filled with warmth.

"Bernard," she whispers, as though she had been waiting for me.

I fall to my knees before her, bowing my head. "Grandmother." My voice breaks. "Forgive me. I should have come sooner."

Her hands, frail yet sure, lift my face. She smiles, lines deepening around her mouth. "You have come now. That is enough."

She leads me inside. The cottage is simple, filled with the scent of herbs and woodsmoke. The fire glows low, a pot simmering. She settles me at her table, pours water, tears brimming in her eyes as she studies me.

"You wear the robe of a priest," she says softly. "I knew you would. You always longed for God."

I bow my head, my throat tightening. "I longed… yes. But what I found, Grandmother…" I stop, unable to speak it.

Her hand rests over mine, light as a bird. "You will tell me when you are ready. For now, let me look at you. My boy, grown into a man."

For the first time in years, I feel seen — not as Father Bernard, priest of the Church, but as the boy she once held close, the boy who once believed God's love was simple and sure.

She sets a bowl before me, steam curling from a simple stew of beans and leek. The spoon is old, smoothed thin by years of use. I turn it in my hand and recognize a nick near the handle.

"You made that," she says, catching my glance. "With your little knife. You were eight and very proud. It was crooked then, too."

I smile before I can stop myself. "You kept it?"

"I keep what is given in love," she answers, as if it needed no saying.

We eat without hurry, the way she always taught me—to taste, to bless, to listen to what the day has placed in our hands. When we have finished, she wipes the table with the heel of her palm, a gesture so familiar it aches. She heats water, rinses the bowls, sets them upside down to dry. The stream outside speaks in the same voice it used when I was a boy.

We speak of the small things first. Who married whom. Whose cow wandered into the miller's field. Which winter was hardest, and which harvest surprised us. She names neighbors I half remember, adding, "He limps now," or, "Her laugh is gone since her sister died," as if sorrow and resilience were as ordinary as bread.

"And you?" she asks at last, not prying, only inviting. "Where have your feet carried you all these years?"

"North and south," I say. "Through towns I do not miss and monasteries that should have been kinder. The roads are long. The Church is… vast."

"Vastness does not warm a bed," she murmurs, laying another log on the fire. The flame takes slowly, then brightens. "Sometimes a small light is the one we need."

I step to the door and fetch in the last of dusk—the cool of it, the sound of the water, the smell of damp earth. A cat slips past my ankles into the cottage as if it owns the place. It always did. It leaps to the hearth stool, curls into itself, and sleeps.

"Do you remember the oaks?" she asks.

"I passed them today."

"You used to whisper into their bark and tell me they answered."

"They did," I say, and hear how it sounds—like a man admitting to a child's dream. But she only nods, as if the oaks had indeed been listening.

She brews an herb tea—chamomile and a sprig of mint—and we cradle the warm cups. She hums a tune without words, something she used to sing when I could not sleep for storms. I find myself humming the second part, the old harmony we made together, and when the last note fades, it leaves a quiet so soft it feels like a hand on the brow.

We do not touch the deep places. Not yet. She asks instead about the roads, the weather, the shape of the churches where I said mass. I describe a hilltown with bells that cracked in winter, a chapel where the roof fell in but the people gathered anyway beneath canvas, singing so loud I felt the rafters we did not have. She laughs at the image, then grows still.

"And your health?" she asks.

"I walk well enough."

"And your sleep?"

I do not answer. She does not press.

Night edges in. She lights a tallow candle and speaks a blessing over the room—not Latin, not rote, but the small, homely prayer she always spoke at day's end. It asks for nothing clever: bread for tomorrow, strength for work, peace for quarrels, safe passage for the departing. When she says "Amen," she adds, as she did when I was small, "And for my Bernard, a clear heart."

Something catches in my throat. I busy myself with the fire.

She spreads an extra blanket on the pallet by the hearth. "You'll take this," she says. "Your bones will not forgive me if I put you on the bench."

"I have slept on worse," I tell her.

She smiles. "I know. That is why you will sleep here."

Before she retires, she chooses from a bundle of dried herbs hanging from the rafters and crumbles a pinch into a small dish. "For the night air," she says. "It keeps the damp from the lungs." The scent lifts—thyme, a little lavender—and for a moment I am ten again, listening to rain knock at the shutters while she tells me stories of saints who were not always saintly, and of God who loved them anyway.

At the doorway to her little room, she pauses. "When you rose from the table," she says, "you put your chair back without scraping it. You did that as a boy, too. You thought no one noticed."

"I thought *you* noticed everything."

"I tried." She rests her hand on the doorframe, steadying herself. "We will speak more tomorrow. There is time."

She leaves the door ajar the way she used to, so a strip of candlelight lies across the floor. I lie on the pallet and watch the light tremble with her movements. The stream keeps its slow counsel. The cat sighs.

Out on the road, in churches far from this one-room home, my voice has carried judgment and mercy in measures I believed were fixed. Here, the measures are different—bread, warmth, the naming of small things, a chair set back with care. I feel something loosen in me, not a certainty, not yet, just a slackening of the cord that has pulled me taut for years.

I do not dream of fire. I do not dream at all.

The candlelight narrows, then goes out, and the darkness is not a threat but a blanket. Somewhere beyond it, a woman in chains forgives me. Somewhere within it, an old woman hums the tune that taught a boy to sleep.

I breathe, and the room breathes with me.

I wake to the sound of the stream and the soft knock of her spoon against a clay bowl. Dawn sits pale in the window. The cat has migrated to my ribs and refuses to move. When I shift, it thumps to the floor, offended, and stalks to the hearth.

"Up, then," Grandmother says, not turning. "The dough is ready for a pair of hands that remember."

I wash at the basin, the water cold enough to sting me awake. She passes me a cloth and the bowl. The dough is sticky, alive under my fingers. I work it as I did a lifetime ago, folding, turning, pressing the heel of my palm until it smooths.

"You haven't forgotten," she says.

"Some things keep," I answer.

We set the loaves near the fire to rise. She pours thin porridge, and we eat with a heel of yesterday's bread. Only then does she sit back, studying me the way she studies weather. Not prying—measuring.

"Tell me your life, Bernard," she says. "Not the miles. The life."

I wrap my hands around the warm cup. "I took vows at twenty. I was certain." I search for plainer words. "Certainty felt like a roof in a storm."

"And the storms?" she asks.

"Many," I say. "Some outside. Some… within." I look at the knotted grain of the table. "I learned the rule and what to do when others broke it. People wanted answers. I gave them. Sometimes I believed myself wise."

She waits. It is the waiting that loosens my tongue.

"I traveled with men who loved God, and men who loved power and called it God." The words taste dangerous and true. "In the beginning, I told myself there was no difference. Later, I told myself I could not tell. Lately—" I stop.

"Lately?" Her voice is soft, a hand not yet touching a bruise.

"Lately, I hear my own answers and they sound hollow in my mouth." I rub my thumb along a flour crack on my skin. "I serve, Grandmother. I do what I was taught. People kneel. I bless them. Often they rise lighter. I am glad for it. But there is a place in me that stays heavy."

She nods as if I had said the name of an herb she knows well. "And the heavy place—did it begin on the road to me?"

"No." I let the truth out on a breath. "It began when a woman in chains forgave me."

She does not startle. "Ah," she says, and nothing more.

We lift the risen dough to the hearthstone. The smell of yeast and ash mingles as heat takes hold. She brushes flour from her palms and sits again.

"And before the chains?" she asks, turning the bread with a stick. "Before vows, before Latin words. What was your life then?"

"A boy who ran to your door," I say, and the answer warms me. "A boy who listened to oaks, and believed they listened back."

"And God?" she asks.

"I thought He was near," I say. "Near like breath." I meet her eyes. "Then I learned to speak to Him through walls—words, rules, men with keys."

"Keys are good," she says mildly. "But doors are not the only way out of a room."

We fall quiet while the crust browns. I watch her hands—work-worn, deft. They have stitched, kneaded, blessed a thousand small things that never made a sermon.

She breaks the first loaf and sets half in front of me, steam rising. "Eat," she says. "You can talk to me with your mouth full. God understands."

Between bites, she asks little questions that carry much: "Do you sing when you pray?" (Sometimes, in my head.) "Do you sleep?" (Less than I should.) "Do you forgive yourself?" (I do not answer.) She does not press that one.

When the bread is half gone, she reaches across the table and lays her fingers over mine. "Your life is not wrong because it is heavy," she says. "But if the heaviness is all you know, you are carrying it the wrong way."

"What is the right way?"

"With someone," she says simply. "God, if you'll let Him. Failing that, an old woman will do."

I laugh, and the laugh surprises me; it has been a while since I heard my own sound without iron in it.

She smiles, victorious in some small plan I cannot see. "Later, we will walk by the oaks," she says. "You can tell me if they still answer. And you can tell me, slowly, what that woman said to you. Not now. When the day grows warm."

I nod. "Slowly," I agree.

"Slowly," she echoes, and pours more tea.

The stream keeps speaking. The crust crackles as it cools. I sense how this day will go—work, a walk, the naming of little things, and room enough for a larger thing to come when it is ready. I have told her parts of my life. The rest sits in the room with us, like another chair pulled to the table, waiting its turn.

I take another piece of bread. It tastes of fire and patience.

Chapter Twenty-Three

WE CARRY A heel of bread between us and follow the path that braids the stream. Sunlight lifts through alder leaves in coins. The grass is wet enough to darken the hem of her skirt. I offer my arm; she takes it, not because she must, but because it pleases us both.

We do not speak at first. The day makes its own small talk—the water over stones, a thrush trying three notes until it likes the fourth. The oaks come into view, older than my questions, their bark ridged like river maps. I lay my palm on the nearest trunk. It is cool, and it remembers me.

Grandmother breaks the bread and gives me the larger piece. "Your father," she says, like a door opened on a room we both know.

I chew, swallow, nod. "He filled the house," I say. "Even when he was gone."

"How did you live inside that bigness?"

"Quiet," I answer. "And small. If I could be part of the wall, I could be safe. I learned the creak of each floorboard. I learned his tread on the lane. I learned when to be useful and when to vanish."

She waits.

"I hid here, some days," I add, patting the oak. "Or at your hearth. Or in the church when the sacristy was warm. I told myself I liked the smell of wax and wood. Maybe I did. But mostly I liked the door that could be barred."

"And in yourself?" she asks gently. "Where did you hide there?"

I let out a breath. "In rules," I say. "In doing everything the right way the first time. If I folded the cloth square, if I said the prayer without stumbling, if I held my tongue, perhaps—" I stop, because the boy finishes the sentence for me: *perhaps he would not see me.*

She nods as if she hears that sentence anyway. "You were a clever child," she says. "Clever children often survive what should not be survived."

A breeze moves through the leaves. I watch their undersides flash pale, like fish turning in a current.

"I hated him," I say, tasting the old metal of it. "Then I hated myself for hating. Then I hated God for giving him to me. Then I hated my hating God. It was… a wheel."

"And when he died?"

"I felt relief when I learned of it only yesterday," I say. "And shame about the relief." I press my thumb into the bread until it dents. "No one was sorry. That shamed me, too. A son should mourn."

"A son should be safe," she answers, not arguing, only setting a truer measure on the table between us.

We walk a while without talking. My steps find the old rhythm: two of mine to one of hers. She points with her chin to a stone I used to jump from to the far bank. I do not jump it now.

"What did you feel in the church as a boy?" she asks.

"Order," I say. "A place where the rules were printed and the punishments predictable. If I did what they asked, something opened—a little door. I mistook the door for God."

"And was God there?"

"Yes," I say, surprised at how quickly the certainty rises. "But I put Him behind the door. It was safer to keep Him there."

We reach the farthest oak, the one with a scar along its belly where lightning once spoke. I rest my shoulder against it and feel the roughness through my robe.

"I wanted a Father who would not turn," I say. "So, I chose one made of stone and words. I thought if I served perfectly, He would keep still."

"And now?" she asks.

"Now I have met a love that moves toward me," I say, the confession like water finding a crack. "It did not wait for me to be perfect. It came into a dungeon and did not recoil from filth. It forgave me without asking who I was to deserve it." My throat tightens. "I do not know what to do with that."

She studies the scar in the oak as if it were a line of scripture. "You received what you were starved of," she says. "It will be hard to chew, even if it is bread."

"I am afraid," I admit. "If I let that love in, what becomes of the walls that kept me safe?"

"Safe from whom?" she asks.

I look at the stream. "Once, from him. Then, from everyone. Lately… from God."

We sit on a root that offers itself like a bench. She takes my hand the way she did when my feet were smaller and the world larger.

"Bernard," she says, "you learned to make yourself small to survive a man's wrath. It was a holy trick for a child. But holy tricks have lifespans. You are forty now. The room you hid in is too tight for the size of your soul."

I blink, and water blurs the trees. I let it. She lets it.

"I do not know how to live big," I say.

"Practice," she answers. "Start with one thing. Breathe bigger. Pray bigger. Forgive one small piece bigger than you think you can."

"And my father?" The question is gravel in my mouth. "What do I owe him now?"

"You owe him nothing," she says. "But you may lay him down." She nods toward the water. "Tell the stream one true sentence about him, and let it take the weight you've been carrying alone."

I face the current. The first sentence will not come; they all crowd the door, jostling. Then the smallest one steps forward, plain and strong.

"He was not able to love me," I say. The words strike the surface and go under.

The stream answers the only way it knows—by passing on.

I stand a little straighter. The air moves cleaner in my chest.

Grandmother squeezes my hand. "Come," she says lightly, as if we had done nothing more than mend a fence. "There is broth to skim and a cat to scold for stealing it. And later, if you like, you can tell me about the woman who forgave you. Not everything. Just the part you can say without breaking."

"I will try," I say.

"We are not in a hurry," she reminds me.

We walk back the way we came, two lengths of shadow threading the path. The oaks keep their counsel. The stream carries what it was given. And somewhere behind the walls I built, something expands by a finger's width, enough to notice, not enough to frighten.

We are almost to her gate when three villagers turn from the lane and spot my robe. A woman with flour on her sleeves, a boy out of breath, a man twisting his cap in both hands.

"Father—pardon—Father," the man says, stepping forward and half-bowing, half-reaching. "Old Marthe is failing. She asks for the sacrament."

The woman adds quickly, "And if you can… the baby—my sister's —he was born weak last night. We hoped—" She cannot finish.

My grandmother's hand loosens from my arm. She tips her chin toward me, the smallest nod: *Go.* Then, to the woman, she says, "I'll sit with the baby's mother till he returns." She turns home without fuss, trusting the world to be mended in the order it presents itself.

I follow the villagers to the church. Its door sticks as always; the boy puts a shoulder to it, and it gives. Cool stone breathes out to meet us. Dust drifts in light shafts. The bell rope hangs like a vein.

First, the sacristy—oil, stole, a small pyx. My fingers know where everything is, though twenty winters have passed. I move without hurry; haste dishonors the holy. The man waits in the nave, cap wrung to a rope.

"At once," I tell him, and we go.

Old Marthe's cottage smells of nettle tea and old wool. She lies small beneath a blanket, eyes filming, breath thin and sticky. A girl —granddaughter, perhaps, stands stiff as a fencepost by the bed, afraid to blink and miss the moment.

"Marthe," I say, kneeling where the light finds her cheek. "It's Bernard." The name surprises me in my own mouth; it surprises her face too. A smile swims up slowly from some deeper layer.

"Little Bernard," she whispers. "You stole pears from my tree."

"I did," I admit. "You looked the other way."

"Waste is a sin," she murmurs. "Even pears." Her eyes close, open. "Will you...?"

"I will," I say.

The rite moves through me like a river along a bed it knows. *Confiteor Deo omnipotenti...* She cannot say much, so I lend her my breath. I anoint her forehead, her hands, the faint blue map of veins. Oil gleams; the room smells briefly of olives and old summers. The granddaughter begins to weep soundlessly, as if not to disturb the sacrament. Marthe's fingers find mine with the accuracy of the blind.

"In pace," I whisper. "Go in peace."

When I finish, the granddaughter leans, kisses the oil on her brow. "Thank you, Father," she says to me, but her eyes are on Marthe, as they should be. I leave them to their parting.

Outside, the boy tugs my sleeve. "The baby," he reminds me, already running.

We cross two lanes to a low house where the air is warm and wet with breath. The mother lies gray with effort, the father hovering as if he dares not touch either of them for fear of breaking both. The baby's cry is a thread—thin, frayed, but there.

I wash my hands in a basin, ask the name they have chosen. "Étienne," the father says, then adds, "if he should live." I look at him,
and in his face I see every man who ever needed a door to open
quickly.

"At the font or here?" I ask.

"Here," the mother whispers.

So I bend over the small chest, rising and falling like a sparrow's. I
take water in my fingers, trace the cross upon a forehead scarcely
big enough to bear it. "Étienne, I baptize thee in the name of the
Father, and of the Son, and of the Holy Spirit." The baby startles,
makes a sound a little stronger than the one before. The mother
sobs once and laughs in the same breath. The father covers his
face, shoulders shaking.

When the room settles, the woman with flour on her sleeves
lingers. "Father," she says, voice low, "if… if he hadn't lived to be
baptized today, would God have—" She cannot shape the rest.

Once, I would have given her the safest sentence I owned, a wall
made of words. Now Clara's dungeon breathes in the corner of the
room, and my grandmother's prayer warms my back.

"God loved him before you knew his name," I say. The truth feels
like stepping onto a floor that does not give. "He is not stingy."

The woman's mouth opens—startled, then relieved. She nods
quickly, as if she has just set down a weight she had no hands left
to carry.

Back at the church, I hear confessions until my knees complain. Ordinary sorrows, ordinary cruelties, ordinary mercies. A man who struck his brother when the cider ran out. A girl who pocketed thread and then returned it, too ashamed to speak. A widow who cannot forgive God for winter. I listen as if each were my first penitent. I absolve as if each were my last.

For a time, I am simply a priest in a place that remembers me. My hands are steady. My voice does not tremble. The rope of the bell prints its old roughness into my palm when I pull it once at dusk and let the sound lie over the fields like broadcloth.

Only when the door is bolted and the last candle snuffs itself with a sigh do I feel the ache return—not a wound reopening, more like a seam that has been stitched too tight and now longs to breathe. Clara's words rise, less as a sentence than as a presence.

Even for you.

I step outside. Evening gathers like a shawl. Across the lane, a small figure is waiting, her hands folded into her sleeves against the chill. My grandmother.

"You served them," she says, not as praise, just as a fact set gently on the table of this day.

"I did," I answer.

"Come home," she says. "There is stew enough for two and a story I forgot to finish thirty years ago."

We walk together through the bluing light. The church behind us keeps its watch. The village settles. The stream will be speaking when we reach the door. And in my chest—under stole and habit, under years and ash—something faithful and old keeps time with our steps, not healed, not resolved, but undeniably alive.

The cottage is warm again. She has coaxed the stew to a soft bubble and set two bowls to the side where the heat won't bully them. The cat patrols the rim of the hearth, pretending it has business with the kettle.

We eat with the same unceremonious grace as noon: bread passed, bowls refilled, a pinch of salt between fingers. When we are finished, she wipes the spoons and lays them on a folded cloth, then settles into her chair with a tidy sigh, hands resting one upon the other.

"I told you once a story I did not finish," she says, looking at the window as if the rest of it has been waiting in the glass all these years. "About the hawk."

I remember the beginning—the winter wind, my small hands blue with cold, the bird under the hedge, wing at a wrong angle. "You wrapped it in your shawl," I say. "We hid it from my father."

She nods. "We fed it bits of liver and set its wing against a splint made from a willow switch. You wanted to keep it."

"I wanted to keep everything that did not hurt me," I say, and she makes a soft sound that could be a laugh or a blessing.

"It stayed three weeks," she continues. "Then one morning it thumped against the shutter as if to say, 'Enough.' We opened the window and out it went, ragged but determined, and you cried until you tasted salt in your teeth."

"I thought kindness ought to end with keeping," I admit.

"Ah," she says, as if the word itself has warmed her. "There is the part I never told you. Two winters later, when the snow was honest and the woodpile low, I heard that same fool thump at the shutter. I opened it, scolding like an old crow, and there he was on the sill, fat with luck. He hopped once, twice, then shook out a feather and left it there—payment, I suppose." She tilts her head. "It was not a miracle. Birds molt. But the timing was tidy, and I took the feather anyway."

"Did you keep it?" I ask.

"I keep what is given in love," she says, and reaches to the mantle. From a clay jar, she draws a narrow length of pale brown—barred, clean, the quill still strong. She lays it on the table between us.

I lift it as if it could bruise. "You kept it all this time."

"All this time," she says. "I meant to tell you the end of the story when you were old enough not to turn it into a sermon. Then you left." She smiles to take the sting from it. "So, I tell you now."

"And what is the story's end?" I ask, though I feel it before she speaks.

"That we do not own what we save," she says. "We are visited by it."

The cat tests the edge of the feather with its nose and sneezes, insulted. She shoos it with a flap of her hand, and it retreats to dream of better prey.

She pours us each a little of last year's cider, just enough to shine in the cup. We drink slowly. The stream keeps to its line. A log collapses inward and turns to orange cities for a heartbeat before settling into coal.

"Your father hated the hawk," she says after a time, no venom in it. "He called it a thief. I told him we all steal something to live. Bread from the oven. Heat from the wood. Time from sleep. Only the hawk is honest about it."

"I remember," I say. "He called you soft."

"I was," she answers, pleased. "Soft holds. Hard breaks."

We sit with the feather between us like a third hand laid open. I feel the day we walked under the oaks moving through me, loosening knots I had forgotten how to name.

"Why tell me now?" I ask.

"Because you have come home with a hurt wing," she says simply. "And because you cannot be kept. You were never meant for cages, my boy. Not even gilded ones." She glances at my robe without accusation.

The candlelight lifts the lines at the corners of her eyes. She does not reach for me; she does not have to. I feel the reach anyway.

"When you are ready," she adds, as if discussing nothing more perilous than weather, "you can tell me about the woman who forgave you. You can tell me a little tonight or none at all. We have winter enough for the rest."

I look at the feather, at the small house that has always been larger on the inside than the world outside it, at her hands folded like prayer made flesh.

"She said four words," I manage. "And they have not left me."

Her mouth softens. "Then let them sit," she says. "Words are like seeds. They don't grow faster because you stare."

We tidy the table. She leaves the feather where it is. At the doorway to her room, she pauses, the same pause as last night, the same strip of candlelight falling across the floor. "Sleep," she says. "If it comes. If it does not, sit with the stream. It never minds company."

When the door closes, I stay where I am, the feather under my palm, the room remembering the winter I wanted to keep a thing that could fly.

Outside, the water works on its single task. Inside, a sentence I did not choose stands up in me and stretches, not yet ready to speak itself aloud—only to be true.

We are visited by what we save.

Sleep comes like a door that was never locked.

I am in the field behind the oaks. Snow, but it is spring; the world can't decide. A hawk crouches in the drift, one wing canted like a sail that will not catch. Its eye is fierce, not begging. I kneel, offer my wrist. It steps up—light as a word I have not spoken—and the broken wing brushes my throat. Warm. Alive. Waiting.

My father stands at the fence. Not young, not old—exactly the age he was the day I first feared him. He holds his chest as if the bones there are a basket with a hole, something precious falling through. He does not look at me; he looks at the hawk, and in his face there is envy so clean it hurts. He wants what flies. He does not know how to want what loves.

Behind him rises a church I know and do not know. The stones are mine, the bell rope mine, the altar mine. A wind moves and a banner snaps: *Vocation.* The cloth is fine and bright, stitched with promises in a hand I recognize as my own. I walk toward it, carrying the hawk, and the letters loosen in the gust, thread pulling, a seam parting with that soft, traitorous sound linen makes when it yields. The word breaks where I thought it was strongest. The banner keeps flying, but something essential has torn.

The hawk shifts, testing the ruined wing. My father sags, both hands to his ribs, as if to keep himself from spilling. The church doors open of their own accord, and all the pews are empty, clean as the inside of a shell.

I say aloud, "Three things are broken," and the air answers with my grandmother's voice: *Soft holds. Hard breaks.*

So, I stop bracing.

I crook my arm and make a cradle of it. The hawk settles. I do not splint, I do not bind. I only carry. My father lifts his head and, for the first time in any year of my life, I see him ask for help without making it an order. I cannot mend his heart, but I can set down the fence between us. I do. He does not cross it, but he sits on his side while I sit on mine, and we are nearer than we have ever been.

At the church threshold, I take the banner in my hands. The torn edge flutters, not accusing, only honest. I knot the loose thread to it-self, not to hide the rip, but to keep it from running further. The word is changed now. It reads like a sentence missing a letter you can still hear. I hang it back in the wind anyway.

The hawk steps from my arm to the lintel. It lowers its head and presses the good wing against the bad, as if body can teach body what it has forgotten. It looks at me with that unblinking gold, and I understand: flying will come or not, but holding is already here.

Snow turns to thaw. The oaks shake down a small rain that smells of green wood. My father stands, one hand still at his chest, the other lifted in a gesture that is not quite blessing and not quite farewell. It is enough.

I wake with my palm over the feather on the table, as if I have kept vigil for something that did not need me to keep it.

The stream is saying what it always says: *Go on, go on.*

In the half-light, I whisper back, "I will carry what is broken until it remembers how to be whole. And if it never does, I will carry it still."

Chapter Twenty-Four

BEFORE THE SKY admits it is morning, I take the path to the water. The air is a cool kiss on my face. Mist hangs low, tasting of
stone and leaf. The stream moves with its small, tireless courage.

I walk until the cottage is a bend behind me and the oaks lean
closer to hear themselves. I stop where the bank shelves gently,
where child-Bernard once launched stick boats and swore oaths to
no one.

Across the water, a deer stands in the half-light. Not startled, not
poised to flee—only present. Its ear turns, that delicate cup receiv-
ing what I cannot hear. Its breath ghosts from its nostrils and vanishes. We look at one another as if there were nothing to solve.

It chews a sprig of last year's something, lifts its head, and simply
is. The world hangs from that stillness as from a peg: sound, scent,
the thin thread of dawn. No lesson, no parable offered. Only a
body sure of its place.

I feel the old reach of my mind toward meaning—the habit of
coaxing everything into scripture—and I let my hands fall empty.
The deer does not instruct me. It keeps me company.

I notice, then, the things it has taught without trying: how the
hooves are dark with damp, how the ribs do not show, how the tail
flicks once and rests, how the muscle along the shoulder ripples
when a fly dares, how life can be alert without fear, open without
invitation, sufficient without praise.

The stream speaks between us. *Go on, go on.* The deer lowers its head to drink. The water takes its reflection and breaks it into a thousand moving coins, then gives it back, untroubled.

A breeze comes thin from the east. The mist thins with it. The deer looks once more in my direction, not weighing me, not measuring me—acknowledging, as a tree acknowledges shade. Then it steps into the understory and is not there, which is different from being gone.

I stand a while longer. My feet find the stance that asks nothing of the ground. The breath goes out of me and comes back of its own accord. Nothing has changed. Everything has.

When I turn for the cottage, the light has found the window. I think of my grandmother stirring the fire, of bread deciding whether it will rise, of a feather that has waited years to be held again. I think of a woman who forgave me in a room where nothing was clean and love did not care.

I walk home without hurry, carrying nothing I can name, and more than I can hold.

The door answers my hand before I touch it. Warmth comes first, then the smell of barley porridge and woodsmoke, and the faint ghost of mint she dries over the lintel. My grandmother stands at the hearth with a wooden spoon and the calm of a clock that does not hurry because time belongs to it.

"You were with the stream," she says.

"I was," I answer, and the word carries more than place.

She sets a bowl before me. Steam lifts, a soft flag. She places honey on the table, the small crock I remember with the hairline crack along its lip, and a dish of salt. We eat without speech. It feels like prayer done properly: the world received, not wrestled into meaning.

When the bowls are empty, she ladles a little more, and I do not refuse. She does not ask questions. She waits as she would for bread to rise, trusting yeast to be yeast.

"I think I can speak," I say at last.

"I think you can, too," she says, and reaches for the kettle to pour us each hot water brightened with a leaf of mint. She sits, hands open on the table as if to show me they carry nothing I need to defend against.

"The dungeon," I begin, and see it—stone sweating, air thick, the guard's torch scraping light along iron. "I went in as I always have. With the rite ready in my mouth. With obedience like a board across the door of my heart."

She nods once, not to move me along but to say she is walking beside me.

"She was chained, filthy," I say. "I have seen that before. I spoke the words I always speak. Renounce. Repent. Return." The spoon on the table is very still. "She asked me a question."

"What did she ask?" Grandmother's voice is the softest tool— sharp enough to open, gentle enough not to tear.

"Whether God desired the fire," I say. "Whether love wanted what justice called for." I feel the old training rise to answer, and the answer fails again. "I told her what I have been taught. That the flame purifies. That obedience saves."

"And then?" she asks.

"She did not argue," I say, hearing again the steadiness of that room. "She did not plead. She moved closer so the torchlight found her face, and she said—" The words stand at the door of my mouth the way a guest stands with traveling dust on their cloak, uncertain if they are welcome. "She said, 'I hold no hatred—not for them, not for you. Even for you.'"

Silence sits with us like a third person who has taken off their shoes and intends to stay.

"I could not answer her," I say. "The rite was still in me, but my tongue could not lift it. Her words were… larger. They did not leave room for mine."

"Do you believe her?" Grandmother asks.

"I do not know what believing means, if it does not mean her," I say, surprising myself with how cleanly that arrives.

She exhales, not satisfaction, not relief—recognition, perhaps, like a midwife noticing the right color in a newborn's face. "And since then?"

"Since then, I have tried to stand in the old doorway," I say. "I have said mass, absolved the ordinary griefs, walked roads that feel like rosary beads under my feet. I have felt useful. Even, sometimes, glad. But when night comes, I hear her voice in a room where everything else is quiet. It does not accuse me. It does not ask me to change. It simply keeps being true."

Grandmother lifts the cracked honey crock, runs her thumb over the fissure, then sets it down again. "Some vessels sing more clearly after they've been cracked," she says. "The sound has more room."

I turn my cup in my hands. "If her love is true," I say, "what does that make of my life? Of the things I have done in God's name?"

"It makes them your life," she says, "and the things you have done. And it makes this morning what it is: you at my table, speaking truth to a woman who has no power to reward or punish you."

"It feels like a beginning," I admit.

"Beginnings are thin-skinned," she says, smiling. "We will carry it carefully."

I look at her, the person who once shielded a hawk with a shawl and a boy with a song. "What do I do with her words?" I ask. "They do not fit in any prayer I have."

"They *are* the prayer," she says. "Try them on your tongue the way you try bread for doneness. See where they stick. See where they melt."

I close my eyes. "Even for you," I say, and the words warm the roof of my mouth like wine. They move down my throat and take a seat where shame has sat for years. Shame does not rise. It does not leave. But it is not alone.

Grandmother pours a little more hot water into my cup. "You will go to the church today?" she asks, as if discussing the weather.

"If they ask," I say. "If they don't, I will still go. The nave knows my feet."

She nods. "When you stand at the altar, say what you have always said. And somewhere between the Sanctus and the blessing, set those four words beside the others. Let them keep company. Words teach each other how to be truer."

I breathe, and the room breathes with me. Outside, a cart passes, a wheel complaining in need of grease. The ordinary world clears its throat and begins its work.

"There is one more thing," I say.

"There often is," she replies, pleased.

"In the night," I tell her, "I dreamed of a hawk with a broken wing, my father with a broken heart, and my vocation with a broken promise. I did not mend any of them. I carried what I could. I knotted the torn place so it would not run, and I let the banner fly again, honest about its wound."

She considers, then nods as if the dream has just poured her a chair. "Good," she says. "We will not pretend wholeness. We will practice it."

I stand to clear the bowls. She lets me, another patience. When I set them by the basin, she touches my sleeve. "Bernard."

"Yes?"

"Today, if you can bear it, leave the church door unlatched when you go in. Close it if wind demands—but don't bar it. Let the outside air remember its way inside."

I understand more than her words ask. "I will."

She squeezes my wrist once, the way she did when I was small and courage had to be lent by hand. "Then go, my boy," she says. "Bring the people what you have. God will bring what you do not."

I step into the light that has finally decided to call itself morning. The stream keeps its faithful counsel. The oaks stand exactly where they are most themselves. I carry four words that do not feel like mine and know, somehow, they are what I have most to give.

I leave the door unlatched.

The nave holds its cool like a kept promise. Dust swings in beams of early light. I set the missal, fold the corporal, check the cruets. The church makes its small throat-clearing sounds—wood easing, rope breathing in its pulley, a swallow scratching in the rafters.

The door lifts a whisper. A woman steps in with a boy on the verge of twelve. She dips her fingers at the stoop and presses water to his brow, then to her own, smiles at me as if I were a lamp relit.

"Father Bernard," she says. "Welcome home."

"Thank you," I answer, and mean it.

The boy is all elbows and earnestness. He bows too low, almost drops his cap, recovers it with a grin that shows the child still inside the almost-man. He looks at the altar the way some look at mountains.

"May I… help?" he asks, half to me, half to the air.

"You may ring the bell before the people come," I tell him. "Three times, with breath between, so the valley has time to listen."

His eyes spark. I show him the rope's roughness and the knot that saves palms. He takes it solemnly, then looks back at me as if to ask permission to be glad. I nod. He pulls. The first note rises, round and sure, and rolls away. He waits, breathes, pulls again. By the third, I can feel the sound in the wood under my feet.

When the rope stills, he does not let go right away. He watches the bell settle, as if he has woken something and wants to be sure it goes back to sleep properly.

His mother touches his shoulder. "Tell Father what you told me," she says, with the tender mischief of one who pushes a bird from the nest knowing it can fly.

The boy sets his cap between his hands like an offering. "I think," he says, choosing words as if they might break, "that I would like to be a priest. Like you."

"And why is that?" I ask, steady as I can make myself.

"So I can get to heaven," he answers, quick with relief now that the hard part is spoken. "It seems the surest way."

There is a time in my life when I would have praised his prudence, handed him a ladder of rules, and taught him to climb. I feel the old reflex reach for my tongue and stop it with a breath.

"Come," I say, and lead them forward to the front pew where the light falls warmest. We sit as if we were three at a kitchen table. The church accepts our arrangement and does not ask for ceremony.

"It is a good thing to want heaven," I tell him. "But heaven is not wages for work well done. It is home to love that has always loved you."

He blinks, uncertain whether I have answered his answer.

"Being a priest won't buy you a safer road," I go on. "Sometimes it brings you through rough ground first. The vestments are not armor. They are a promise to stand where love is needed."

The mother's eyes flick to me, quick with attention, not alarmed.

The boy frowns, thinking hard. "Then why are you a priest?"

I look at the altar, at the cloth smoothed by hands older than mine. "When I was your age," I say slowly, "I liked the church because the doors closed and the world grew quiet. I thought God was the quiet itself." I let the honesty stand upright between us. "Later, I found out God is also the voice that calls from the other side of a door you forgot to open."

He tips his head. "What does the voice say?"

"Sometimes nothing," I admit. "Sometimes only your name." I find a smile I do not have to make. "Sometimes it says, 'Come help me love these people.'"

He glances at his mother, whose mouth softens at the sound of that sentence.

"And heaven?" he presses, because twelve is the age that still believes in maps. "What if I do not become a priest? Will it be farther away?"

"No," I say, and feel how much I mean it. "Heaven is not a distance. It is a presence. A priest's work is to point to it. So is a mother's. So is a stonemason's and a shepherd's and the boy who rings the bell so the valley remembers what time is." I touch the rope with two fingers. "You rang well."

He brightens, then reins himself, trying on the seriousness he thinks belongs to holy things. "What should I do, then, if I still want—maybe—not for safety, but…" He hunts for the end of the sentence and cannot find it.

"For love?" I offer.

He nods, startled by the word and relieved by it.

"Then begin with what is near," I tell him. "Help your mother where no one sees. Tell the truth even when it costs you your small pride. Learn the psalms until they know your voice. If you are to be a priest one day, it will be because love has already been your work, not because you wanted a key to a locked gate."

He mulls this, measuring it against the ladders he has imagined. "May I watch you say mass?" he asks, as if it were a craft he might apprentice.

"You may," I say. "But first—would you carry the cruets to the credence table? With both hands, like something that can spill."

He rises with glad gravity and does as he is told, placing water and wine where they belong. When he returns, he sits straighter, as if the pew has adopted him.

His mother lingers a moment after he looks away. "What you said," she murmurs, "about heaven being presence—my sister lost a child. She has not believed that since." A question stands in her eyes with boots muddy from the path.

"Tell her God loved him before anyone did," I answer softly. "Tell her love does not unmake itself. And that she may rage as long as she needs, and love will not be offended."

Tears find her quickly, then go no farther than the rim. She nods, the way people nod when they have heard a sentence they can carry without dropping.

Others begin to arrive, shoulders dusted with flour or dawn. The nave fills with the sound of benches deciding to hold weight. The boy looks at me as if to ask whether the moment is over. I shake my head—no; the moment is the whole thing.

When I step to the altar, I feel the four words standing where I place the chalice, small and steady: *Even for you.* I do not speak them aloud. I do not need to. They keep company with the Sanctus, and nothing in the room protests.

Before the opening prayer, I glance toward the door—still un-latched. A strip of morning lies across the threshold like a blessing.

The boy meets my eyes and, with conspirator's care, lifts the bell rope one finger's width, as if to show me that he remembers how it felt to wake the valley. I incline my head in thanks and turn to the people who have come for bread and for the news that love keeps happening.

I begin, and for once the words feel sized to the room.

I read the Gospel and close the book. The hinge of the church breathes. I look at their faces—bread makers, field hands, a child with ash on his cheek, a widow whose hands never quite rest. The boy sits near the rope, bright and trying not to be.

I do not climb far into thought. I stand where I am and speak from there.

"Brothers and sisters," I begin, "I have come home with a quiet in me I did not earn and a question I do not know how to answer. I think both are from God.

"When I was a boy in this village, I believed God loved me be-cause I could be good. When I grew, I learned to be good with such care that I could hardly breathe. Some of you know that feeling.

"This week I have watched your lives again—your work, your patience, the way you forgive each other in small pieces. I have also listened to the stream before dawn. It says only one thing, over and over: *go on.* Not *prove yourself.* Not *be perfect. Go on.* It sounds like God to me.

"Today's Gospel tells us love keeps its door open. Not because it is careless, but because it is confident. Love believes it can afford to be generous. Love is not stingy with welcome, or with forgiveness.

"I will tell you something plain: God is not waiting until you are holy to be near you. God is near, and that nearness is how we become holy.

"If you have wronged someone, make it right if you can. If you cannot, ask for mercy, and you will not be mocked for asking. If you are tired, rest. If you are hungry, come to this table as to a field already sown. If you are afraid of God, tell Him so. He is not offended by honesty. He would rather hear the truth in your cracked voice than the right words in a voice that is not yours.

"And if any of you have been told that heaven is a place you must purchase with finely counted coins, let me say it as clearly as I can: heaven is what love does when nothing is in its way. It starts now. It starts here. It starts with how we carry each other."

I stop, not because I have run out of sentences, but because I have reached the one that does not require another after it. The silence that follows is not empty. It feels like water settling in a basin.

We go on: the Creed as a wheel that turns without grinding, the prayers that know their own path, the table set with the old care. I lift the bread, lift the cup, see my hands not as instruments of power but of giving. When I whisper the blessing, four quieter words stand beside it like witnesses: *Even for you.*

Communion is unhurried. A man limps and I wait; a child holds out both hands like a bird opening its beak; a woman cries without wiping her face. I do not hurry any of them.

At the dismissal, I make the sign of the cross and say, "Go in peace." I expect the usual scrape of benches, the rush of errands taking back their people.

They do not move.

They stand as if the room has become larger, and no one wishes to find the edge of it yet. A murmur runs like wind in wheat. Then stillness again. I can hear the rope breathe. I can hear my own heart, not hammering—listening.

A man who never meets anyone's eyes meets mine. He does not speak. A girl comes forward and asks if she may light a candle "for no reason." I nod. She lights it and then lights another, as if one were for asking and one for thanks. The flame is small and stubborn.

The boy edges to the sanctuary step. "Father," he whispers, "may I ring the bell *once* more? Not to call them, but to say… we heard."

I look at the people. They are not finished being here. I look at the door—still unlatched, a thin line of day stretched across the floor like linen. "Once," I tell him.

He pulls. The sound lifts its round body and rolls across us. No one flinches. Some close their eyes. A woman who has not taken Communion in years kneels without fuss, as if she had simply remembered how.

The mother of the weak-born child finds me near the font. "He breathes stronger," she says, and then, almost shy, "and I do, too."

Old Marthe's granddaughter stands at the back, unmoored but not alone. I press oil to her brow without ceremony and say nothing. She nods as if I have said exactly enough.

People begin to speak to one another the way they usually speak to me after mass: in low voices, about true things, as if the nave itself were a confessional that absolves not by secrecy but by shared bearing. No one wants to leave first. When finally they do, they go slowly, as though stepping from warm water into air.

I am left with the boy and the echo of his bell, the open door, the smell of wax. I sit on the front pew and feel something I have not felt at the end of liturgy in years: I am not emptied. I am filled.

My grandmother appears in the doorway, not coming in, only making sure the world is still attached to its hinge. She smiles in that way that forgives a man for not understanding how his own face has changed.

"Father," the boy says suddenly, earnest with a new kind of hunger, "what should I do now?"

"Begin," I tell him, and he does not ask with what. He sets the missal straight, retrieves a stray palm from under the bench, rights a candle that leans. He is learning the grammar of care, which is the only language I trust today.

The last of the people drift into the lane. I stand, look once more at the door, and leave it as it is, as a little draft lifts a candle.

Afternoon leans warm against the window. We sit with mint water cooling between our hands.

"What were the words she gave you?" Grandmother asks, as if asking the hour.

"Even for you," I say. Speaking them changes the room.

She nods, counting on her fingers the way she once counted stitches. "Three," she says, and lets silence pull up a chair.

Her thumb strays to the crack in the honey crock. "And the one she saved her breath on?"

I search the space between *even* and *for*. Something waits there, shaped to fit.

Grandmother looks up, eyes bright with the pleasure of naming what is already true. "Love," she says gently.

The word settles like bread on a board.

"Four, then," she adds, pleased. "Enough to feed you a while."

We do not say them again. We don't need to. They sit between us, whole now:

(Love,) even for you.

Chapter Twenty-Five

WE ARE LAYING kindling for the evening fire when someone runs down the lane and stumbles at the threshold. It is the miller's boy—red-faced, panting.

"Father Bernard," he blurts, then ducks his head at Grandmother, remembering himself. "Pardon. Men at the lower bridge—two riders, black crosses on their cloaks. They're asking in the tavern who keeps to the old ways here, who does not come to mass, who visits the midwife after dark." He swallows. "They said they'll seek you at the church for names."

The air in the cottage thins. The old door in me swings on its hinges by habit—*obey, assist, preserve the flock*. I feel the board lifting to bar my heart.

Grandmother sets down a stick of kindling as if it were a chalice. She does not touch me. She does not need to. Four words stand up in the room and take their places.

"Did they give their names?" I ask the boy.

"Sergeant Alain and a clerk," he says. "From the bishop's men, they said. They'll come at vespers."

"Thank you," I tell him. "You've done right."

He nods, relieved to have laid his burden down, and vanishes back into the lane.

I stand very still. I hear the stream repeating itself: *go on, go on.* I hear, too, the old lesson: nets for fish, nets for men. I have thrown them before.

Grandmother tends the hearth. "You will meet them," she says, making it not a question but a path. "Decide now what you will not carry for them. It is easier to refuse a burden before it is on your back."

"What if refusal harms the village?" I ask. "What if I bring the net down tighter by standing aside?"

"What if you help them tie it?" she answers, mild as rain.

I breathe. I remember the boy at the bell, the widow's hands, Étienne's thin cry, and the way it strengthened. I remember Old Marthe's oil-sheened brow. I remember a dungeon where love did not flinch.

"I will not make lists," I say aloud, so the room can hold me to it. "I will not name the missing as if absence were guilt. I will tell them the church is open to sinners and saints and that I do not sort them at the door."

"And if they ask who midwives in the village?" she says, testing the seam.

"I will say that life enters this village by many doors," I answer. "And that I am keeper of one—nothing more."

She nods, satisfied. "Eat first," she advises. "Men think better with broth in them, even when they must say hard things."

We sip in quiet. I take my robe from its peg, lay it across my arm, and feel how light it is compared to what I feared. When I step into the lane, the sky is the color of iron cooling. I leave Grandmother in the doorway, her hand lifted not to bless, not to hold me back— only to be seen.

At the church, I do what she asked: I leave the door unlatched. Candles quicken. The bell rope waits with endless patience. In the nave's hush, I set the missal, touch the altar stone, and practice the sentence that will not fit in any report:

(Love,) even for you.

The boy takes the rope with care; three notes, breath between. The bell speaks the hour, and the village answers. A handful come— those who always do, those who never did until this week. I begin the psalms. The nave makes its small harbor of sound.

They enter on the second antiphon: two riders' boots, cloaks dark, crosses stitched black-on-black so the thread only shows when it catches light. The older is broad in the shoulders, a soldier's gravity—Sergeant Alain. The other, ink-stained fingers, eyes that add and subtract—the clerk. They stand in the back as if not to interrupt prayer. They interrupt it anyway.

We finish the psalm. I give the blessing. No homily. No flourishes. The people do not hurry to leave.

Alain steps forward, removes his cap—respect, or the appearance of it. "Father Bernard," he says, voice fit for a yard of men. "By warrant of the bishop's office, we ask your aid."

"I will hear you," I answer, and step down from the altar. I make no move toward the sacristy. We will speak where everyone breathes the same air.

The clerk unrolls a ribbon of parchment. "Names," he says, brisk. "Those who absent themselves from the mass without cause. Those known to visit one Jeanne, called a midwife, at irregular hours. Those rumored to keep doctrines contrary to Holy Church. We are told you are newly returned and will know who has strayed."

The church grows very quiet, the way fields do when a hawk circles. I can feel the village holding itself still behind me—bread makers, field hands, the boy with both hands on the rope as if it could steady the world.

I keep my hands visible, empty. "I am newly returned," I say. "I know who is hungry. Who is widowed. Whose child breathes easier today than yesterday." I meet the clerk's eyes. "I do not keep ledgers of suspicion."

Alain's mouth tightens—not anger yet; the preface to it. "We ask only the shepherd's knowledge. Wolves have been among these hills."

"Wolves are among all hills," I say. "Some wear fleece. Some wear law." I let the words stand and do not press them harder than they can bear.

The clerk scratches a note, perhaps of my insolence. "The midwife, then. Jeanne. We are told she receives women late. What medicines? What counsel? What rites are performed in secret?"

I feel the old board lift toward my heart; I set it down. "Life enters this village by many doors," I say. "Jeanne keeps watch at one of them. I keep watch at another. Neither of us bars the other's work."

Alain steps closer. He smells of leather and iron and the long road. "You served at the fortress," he says, testing. "You know what harm heresy does when it is permitted to root."

"I have seen harm," I answer. Clara's eyes rise, and do not accuse me. "I am careful with the word."

He studies me the way a man studies a ford before a charge. "Father," he says finally, quieter, "we are not your enemies."

I let the sentence reach me. "I do not choose enemies," I say. "I choose what I will carry."

"What will you carry for the bishop's men?" the clerk asks, impatient.

"Bread," I say. "Blessing. Confession, if you seek it. I will carry no lists."

A stir moves the benches. It is not applause. It is breath returning.

The clerk's face hardens. "Your refusal may be written as obstruction."

"Write what is true," I say. "Write that I leave the door unlatched."

Alain's eyes flick there—the door ajar, dusk pooling at the sill like blue water. Something in him shifts, a grain's width. He looks past me at the people and finds not defiance, only bodies that have worked all day and come for words that do not wound.

He clears his throat. "We will speak with Jeanne," he says to the clerk, not quite a retreat, not quite a threat. To me: "And if we find wolves, Father?"

"Then may your hands be gentler than your orders," I say. "And may you remember who taught you to tie a bandage before you learned to tighten a rope."

The clerk half turns, disgusted, but Alain holds him a heartbeat, measuring me. "You have changed since fortress days," he says.

"Perhaps I have remembered," I answer.

"Remembering is not always safe," he warns.

"No," I say, and the words arrive as if someone else has carried them to my lips: "(Love,) even for you."

I do not intend to say it aloud. I have. The sentence hangs between us like a bell's last note. The boy looks at me as if he has seen lightning without thunder.

Alain does not flinch. He closes his cap in his fist, jaw working as if at tough meat. Then he nods once, to me or to the air, I cannot tell. "We will call again," he says, and turns. The clerk follows, parchment snapping like a pennant in a petty wind.

They leave the door ajar, as they found it.

No one moves for a long breath. Then the mother of the bell-boy crosses herself, not out of fear. Old Marthe's granddaughter lifts her chin like a woman who has decided something about the way she will carry her grief. A midwife's name travels the room without lips moving.

My grandmother is there at the very back, a shadow beside the jamb. She does not smile. She stands as if to say: *You did not trade anyone else's safety for your own. Good. Now wash your hands. There is flour on the table and stories to finish.*

The boy edges near, whispering, "Father, should I—?" He gestures to the rope, unsure whether the valley should be told.

"Not yet," I say. "Let the silence have its turn."

We sit with it. It holds.

When the people finally drift out, they are not hiding. They are simply going on. The stream outside keeps its counsel. The oaks are exactly where they were. I feel my heart do a new thing—open without a bar—and stay that way long enough to notice I can still breathe.

I snuff the last candle, leave the door as it was, and step into the evening.

The lane gives me back to the cottage. Light stands in the window like someone waiting with good news that is not loud. Grand-mother has set two bowls, a heel of bread, and a little dish of salt. The feather lies where we left it, keeping its quiet.

"You met them," she says.

"I did."

She tastes my face as if it were a stew not yet seasoned. "And you did not carry what was not yours."

"I tried not to."

"Good," she says, and nothing more. She gestures to the bench. "Eat before the story escapes. Stories keep better with broth."

We eat. The broth is simple—barley, onion, a piece of carrot that has outlived winter. She breaks the bread with her thumb, gives me the larger piece with the same thoughtless generosity that once divided apples on the path from market.

When the bowls are half-empty, she begins.

"Jeanne," she says, as if the name were a cup set gently on the table. "You heard it this evening, like everyone did, so you should hear it from me, too. She was born in lambing season. Her mother died three days later, and the village decided it would keep the child. I was younger then, with more walking in my legs, so I took some of the keeping."

She stirs the memory with her spoon. "She watched the goats first, then the women, then the breathing of the new ones that don't know how to breathe yet. Learned to look and not panic. That is the heart of midwifery, and half of priesting besides."

I smile without meaning to. "Looking and not panicking?"

"And knowing when to call for more hands," she says. "You'd be surprised how often that is the miracle—one more pair of hands."

She dabs the table with a cloth as if tidying the past. "They will come for her with questions," she adds. "Not for crimes. Questions unsettle men who like answers more than people."

I hear the clerk's parchment in the way the air moved when he breathed. "Will she be safe?"

"She is not foolish," Grandmother says. "She is careful with herbs and words. But safety is a bag with a hole." She looks up. "You spoke with them without tying any knots around your neighbors. That mends a little of the hole."

The cat reappears to argue with the hearth. She flicks it a crumb. It forgives us both.

"Tell me your story now," she says, turning the evening gently toward me. "Not the riders'—I was there for the shape of it. Tell me the inside."

"I said the four words," I admit. "The last aloud."

"Mm," she hums, pleased the way a baker hums when the loaf sounds hollow in the middle. "How did they wear, spoken in the open air?"

"As if they had been waiting there," I say. "They did not make the clerk kinder. They made me true."

"That is their first work," she says. "The second is none of your business."

We sit with that until the bowls are empty. She brings out a sliver of cheese saved from a market week, cuts it into unfair halves, slides the unfairness my way. "I am old enough to be generous," she says.

"Tell me another," I ask. "From before I could carry the ending."

She leans back, eyes on the rafters where the herbs hang like small green comets. "When your mother was a girl," she begins, "she found a hedgehog by the path, rolled tight as a fist. She wanted to open it with kindness. I told her, 'Some creatures open when the dark is dark enough and the quiet is quiet enough. Kindness is not a pry bar.' She sat beside it and waited until the stars came out. When she stopped wanting, it uncurled and toddled off like a gentleman late for supper."

She looks at me over the top of the story. "Not everything opens because you persuade it, Bernard. Some things open because you stop trying."

I think of the church door unlatched. Of the people who did not rush to leave. Of my own chest.

We tidy without rush. She hums the tune from my boyhood—the one that never learned words because it didn't need any. At the doorway to her room, she pauses as always. "Tomorrow," she says, "if Jeanne comes by, you can take a walk with her where the hedges are tall. Ask her what help she wants, not what help you have." She smiles. "Bring two pairs of hands."

"And if the riders return?"

"Bring the same," she says. "Hands that bless. Tongues that do not list."

She closes her door partway, leaves the strip of light. I sit a while with the feather and the taste of onion and thyme. The stream keeps saying what it says. In my mouth, the four words sit like bread that has decided to be food.

Before I bank the fire, I speak them once to the empty room, not as a lesson, not as defiance—just as the truth that found me and intends to keep finding me.

"Love, even for you."

The house hears and does not argue.

Morning is still deciding what to be when Jeanne comes up the lane. She walks like a woman who has places to get to and the time to get there—a pace that trusts the road. A basket hangs from her arm, lidded with cloth; the shape of jars and a coil of cord press against the weave.

"Father Bernard," she says, as if we last spoke yesterday and well. "I'm bound for the west field cottages. A woman there lost blood with her second and keeps fearing the third. If you walk that way, walk with me."

"I walk that way," I answer, and do.

We take the footpath where the hedges thicken. Hawthorn and bramble stitch the borders, white blossoms blown with bees. She names plants as we pass them—not to teach, simply because things like to be called by their names. Yarrow for bleeding. Motherwort for fear that barrels in the chest. Pennyroyal, *not for this one*, said firmly. Shepherd's purse, good for after.

I carry the basket when the path narrows to a squeeze. It is heavier than it looks, full of help.

"You were small and watchful," she says after a while, not looking at me. "A boy who listened to doors and streams."

"And you were everywhere," I say. "Half the village was born in your hands."

"A third," she corrects, amused. "Your grandmother taught me to keep count in kindness and not in pride."

We walk. Larks make small rope ladders of song into the sky. The hedgerow shows us the quick and the ordinary: a stoat, a feather snagged and left, a spider busy with her arithmetic.

"You heard my name last night," she says, as if remarking on the weather. "Carried thin and far by men who prefer lists to faces."

"I did," I say.

"And will you help them find me?" she asks, light as if asking whether I like my porridge salted.

"No," I answer.

"That a vow?" she asks.

"It is," I say.

She nods once. "Then if they press you for other names, you can tell them mine again. It will save our neighbors the trouble of being brave."

I almost stumble, not at the sharpness but at the generosity in it. "You would stand in front of them."

"I stand where I already stand," she says. "At the door where life comes in." She glances at me. "And you?"

"At another door," I say. "I will not turn yours into a trap."

"Good." She taps the basket with two fingers. "Two doors are better than one, for air."

We reach the cottages. The woman's house is neat, swept with the kind of care that tries to keep fear from settling. Her belly is a new moon under her dress; her eyes are tired from nights not sleeping. Jeanne's voice turns to water that knows the way around stone.

"Let's see the breath first," she says. "And the pulse that drums in your wrist. And the color in your gums. And the thoughts that don't let you eat."

She looks and does not panic. She asks and does not pry. She touches without taking. I watch the room change its breathing to match hers.

She sends me for water twice and for wood once, and for a chair that will keep the patient from standing to be polite. I am useful exactly as I am asked to be, no more. When a flutter of worry shivers the woman's hands, Jeanne gives her motherwort steeped with truth. "You have done this before," she says. "Your body knows the path. Fear makes shadows longer than the thing that casts them."

The woman's husband stands with his cap in his hands, lost in the way men are lost when they cannot mend what matters. Jeanne gives him a task so the lostness has something to carry—counting cups, warming linen, telling the baby in the next room that the world is kind.

When at last we leave, the woman's breathing moves lower and wider. The husband's shoulders sit nearer where shoulders belong. Jeanne leaves a small packet on the shelf and a larger calm in the air.

Back on the path, she lets the silence use its legs. Then, "You were careful with your words in there," she says. "Priests sometimes spill them like grain and wonder why mice come."

"I am learning to measure," I say.

"Good," she says again, which from her is worth more than a page of praise. "There is a girl at the ridge cottages with a belly that does not belong to her husband. When the time comes, if the riders are still sniffing, I will need you to be very poor at remembering how to spell names."

"I will forget the alphabet," I say.

She grins, and in that brief unguarded curve I see the child lambing-season left behind and the woman winter made.

We stop where the hedges lean close enough to make a green chapel. She lifts the basket lid, checks a jar's cork, then glances at me sideways. "They say you changed at the fortress."

"I remembered," I answer.

"That is the harder work," she says. "Changing is a trick. Remembering is a pilgrimage."

We start again. A gust lifts the hedge-blossom and snows it over us. She shakes petals from her hair like a girl at a feast. "Your grandmother keeps counsel with me," she adds, as if to tell me where my footsteps fall. "She said you'd learned four words."

I touch them where they live now, not in my mouth but in the room that is larger than my chest. "I did."

"Keep them," she says, "for me as well."

"For you as well," I say, and the fourth steps in by itself.

We come at last to the lane where our paths split—hers to the next door, mine back toward the church. She lifts the basket from my hands.

"If the riders find me before you do," she says, matter-of-fact, "do not argue theology with them. Argue time."

"Time?"

"Tell them we were busy keeping someone alive. It is the one debate men with swords sometimes understand."

I nod.

"And Father," she adds, starting away, "leave your door unlatched."

"I will."

She goes, the hedge swallowing her stout figure and her certain stride. I stand a moment longer in the green hush, feeling how two doors can make a house, and how a house can be anywhere love keeps happening. Then I turn toward the bell that needs ringing and the table that needs setting, carrying less than I brought and more than I can say.

Chapter Twenty-Six

I COME UP the lane as they turn the corner—Sergeant Alain and the clerk, dust on their hems, purpose riding before them like a standard. The church stands open. I put my hand to the door and widen it as if for friends.

"Come in," I say. "You look ridden out. The nave keeps a cooler air."

Alain inclines his head. The clerk measures the threshold with his eyes before stepping over it, as though traps were a sacrament.

Candles hold a steady light. The bell rope rests. The missal waits where it should. The room makes no fuss about men with warrants.

I set a pitcher and two cups on the front pew. "Water," I offer. "There's salt on the tongue after long roads."

Alain drinks. The clerk does not.

"We seek Jeanne," the clerk begins, parchment already pawing at its leash. "Reports say she—"

"Is presently busy keeping a woman alive," I say, exactly as Jeanne taught me. I don't raise my voice. "If your questions can pull a babe from the womb, we'll walk to her together."

Alain's mouth twitches—almost a smile, almost a wince. The clerk bristles. "We have authority to compel her appearance."

"And I have a basin for blood if you prefer the law to the life in front of you," I answer, mild as rain. "Or we can sit. You can tell me what harm you hope to prevent, and I can tell you where there is no wolf in sight."

Alain takes the second cup—this time for the clerk—and presses it into his hand without looking at him. "Sit," he says, and does. The clerk perches, spine like a spear.

"We were told," Alain begins, "that certain practices—herbs, bathings, lay-hands—mask darker doctrines. We were told men here avoid mass and meet by night."

"Men avoid mass everywhere," I say. "Ale and sleep are old heresies. As for herbs—" I nod toward the fields. "God stocked this parish with pharmacy before your fathers learned their letters."

The clerk scratches at the air. "And the midwife's counsel?"

"She counsels breathing," I say. "And eating when fear knots the belly. And sleeping when grief refuses to lie down. You could try all three and be holier for it."

Alain studies the floorboards—how they've learned to hold weight without complaint. "You spoke last night of leaving your door un-latched," he says. "That is not a common boast."

"It isn't a boast," I say. "It's a way of telling the truth about God."

The clerk snorts—a small horse behind the teeth. "Truth," he says, as if the word were a coin that needs biting.

"Truth," I repeat. "Sometimes it looks like a priest saying, 'I do not have the names you want.' Sometimes it looks like a midwife saying, 'Breathe now; the worst you fear is not what's happening.' Sometimes it looks like a sergeant who knows when orders need a gentler hand than the one that gave them."

Alain's gaze lifts to meet mine. We stand on that small bridge between men who remember other rooms. His jaw works; he swallows whatever wanted out first. "Were you with her?" he asks. "With Jeanne?"

"I carried her basket and counted cups," I answer. "The woman's color improved. The husband remembered that his own house was not the enemy. If you need more particulars, ask me whether the linen was warm enough or if the kettle needed another stick. I am rich in such data."

The clerk opens his mouth to protest that such data is not the sort his ribbon expects. Alain lifts a hand. "No lists, then," he says, almost to himself, as if repeating an instruction he didn't know he'd obey.

"Father," the clerk tries again, sharper now, "the bishop's office will not be satisfied with—"

"With life," I finish for him. "No. It rarely is."

The words hang. The nave accepts them and does not echo.

I rise and gesture toward the confessional, not as a threat, as a mercy. "You're welcome to pray while you wait," I say. "Or to wash and eat. There's bread in the sacristy. If you insist on questions first, ask me yours here—in the open. I will answer what I can carry.”

Alain stands. He walks a slow circuit to the door, touches the latch, then lets it go—unmoved, unmoored. “We’ll return at dusk,” he says, looking not at me but at the rectangle of day. “If there is harm, Father, you will have said nothing to prevent it.”

“If there is harm,” I reply, “I will be where harm is, and so will she. That is the prevention we know.”

He takes that in like a man learning a new drill, one that does not require marching. The clerk gathers his ribbon, makes it snap because something should.

At the threshold, Alain pauses. “You speak softer than fortress men,” he says. “But you do not move.”

“I am learning to stand,” I say. “It is new.”

He nods once, not agreement, not refusal—recognition edged with worry. “Dusk,” he repeats, and they are gone, their boot-sound taken by the lane.

The church exhales. I pour the remaining water back into the pitcher, set the cups aside for washing. The boy appears at the side door as if grown from stone, eyes wide with questions he will not yet ask.

“Ring once,” I tell him, “for the woman in the west fields. Then fetch my basin and clean cloths.”

He nods and runs. The bell lifts its single note and sets it gently on the hedges, the roofs, the road where two riders are learning the shape of an unlatched door.

At the altar, I set the corporal and whisper the four words where only the wood can hear them.

(Love,) even for you.

The bell's single note hasn't finished laying itself over the roofs when a woman edges in with a basket of eggs. She sets it on the front pew, nods once—apology and gratitude sharing one bow— and slips away.

I take the basin and cloths and step into the lane. It is market day for those who have nothing to sell.

At the first corner, a cart lists, a wheel sulking in a rut. The wheel-wright is away; the man bracing the axle is not built for bracing. I lay my shoulder under the rim and heaves become ours instead of his. The wheel climbs out of its argument with the earth.

"You've mass at dusk?" he asks, catching breath.

"Vespers," I say.

He grimaces. "I've not darkened a door in years."

"Doors don't keep grudges," I answer. "Come or don't. If your cart sulks again, send the boy."

He waits for the hook—there isn't one. "I'll send the boy," he says slowly, as if the sentence were new to his mouth.

At the next lane, Étienne's father meets me with both hands empty —on purpose, I think, so I can see they are not trembling. "He ate," he says. "Twice."

"Then you should, too," I tell him. "Bring a heel of bread to your wife when you do. She'll forget otherwise."

He laughs, surprised he has the breath for it. "I will."

Outside the smithy, heat breathes a blessing that doesn't ask for permission. The smith's apprentice—barefoot, proud of his burns —stands with a split palm he's wrapped in a rag. I wash it, prick a blister, lay lamb's-wool and linen, and a blessing that does not name itself as one.

"Should I bring it to the priest?" he jokes, watching me tie the cloth.

"You did," I say. "Try not to open your hand against hot iron for a few days."

He looks at the forge and at me. "I'll open it against something else," he promises, which is exactly right.

Across from the tavern, a woman carries water as if it were an ac-cusation. I take one bucket from her, and we walk crooked in the same direction. She eyes my collar the way cats eye hands.

"I don't come," she says at last, chin lifting toward the church.

"I can see that," I say.

"I don't like muttering I don't understand."

"Fair," I say.

"And I don't like men telling me when to kneel."

"Also fair."

"And I don't like the looks the women give me."

I keep pace. "We could use your voice for the psalms," I suggest. "No Latin required. As for kneeling, do it if your knees wish. As for looks, turn your face toward God and give the women your back."

She almost smiles, which is near enough to a hymn for now. At her door she takes the bucket and says, not quite rudely, "If I sit in the porch and listen, will your God hear me?"

"If you sit on your bed and curse, He'll hear you," I say. "Porches are an easy reach."

She snorts and closes the door softly, as if the snort were the hard part.

An old man with a clay pipe—one of those who never come and proudly—calls me in to read a letter from a son who went north. The letter is short and full of weather. We read it twice anyway. He hands me a coin I will not take. "Then sit and smoke while I do," he commands, and I obey, which is also service.

Near the mill, a boy has folded himself beneath a willow, hiding from a beating he expects and probably earned. I sit with him until the shadow measures us both. We count dragonflies. When he trusts me enough to speak, I walk him back to his mother and accept her storm so he won't have to take it full in the face. Between gusts, I ask her to let the boy ring the bell at vespers. She blinks, then relents, because bells make mothers soft.

Behind the tavern, a man with cider on his breath and a bruise he makes jokes about offers me the apology he won't yet offer his wife. I teach him a prayer that fits in his mouth: "Help me do one right thing." He seems disappointed it is so short. Short things are harder to dodge.

By the hedgerow path, I pass a house whose shutters blinked shut when the riders came yesterday. I knock and wait. A face appears where the latch has earned its splinters—a man who once sat in the back pew and decided the door was a safer church.

"I've bread," he says, suspicion and hospitality fighting a small duel in his eyes.

"I have jam," I answer, which is true—I brought the last of Grandmother's gooseberry in my sleeve on purpose. We eat on the stoop like men at a fair who have lost the fair.

"I don't come," he mutters. "Not since…" He stops before the story can make a fool of his mouth.

"Then don't come," I say. "Walk past. Doors like to be seen as much as they like to be entered."

He chews. "You're different," he says. "For a priest."

"I am exactly the same," I answer. "But the door is unlatched."

He grunts, unsure whether he has been answered or invited. It is both.

When the sun has turned the stream to coin and back again, I find myself at the church steps with hands that smell of forge and bread and gooseberry, and sleeves that remember water. The boy is there, ready to ring early if I let him, and the woman who dislikes kneeling is on the porch across the lane, pretending to count stitches while not quite not-listening. The man with the cart passes and nods as if we share a trade.

Inside, the nave is exactly as God left it: quiet enough to hear the grain in the wood, spacious enough to keep everyone's breath from bumping.

I set the missal. I touch the altar. I say the four words where only I can hear them and where, somehow, everyone will. Then I look at the door and leave it as it is.

By noon, the square smells of yeast and onions. Someone has set a rough board across two barrels, and on it a cloth, and on the cloth a scatter of loaves, a wedge of cheese, three turnips, a crock of beans left without a name. No proclamation. No charity announced. Only a place where food looks less like property and more like weather.

I did not make this table. The porch-woman did, I think, though she pretends she did not. She leans on the church steps with her sewing, counting stitches and not counting people. "Take, leave," she says to anyone who furrows at the sight. "If your hands are empty when you come, let them be less so when you go." It sounds like market wisdom. It is gospel.

I keep to the edge, sleeves rolled, moving a stool, carrying water, mending the wobble under one barrel with a stone that fits perfectly because the earth is full of such stones. People come who never did. Some hover and watch, then find they are hungry after all. Others bring what they can—half a loaf, a handful of herbs, a story that makes chewing easier.

The clerk stands by the well, thin as a tally mark. He writes nothing; he measures everything with his mouth pressed flat. Sergeant Alain is with him, not close, not far: a man who knows how to be present without making a scene of it. He watches the table longer than he watches me.

A child drops a crust and bursts into apology. Alain bows to her as if she were a woman in a hall. "The ground eats too," he says, and the apology dries.

When the first lull comes, Étienne's parents arrive with a pot that steams like prayer. "His breath is strong," the father says, and the mother nods without words. She ladles out stew, then sits and eats her own bowl as if it were a vow kept. The porch-woman slides her a slice of bread with two fingers, never stopping her counting.

I give no homily; the table is speaking. Still, when a small ring gathers at the end of the board—those who would listen if there were words—I keep it simple.

"If you leave something here," I say, "leave what won't turn you bitter. If you take, take without apology and plan to leave another day. The church has many altars. This is one."

The clerk snorts at that, almost imperceptibly. He turns as if to go and finds Alain hasn't moved.

A man who never darkens the door but always knows where the cider is stands across from me, a crust in his hand like a question he is not brave enough to ask. I break another piece and set it on his palm, then break one on mine, then we eat at the same time. It is not a ritual, and it is exactly one.

He chews, looks down, looks up. "I don't pray," he mutters.

"You just did," I answer, and do not force the smile that wants to betray the moment.

A tug at my sleeve. The bell-boy, breathless. "Father, Alain— Sergeant Alain—wants to… talk? But not like last night."

I find him at the well, filling a cup and not drinking it. Up close, his eyes show the nights he has fewer fires than orders and still smells smoke. He nods toward the table. "You will call this mercy," he says, neutrally.

"I will call it lunch," I say. "Mercy is what happens around it."

He lets that sit, then says: "At the fortress I've seen bread withheld to make men speak. Here you use bread to make them quiet. It is… different."

"Does it offend you?" I ask.

"No," he says, surprising himself with the speed. "It makes my work harder to explain."

"Explain it to me," I say.

He tries and stops. The clerk reappears like a rumor one cannot ignore. "Sergeant," he says, "we are not posted to supervise pantries."

"We are posted to prevent harm," Alain replies, not looking at him. He turns back to me. "Father, if harm hides under kindness, will you name it?"

"If harm comes to the table," I say, "it will not eat without shame, and I will see it. If harm comes in lists, I will not help it find a chair."

He studies me the way a soldier studies a map he did not draw. "You are bold for a man who speaks softly."

"I am tired of loud," I say. "It did not save who I meant it to save."

He does not ask whom. He does not need to. His jaw works and rests. "The bishop's letter has been read," he says. "Recall. Do you intend to answer?"

"I will," I say. "I will answer that I am already at my post."

This is not defiance in my mouth. It is location.

The clerk's lips thin. "Your refusal will be noted."

"Then note that the door is unlatched," I say, and I realize I am less explaining myself than reminding myself what I set down and what I will not pick up.

A scuffle near the cart. Two men snapping like dogs over a sack with more debt than grain in it. Before the porch-woman can set her sewing aside, Alain is there—not with hand on sword, with hand on sack. He lifts it, feels the weight, hands it to the thinner man, and looks at the other until looking is enough.

"Make your argument to me when the table is empty," he says to the thicker one. "For now, you are fed."

It is a small act. It is not small.

He returns to the well and only then drinks the water he drew. "If you will not come to the fortress," he says quietly, "the fortress will keep coming to you. It is better when I am the one sent."

"I believe you," I say.

He squints into the street as if measuring the evening. "When it comes hard, I will not always be the one," he says. "Decide what you will do then."

"I am deciding," I answer, and feel how true it is: decision not as a sudden sword, but as the slow lifting of a bar from a door.

He nods once, the way a man nods when the terrain has not changed, but he has learned where the rock shelf lies under it. He tips two fingers to the bell-boy, who stands taller under a soldier's notice than under any cassock's.

By late light, the board is down to crumbs and good fatigue. The porch-woman swats my knuckles when I try to carry too much at once. "Leave some weight for tomorrow," she says. "A priest with no work to do will only make some."

Étienne's father brings the empty pot, apologizes for its emptiness, thanks me for the way it had been full. I show him where the water steams for washing. He takes the rag from my hand and cleans it himself.

The clerk is gone—sent his letter with his face. Alain lingers at the edge, watching the way people leave: not sneaking, not performing, simply going. He catches my glance and does not look away.

"Vespers?" he asks.

"Vespers," I say.

He nods. "We'll come," he adds, and the *we* is not the clerk's. It is larger and older, and may yet include the part of himself that has been listening at a door he did not know was unlatched.

When the square is quiet again, the stream says its sentence and I answer with mine, not aloud, only to the dust and the stones and any soul that still thinks bread is a trick.

(Love,) even for you.

The cry reaches the square before the dust does. Men running from the mill, a cart pitched, the axle split like a bone, and under it Mathieu, the cooper's eldest—breath in him, then not. His brother stands with blood on his hands and someone else's curse in his mouth. The miller stares at the broken gear as if it had committed betrayal.

The crowd gathers around blame the way flies find sweetness.

"It's the pin—cheap iron," one says.

"It's the lad—drunk," says another.

"It's the miller—won't pay for a smith," says the third, loudest because sorrow needs a target.

I put my hand on the cart's rim. "We will not fix grief by choosing an enemy," I say, and it sounds like arrogance until I add, "We will lift him now. Then we will breathe."

We lift. We lay him on his mother's shawl because she insists there is nothing else in the world fit to touch him. The brother staggers away; the miller finds a post and leans his forehead to it like a penitent. The square trembles between rage and collapse.

"Tonight," I say, "the church will be open. We will keep vigil for Mathieu."

The miller looks up, eyes red. "You will judge me," he says, accusation as shield.

"No," I answer. "We will name our sorrow aloud until blame has nothing left to eat."

Word goes like water.

By dusk, the nave is a room that remembers what rooms are for. The boy rings once, slowly, a sound shaped to fit the body of what has happened. The porch-woman takes the threshold with her sewing and then forgets to sew. Étienne's father sets candles without counting. Old Marthe's granddaughter brings oil and linen as if the dead could need tending still.

They come who always come. They come who never come. The woman of the porch stands just inside, hands on the pew in front of her, as if steadying the whole row by touch.

Mathieu lies before the rail, his hair combed, his hands washed and folded. The brother stands at the head like a guard who lost his post. The miller keeps to a side aisle, jaw locked, hat twisting.

I light the first candle. "No homily," I say. "Only psalms and silence and true sentences."

We begin with breath. The first psalm is a plank across water. People step onto it. Halfway through, the door darkens—Sergeant Alain. He removes his cap and stands at the back, not as watcher, as man. The clerk is not with him; paper cannot breathe.

Between psalms, I speak the rule we will keep. "When it is your turn, say one truth you can carry without it breaking you. If what you have is anger, set it down and let us hold it with you. If what you have is blame, say it to God first."

Silence sits, large and patient.

The mother speaks first—"He laughed this morning and said the cart would behave because it owed him"—and her voice tears and mends in the same breath. A child speaks—"He always lifted me to see the bell." The brother tries and fails; the woman from the porch steps to his side and gives him her shoulder until he finds a sentence that is not punishment: "He tied my boot when I was too proud to ask."

The miller stands and shakes with something that wants to be an apology and is not strong enough yet. Alain moves two steps, no more, so the man knows he could lean without falling. He doesn't. He remains upright and says, to the whole room, "I should have shut the mill when the axle sang. I did not. I have learned by the cost." He sits and folds himself like a man who used to be taller.

The room does not applaud. It takes the sentence in and makes space around it.

At the hour, the boy lifts the rope, and the bell says a single note that lands on every shoulder and does not bruise. Between notes, the stream can be heard through the open door, saying what it says: *go on, go on.*

The porch-woman begins a hymn without announcing it, a low tune that needs no book. Others join until the sound is not a performance but a blanket. Étienne's mother hums the under-part; the smith's apprentice, who cannot keep his hands from forging, braids two candles with soft twine.

Midnight brings hunger, and someone remembers bread. The table from noon returns without being asked—the barrels, the board, the cloth. People eat standing and sitting and leaning, because grief is work and work requires bread. Alain carries wood from the sacristy without ceremony. In the corner, he ties a child's dropped shoelace without asking who the child belongs to.

Near morning, the brother finds the miller by the side aisle and they make a clumsy shape that is not embrace and is not refusal. It is the beginning of neither, which is sometimes the first mercy granted.

Before dawn, when candles are noise and the nave smells of wax and human breath, I step to the rail and say only this: "O God, hold what we cannot. Teach us not to find an enemy when we are only afraid. Teach us how to work tomorrow with hands that remember tonight."

We carry Mathieu out at first light, not far—only to the yard where the ground is willing. The grave is not a punishment; it is an answer. The earth receives him without speech. The mother lays her shawl in first.

At the last spade, the bell-boy looks to me. I nod: once, for coming and going. He pulls. The note lays itself over the mill and the field and the house where a man will sit with his hat in his hands until he can stand again.

Alain lingers at the gate. He does not speak. He puts his cap on slowly, like a man who has learned to time his armor. When he turns to go, he touches the latch of the church and leaves it as he found it.

Unlatched.

Chapter Twenty-Seven

THE LETTER ARRIVES with the flour cart—tucked under the strap of a sack, seal intact, red as a wound that has learned neatness. The carter hands it to me like a hot stone and wipes his palms on his apron.

"For you, Father," he says, relieved to have it gone.

The seal bears the bishop's ring: the fisher's net, the Latin band. I break it with my thumb. The script is the clerk's—ink that believes itself a blade.

To Father Bernard,

By authority of the bishop's office, you are ordered to present yourself at the fortress within seven days, to answer for irregularities observed in your cure: unlicensed rites, scandalous toleration of midwifery, failure to report absentees from the Mass, and seditious public assemblies held in the nave.

You will return to inquisitorial service pending review.

Come unaccompanied.

In service of the truth. By the bishop's hand and seal.

— Clerk Matheus

The stream outside says *go on*. The wax on my thumb says *stop*.

Grandmother reads my face when I bring it home. She does not ask to see the letter; she looks at my hands. "Decide what you will not carry," she says, as if we were talking about kindling.

"I will not carry their lists," I answer. "I will not carry names."

"And what will you carry?"

"Lives," I say. "Bread. The door."

She nods. "Then answer them before they answer you."

I sit at her table with the feather beside the ink and the cracked honey crock watching like a benign eye. I keep the words small enough to fit through a keyhole.

To my lord Bishop—

I am at my post. I will remain at my post.

What you name irregularity is the ordinary work of love—birth tended, grief borne together, bread shared, prayers spoken aloud and in silence.

I report that the church door here is unlatched. Any man or woman may enter. This includes your officers.

I will hear confessions, I will say Mass, I will bless the dying and the born.

I will not provide lists of absentees nor names for punishment.

If you require my obedience, know that I am being obedient to the cure entrusted to me and to the God who entrusted it.

— Father Bernard

I sand the page, fold it, seal it with plain wax—no ring—then give it to the bell-boy to carry to the carter. "No shortcuts," I tell him. "Bring back a heel of bread with your news." He grins at the errand, at the bread, at all of it.

In the afternoon, I find Sergeant Alain at the well. He has the look of a man who suspects the shape of a knife without feeling it yet. "You received a letter," he says.

"I sent one," I answer.

He holds out his hand. I place a copy in his palm; the bishop will see the other. He reads slow, lips moving, a soldier's care with words that are not orders.

"You refuse," he says.

"I remain," I correct. "If they come, I will be here to answer. I will not abandon these people to conversations about them in rooms where they are not present."

He scratches his jaw, eyes on the church door. "You know what this makes of me."

"A man at a threshold," I say. "The threshold will need you."

He exhales through his nose—half a laugh, half a prayer that never learned Latin. "There will be a second letter," he says. "Harder."

"I expect it."

"And men," he adds.

"I expect them too."

He taps the page against his palm, thinking. "Father… if that day comes, and I cannot stand where you stand—if orders are orders—conceal the children first. Grief is heavier where there are small shoes under it."

I look at him until the words can go nowhere but in. "I hear you," I say.

He nods once and hands me back the copy as if he were returning a blade to its sheath. "Vespers," he says, only that.

"Vespers," I answer,

The table is out again—less food than yesterday, more hands. The porch-woman has brought a stool for her sewing and a bowl for those who cannot say out loud what they have brought. Coins appear like shy birds, then vanish into the cloth. Étienne's mother has color in her cheeks; his father carries him once around the square like a procession that needs only one saint.

At vespers, I do not speak of the letter. I speak of a psalm that knows the sound of boots and still says *mercy*. We chant until the words borrow our breath and lend it back stronger.

After the blessing, the clerk himself appears in the doorway, alone —his face the same tidy blade, his eyes tired by it. He holds his ground at the sill. "Father Bernard," he calls, voice carrying not like a threat, like a habit, "you will answer for your refusal."

"I am answering," I say, "every day." I take two steps so we are near enough that neither of us must raise our voice. "Stay for bread."

He looks past me at the table, at the people putting cups in a stack with the quiet competence of those who know tomorrow comes. Something in him flinches—resentment, hunger, both. "Your defiance will hurt these people," he says flatly, as if info, not warning.

"My compliance would," I say. "The door will remain as it is."

"Unlatched," he says, like a bad word.

"Yes."

He presses his lips, turns to go, then stops. "You have a reputation for skill with final sacraments," he says, not looking back. "A man in the next parish lies with fever. Their priest is drunk. Will you ride?"

The room leans toward the question without moving. I feel Grand-mother's hand on my sleeve without her being there. Decide what you will not carry; decide what you will.

"I will walk," I say. "Send a boy to Jeanne first, if the fever breaks into raving."

He nods—barely a nod, the kind a man gives when he's agreed with himself not to admit it—and goes into the evening.

Alain has watched all this from a shadow by the font. He comes forward only when the door settles. "There," he says quietly. "That is how it begins to be difficult to despise you."

"Try not to practice," I say. "It might stick."

He almost smiles and fails, but the failure looks like a man who has begun to forget how to scowl.

At Grandmother's table, I fold her a copy of my letter. She tucks it into the honey crock's cracked side as if it were a seed that prefers small dark spaces.

"Good," she says. "Now sleep if sleep will have you. If it will not, the stream will."

I lie on the pallet and hear the water keeping its single promise: *go on*. I think of lists and births and a door that has not learned how to close. I think of a soldier at a threshold, and a clerk who invited me to a deathbed without admitting it was mercy.

In the dark, the four words do their work without me pushing them.

(Love,) even for you.

The storm rolls in without rain—only heat the color of iron. Word runs faster than weather: Jeanne is needed at the ridge cottages; the woman's pains have leapt from counting to flood. I find her already on the lane, basket in the crook of her arm, jaw set the way oaks set their roots.

"Come," she says. "We'll need your hands to be quiet and your voice to be simple."

We take the hedgerow path. Bees stitch their urgent thread through the hawthorn. A lark climbs a rope of its own making. In the distance, the road lifts dust—riders.

At the cottage, the room is small and hot with breathing. The mother labors on a pallet pulled near the door; the husband hovers like a man trying to be wall and window at once. Two neighbor women hold the edges of the world steady.

Jeanne's voice enters first. "Good. You've made space. Water's ready. Cloths warm. You've kept her fed." She nods to me: "Basin. Linen. Then sit where she can see your mouth when you say 'breathe.'"

We work. Not grandly. Cloths and cups. Her hands at the mother's belly, reading it like scripture: "Here it tightens; here it loosens; here we wait." My palm at the mother's shoulder where the muscle knots. My breath slow, hers learning mine for a moment and then taking its own line again.

A sound outside. Iron. The neighbor woman glances at the door.

"Keep your eyes on me," Jeanne tells the mother. "The rest of the world can knock until it learns manners."

Boots on the sill. Sergeant Alain, cloak dusty, with two men at his back and the clerk already reaching for the latch as if a latch were a law. He stops because the door is not shut; it is crowded with life.

"Father Bernard," the clerk begins, voice already shaping an accusation, "we require—"

"Step back," Jeanne says without looking up. It is not rudeness; it is triage. "Unless your questions deliver children. If they do, state them between the next two pains."

Alain's eyes take the room—the sweat, the steam, the breath that wants to bolt. He lifts a hand, and his men stall.

"Is there danger?" he asks, and means the mother, not the law.

"There will be if we argue," Jeanne says. "Fetch clean water or stand on the lane."

I hand Alain my empty basin. He takes it and is gone, and returns before the clerk can decide which paragraph covers carrying water. He kneels to pass it to me without dirtying the rim. His men hover, uncertain whether civilization is permitted.

The clerk tries again, smaller. "There are allegations of gatherings—"

"This is one," I say. "Count us."

The mother cries out, and the room closes around her sound the way sea meets a rock. Jeanne presses her palm and meets the cry with her own quiet. "Good," she says into the wave. "Yes. Now breathe down. Down. The body knows."

"Father," Alain says, urgent but not loud, "if men gather at the square—"

"Then they will have to wait their turn," I say. "Time is not on parchment today."

Another pain takes the mother. She bears it with her teeth and her eyes. Jeanne's hand is all authority and all mercy in one. "Now," she says. "Now we make way for the living."

The child stumbles into the world with a sound like a bell that has never been struck before. Wet, outraged, alive. Jeanne clears his mouth, rubs his back, hears him change keys from fear to breath. She passes him to the mother, and the room becomes suddenly larger because it contains not only what was but what is.

No one moves for a count of three. Then breath returns to people who did not know they had been starving for it.

"Water," Jeanne says again, softer. "Linen. Father, the blessing."

I touch the child's crown with wet fingers, and the sign I have made a thousand times is the newest thing I own. "In the name of the Father, and of the Son, and of the Holy Spirit," I whisper—and then, quieter still, where only he can hear, the four words I do not need to explain to anyone.

Behind me, boots shift. I turn. Alain stands with his cap in his hands as if he were in a chapel and not a doorway. The clerk has lost his next sentence and cannot find it on his ribbon.

"Sergeant," I say, "you wished to prevent harm. Here is the absence of it. You may write that down."

He does not write. He nods—the smallest nod, the kind a man gives when he recognizes a rank older than the one on his sleeve. To the clerk, without taking his eyes from the child: "We will not make arrests today."

"Your authority—" the clerk begins.

"My judgment," Alain answers, not harsh, simply settled. "Fetch the men to the lane. We will wait there until the mother sleeps."

The clerk looks to me as if I had done this to him. I have done nothing to him he did not bring to his own throat. He swallows and goes.

Jeanne tucks the blankets, sets the mother's hair behind her ear with a gesture so ordinary it feels like an altar. "Good," she tells the room. "You can all breathe again. One of you make broth. One of you bring bread. One of you stop shaking and hold the father's hand before he falls over."

They do as they are told because the world is briefly sane.

When the child is bound and settled, Jeanne looks at me over the mother's shoulder. "Walk them," she says, the way one might say, *ring the bell*. "Let the lane see what time it is."

I step to the threshold and lift my hand to the boy who has appeared as if time itself called him. "Once," I say. He runs for the rope.

The bell lifts its single, new note and lays it over hedges and roofs and the road where the riders wait. It tells the valley what the valley already knows: life has entered by one door while another remains unlatched.

Alain stands at the foot of the steps when I come out. The clerk's men keep a restless line; their hands don't know what to do when there is nothing to seize. Alain's face is not soft. It is human.

"I will write that we found order," he says.

"Write that you found a child," I answer.

He considers, then: "I will write both."

The clerk approaches, bristling with the dignity of a man whose quill has been insulted. "This does not discharge our mandate," he says.

"No," Alain agrees. "It fulfills mine." To me, lower: "There will be a second day."

"There always is," I say. "Today we keep this one."

He looks at the cottage where the air has changed shape, at the hedge where petals are stuck to a soldier's boot. "I am beginning to hate lists," he confesses, almost to himself.

"Then you have begun," I say.

We part without more. I go back inside to wash and to be one more pair of hands, which is the precise number love requires.

At dusk, when mother and child sleep and the cottage smells of thyme and milk and the tired holiness of men who have done one thing right, I step out again. The riders are gone. The lane holds their absence the way a cupped hand holds water briefly and then lets it go.

I walk to the church. The door is as I left it.

By the third morning after the birth, strangers appear who aren't. They come with the look of people who have heard a rumor about water and walked until it might be true.

A woman with a scar the shape of a crescent at her temple stands in the doorway and does not enter. "Do you know the words for a child you never held?" she asks. We light two candles and let the flame say their names. She stays through vespers, singing only the last line of each psalm, as if that is all her mouth can carry. It is enough.

A farmer from two parishes over steps in at noon, hat in both hands. "I spoke once," he says, "and a man burned because of it." He waits for a penance the size of his guilt. I give him the hardest one. "Bring bread to a house that will not expect you. And come back at sundown. We will eat it together." He nods, because shame loves a ladder and does not know what to do with a table.

The porch-woman has perfected her post: one foot inside, one foot out; her voice a bridge. She starts a tune in the lane so those who do not cross the sill can still sing. She does not make a point of it. She makes a place.

Jeanne passes like weather that knows where it is useful. She ties a sling for a man with a shoulder gone wrong at the mill; she lays a hand on a widow's chest and shows her how to breathe where panic has hidden the ribs. When asked if she is permitted to work so openly, she says, without losing her humor, "I am not forbidden— only examined," and then cuts bread with an expert disregard for those who have never kept vigil through a night.

At confessions, the line changes shape. Less whispering through wood, more speaking face to face in pews and corners, sentences placed like objects on a table we share: *I am afraid of my child dying; I hate my brother; I drink so I do not strike.* I absolve when absolution is what is needed. When it is not, I say, "Carry this with me for a while; let your arms rest." I am learning the grammar of shared weight.

Sergeant Alain comes midafternoon and stands near the well, where the square can decide for itself whether it wishes to be nervous. He speaks with no one first. He watches the way people's shoulders sit. A child runs into his leg and bounces off; he steadies the child without looking down, and the child does not apologize.

We end up at the board across the two barrels, though it holds more cups than loaves today. He picks up a knife and slices a heel, not as a man entitled to be served, but as a man who has been told to share. "The clerk has been reassigned," he says after a time, as though remarking on the weather.

"By the bishop?" I ask.

"By someone who counts appearances," he says. "Another man will come. Quieter, perhaps. Or more clever. I don't know which I prefer."

"And you?"

He shrugs, a slow lift of weight that has learned its own heft. "I stay until I'm posted elsewhere. Meanwhile, I keep men from mistaking zeal for skill." He glances at the porch. "And I watch doors that I didn't know could be kept open."

"You are changing," I say.

"I am remembering," he answers, surprising himself, then letting the surprise stand.

A rider—this one dusted with honest miles, not mandate—arrives before vespers with a satchel and the posture of someone who knows how to find the right table in a strange town. He asks for Father Bernard, and when I step forward, he pulls a folded parchment from the bag, sealed with wax that has been warmed and cooled too many times.

"From a monk who travels light," he says. "Said he'd pass through again when God's patience allows. Asked me to deliver the letter to a priest who keeps his door the way he keeps his altar."

My hand knows the shape of Cassien's script before my eyes do: spare, inward, like a path that avoids thorns without fuss.

Brother—

Word reached me of a church that does not bar its heart. If this be yours, keep it so. If not, forgive the hope that mistakes.

The fire she left with us does not argue; it illumines. I have not learned to carry it well. I am learning to carry it anyway.

If a wooden lily passes you by, let it. If it returns, do not hold it tight.

— C.

I fold it shut without sealing, the way one covers a bowl to keep flies off, but lets the warm escape. I do not read it to the people; the letter is not for the square. But I set it on the first pew, where anyone can sense that something has been placed and nothing has been hidden.

At vespers, the psalms run like a mill finally greased. The boy rings with a touch that does not overswing. We pray for the unknown priest with fever two parishes over, because even the clerk's errand deserves mercy if it saves a life; we pray for the clerk who is gone, because resentment is a poor liturgy.

After the blessing, the farmer who confessed to burning another by his speech sets down a loaf he did not bake and a coin he cannot spare. He does not look at me; he looks at the table and at the gap where his guilt used to sit. The porch-woman sings one more verse, and somehow it is the right one.

Alain lingers until the square is down to sweeping and small laughter. "There will be a second letter," he says, because that is the world. "And men who prefer doors closed."

"I know," I say. "We will practice opening."

He taps two fingers to the brim of his cap—respect, not salute—
and turns into the lane. He pauses at the church and touches the
latch as if making sure it still knows its work. Then he leaves it as
it should be.

Unlatched.

Chapter Twenty-Eight

SHE BEGINS TO TIRE between spoons.

Not a collapse—nothing dramatic—only the way her hand rests on the table half a breath longer than it used to, the way she lets the kettle talk by itself before answering. She notices me noticing and smiles as if I were checking the latch on a door we both know by heart.

"Bring the stream in," she says one morning, when the light is thin and the cat has chosen her lap over patrol. "In a cup. It will remember the way."

I go with a jar and a quiet. The water comes back tasting of stone and leaf. She wets her lips and hums. "Yes," she says. "That's the sentence."

Jeanne arrives with herbs and the look she wears for friends—no drama, all reckoning. She takes Grandmother's pulse the way one listens to a familiar song played slower. "You're doing it properly," she says. "Growing lighter where it counts."

"I have practice," Grandmother answers. "I have been putting things down all my life."

We keep the days simple: porridge, the tune that never bothered with words, a short walk to the door and back. On good mornings, we reach the bench beneath the window and let the sun count our breaths. On others, I bring the sun in—open the shutters, set the chair where warmth can find it.

"When the hedgehog uncurled," she says once, out of nowhere, "it did not look at us. It simply remembered itself. That is what dying should be for old women. Remembering without apology."

She sleeps a little after that, the cat pinned to her skirt like a seal.

Alain comes to the threshold at noon with a sack of flour that he does not pretend he milled. He removes his cap and stands as if the doorway were a rank he has not earned. "For your table," he says.

"For yours, if you like," Grandmother answers from her chair. "Sit, Sergeant. Let me see the man who kept water in his hands long enough to hand it back clean."

He sits on the edge of the stool, large and careful. She studies him the way she studied my boyhood knife-work, fond and exact.

"You carry what isn't yours," she says. "I can see the marks on your shoulders."

"Some of it I must," he admits.

"Some of it you don't," she returns, light as bread. "Decide before men hand it to you. Burdens are shy once they're refused."

His mouth twists—grief, gratitude, both. "I will try," he says.

"You will practice," she corrects, and pats his wrist once, a commission. He bows, a soldier taught by a grandmother, and goes.

Toward evening, when the stream sounds nearer than the road, she asks for the feather. I lay it across her palm. She strokes the quill with her thumb as if encouraging a small thing to remember that it was made for air.

"Bernard," she says.

"I'm here."

"Decide what you will not carry," she says again, "and what you will never set down."

"I will not carry lists," I answer. "I will never set down love."

"Good," she says. "And shame?"

"I will let it sit where it is," I say, surprised to hear the truth before I polish it. "But I will not feed it. When it grows thin enough to fly, I will open a window."

She smiles. "You learn."

Night brings a breathless spell. Jeanne stays, one hand at Grandmother's wrist, the other on her own knee to remind her body that the world is holding. I sit on the stool and count the length between breaths. It is not fear; it is river-measuring.

"Say them," Grandmother whispers, not opening her eyes.

"The psalm?" I ask.

"The four."

I lean close. "(Love,) even for you."

"For me," she echoes, almost teasing—*of course, for me*—and the room smiles because even the walls know it is true.

Near dawn, she wakes one more time, clearer than the hour. "The oaks," she says. "You will take me there, or you will take them here. Whichever knows my name quicker."

"We'll bring them," I say.

So we do: a branch of leaf, a scrap of bark that remembers my small hand, a pocket of the smell that made prayers easy. I lay them on her blanket. She closes her eyes and inhales once, twice, as if signing a ledger with air.

"Now say the little ending," she murmurs.

"What is the little ending?"

"The one I forgot to tell you when you were ten."

I wait.

"Go on," she says, a smile in it. "That's the whole."

She sleeps. The breath that follows is a kindness, and the one after that is a gift, and the next does not come because she is busy re-membering without apology.

We sit with her. Jeanne sets the feather on the table and smooths the cloth beneath it. The stream says what it says, near enough to hear without listening hard.

I wash Grandmother's hands and face, comb her hair, draw the sheet to her chin. Jeanne lights a candle not for magic, for company. We open the door and let the morning in, and nothing unpleasant happens.

When the village gathers, they do with the competence grief learned at the mill: bread appears, chairs multiply, the porch-woman plants herself in the threshold and keeps the weather from blowing arguments through. Étienne's mother brings soup. The boy brings the bell-rope in his hand as if the sound would be needed and mustn't be misplaced.

We keep vigil as we kept others. No adjudications, no lead-souled eulogies—only sentences set carefully on the table like bowls. "She gave me a thimble when I lied about needles." "She slipped me a pear and told me not to thank her until I'd eaten it." "She made my anger smaller without making me feel small."

Alain stands in the doorway again, cap in his hands, learning how to guard something that cannot be guarded—only honored.

At last, I step to the bed and say the words the Church gave me for endings. They are good words. They fit her. When I finish, I add the smallest of my own: "You kept what was given in love. Now go where love keeps you."

We carry her to the yard when the ground is ready. The people answer with earth, and the sound it makes is the sound of things finished properly.

Afterward, I walk to the stream with the jar and bring it back, and everyone drinks a little, the way we did when she was here, because the sentence is still the sentence.

That evening, the house is quiet in a different way. Jeanne tidies and leaves with a touch to the doorframe like a signature. The cat patrols the empty chair once and chooses the hearth. I sit at the table and learn how to be a man whose grandmother has gone where my hands can't carry her.

I light one candle and leave the other unlit, a place for absence to sit without being scolded. At last, I speak the four words, not as a shield, not as a bell, only as a fact that has learned how to breathe by itself.

(Love,) even for you.

Outside, the stream keeps its counsel. Inside, the house does not argue. And in me, something settles that had been waiting for permission.

Chapter Twenty-Nine

THE NOTICE ARRIVES nailed to the tavern post at dawn—tidy script that wants not to be torn.

By order of the bishop's office:
Clerk Matheus is reassigned to duties in the city.
Sergeant Alain will continue civil oversight in this parish.
Matters of doctrine to be observed with prudence and charity.
— For the good of souls.

Someone has taught the words to sound merciful. The porch-woman reads them aloud once and then ties her apron tighter, which is her way of blessing what cannot be improved by blessing.

Alain stands a step back from the post, unreadable as stone that has remembered rain. "Prudence," he says, tasting the word. "Charity." He does not look at me when he adds, "The quieter knife cuts, too."

I nod. "Then we will watch the hand that holds it."

He tips two fingers, the new salute that means *I heard you.*

By noon, a man I do not know is waiting at Jeanne's gate—travel coat, city boots, a satchel with neat corners. He holds himself like someone who believes fairness is a skill you can learn from books.

"Good day," he says as she returns from a birth with straw in her hair and triumph somewhere under her ribs. "I am Master Hervé, deputed by the bishop's physician. We are regularizing midwifery."

Jeanne lifts an eyebrow. "Am I irregular?"

"Unlicensed," he answers, kindly as a clean ledger. "We seek to correct that. We value your… field experience. We would prefer cooperation."

"Prefer," she repeats, amused. "Cooperation in what?"

He opens the satchel. Papers. A seal. A small packet of silver laid where eyes can see it without effort. "Instruction in proper baptisms when necessary; an oath not to dispense certain herbs; and"—here he schools his face to neutrality—"timely notice to my office of any households persistently absent from Mass or known to meet without priestly oversight."

She doesn't look at the silver. "I am not forbidden, as you know well," she says, pulling one burr from her sleeve. "Licenses are a kind of looking. So are oaths." She wipes her hands on her skirt. "But this third—who gets to be your neighbors—that is not my job. I cannot keep both kinds of lists and still have hands free for birthing."

He breathes once through his nose. "You misunderstand. We do not require denunciations. Only… vigilance."

"Then stand in a room with a woman giving birth," she says mildly, "and tell me if vigilance wants a seat nearer the door or the bed." Her voice softens a notch. "Master, you have the look of a man who chose books because he loves order and because people scared him young. I am fond of both reasons. But if you ask me to tie women to your comfort, I will send you home with your tidy satchel and a very untidy conscience."

He reddens—not rage; shame at being seen. "You refuse my license?"

"I refuse your leash," she says. "Bring me one that lets me run my road and I will sign it."

He closes the satchel, more gently than he opened it. "I will… consult." He glances toward the lane. "And Father Bernard?"

"In church," she says. "With the door."

Hervé hesitates. "He will refuse, too."

"Perhaps," she answers, eyes kind because kindness is a habit she cannot break. "But if you bring him something that smells of mercy, you may find him braver than your paperwork."

He goes. She watches him to the corner, then shakes the last straw from her hair and turns toward the next door that needs knocking.

I find Sergeant Alain at the well, drawing water by the rope he could order a boy to pull. He drinks, then says without preface: "I watched your friend turn a license on its hinge."

"Will he return with a gentler chain?" I ask.

"Likely," Alain says. "He is not cruel. He is convinced. Convinced men, when wrong, are worse than cruel ones."

"And you?"

"I am less convinced of many things," he says, not proudly. "It confuses the men under me. Confusion is hard to drill."

"Confusion can be honest," I say. "Honesty can be drilled. It looks like not lying to yourself in front of your soldiers."

He huffs, almost a laugh. "You would have made a captain."

"I failed at being a confessor first," I answer. "I am still at it."

He sobers. "Your grandmother," he says.

"She remembered," I say. "Without apology."

He bows his head. "Then may I stand a while where she stood?" He nods toward the threshold of her cottage.

"You already do," I tell him.

The bell-boy shadows me all afternoon, hands never far from the rope, as if sound were a tool he is learning to use with care.

"Father," he says at last, "am I allowed to ring when no one is dying or praying?"

"What would you ring for?" I ask.

"So the valley doesn't forget what it sounds like to be called," he says, embarrassment flushing his neck.

"Then find one reason each day," I answer. "Not for noise. For re-membering." I see him grow an inch on no bread at all.

He will make a priest who does not count ladders. Or a miller who shuts the mill when the axle sings.

The porch-woman has gathered three others who share her distrust of kneeling and her love of tunes. They call themselves nothing and practice everything: the last line of each psalm, a drone under the Sanctus, a way of singing from the threshold so the lane hears itself as invited, not measured.

"Do we bother you?" she asks, which means, *Do we belong?*

"You hold a door I cannot," I say. "I will not ask you to move from the place where you are most useful."

She blinks hard and calls me a fool, which is her best blessing.

At dusk, Master Hervé returns—without the silver, without the leash. He carries a single page.

"I cannot give you what you want," he tells Jeanne in the square, "but I can remove what you won't take." He reads: "Midwives in this parish may act according to conscience in emergency baptisms and ordinary care; no reporting of absences required; avoidance of abortifacients advised but not adjudicated by this office." He folds the page. "It is not the license you asked for. It is less. But perhaps less is more."

Jeanne considers him, then nods—once. "Bring me the book you read to write that," she says. "I will teach you which parts smell of kitchens and which of courtrooms. You should know the difference."

He smiles—tired, relieved, younger than his boots—and breathes like a man whose satchel has been set down. "Tomorrow," he promises, which is a brave word for a man who works for bishops.

Alain has watched from the well with his new habit of witnessing without owning. He meets my eye and does not speak.

The bell-boy looks at me. I nod: once. He pulls; the note rises—a simple call that says only what it needs to: come.

We begin. The nave fills the way fields do: slowly, then all at once. The skeptic choristers take the porch and hold it like a small fort that belongs to everyone. Étienne's mother sings with the under-part again; his father, who thinks he cannot sing, does anyway and is not struck dead.

My homily is as thin as I can make it without snapping. "Today we have practiced less," I say. "Less fear. Fewer lists. Lighter hands. Doors that ask for no password. If we keep at it, the more will take care of itself."

A murmur—not of doubt, of recognition.

After the blessing, Hervé stays. He kneels in the last pew and says nothing at all, which is the first good confession some men make. Alain stands at the back with his cap in his hands and does not look like a watchdog; he looks like a neighbor.

The boy waits. I let the silence have its seat; then I nod. He lifts the bell once, and the note lays itself over the village like a linen sheet on a bed that's been made for the first time in a long while.

At the door, I touch the latch and leave it as I found it.

Morning braids the square and the nave together. Stalls lean toward the church steps; the church steps lean toward the stalls. Turnips sit beside candles; skeins of yarn beside prayer. No one planned it. It happened the way bread rises when hands leave it alone.

Jeanne trades thyme for thread and refuses coin. "It grows back," she says, and no one argues which *it* she means.

Master Hervé walks the row with a satchel that looks lighter than last night's—papers inside, yes, but also a loaf someone put there when he wasn't looking. He stops twice to watch Jeanne's hands bind a wrist and to ask a grandmother which psalm carries sorrow best when breath is short. He writes down neither answer because he has begun to learn that the ones that matter cannot be quoted.

The porch-woman has set a small plank across two stools at the threshold—a place for cups. "So singers don't faint," she says. She has gathered three more throats; they practice a low line that can be sung by those who fear heights.

Sergeant Alain arrives without men, as if the uniform came today to learn rather than to warn. He buys a small jar of honey and pretends he doesn't know he bought it for my table. When children careen with the ferocity of the well-loved, he steadies them with a hand that has forgotten how to be only a soldier's.

The bell-boy hovers, full of sound and patience. He has found his daily reason to ring: "For those who believed they were not invited," he tells me, already blushing. "May I pull once before mass?"

"You may," I say. "Then stay and listen to what you called."

He pulls. A single note rolls down the lane and under the market like a coin a child drops and decides not to chase because it will show up again where it's needed.

We begin.

The nave receives the square without fuss. A basket of apples appears on the back pew. A shawl slides off a shoulder and becomes a blanket for a sleeping child. I place the missal and feel in the wood a heartbeat not mine alone.

"Brothers and sisters," I say at the homily, "today I will not preach long. If you leave with a command, let it be this: *Carry one thing for someone else, and leave one thing you can't carry here.* We will tend it together until it weighs less, or until we learn to be strong where we are soft."

I could say more. I do not. The porch-chorus answers with a line that sounds like walking: steady, sane.

Communion is a moving village. Those who never kneel stand; those who always kneel do not notice they are flanked by those who do not. Étienne's parents bring him forward, round with milk, eyes open as if this were the first day the world allowed itself to be seen. I trace the smallest cross on his brow, and he accepts it as naturally as breath.

At the back, Hervé puts his hands together in the old way and does not come forward. He sits after, head bowed, as if learning how to pray where words have not been approved. Alain steps to the rail—

not to receive, not yet—but to stand where standing says: *I am here among you and not outside you.* It is enough for today.

"Go in peace," I say at the end, and no one bolts. The square continues inside for a time—bread cut, a spindle offered to a woman whose hands need work more than comfort, a letter read aloud for old eyes.

On the steps, I unfold Cassien's letter again. I do not read it to them; it isn't theirs. But I set it on the ledge where the sun can warm wax and words alike. A passerby asks, "From a friend?" I answer, "From a man who remembers," and that is all the explanation anyone needs.

Jeanne finds Hervé by the well. "The book you promised?"

He holds it up: a physician's manual and a psalter tucked between its pages like a spare pair of lungs. She laughs softly and begins to teach him which herbs want caution, and which words want more air. He listens. It looks like penance done properly and like apprenticeship without shame.

Alain comes to me with the jar of honey. He tries to hide it behind a question and fails. "For the table," he says.

"For yours," I reply. "Share it with your men before they learn to despise sweetness."

He tilts the jar in his palm as if weighing his future. "If a harder letter comes," he says at last, "I will ask to be the hand that brings it. The door between will need to know a man who has walked through it both ways."

"You will be that man," I say, and mean it. He nods, relieved and resentful in equal measure—a sign he is still honest.

Afternoon turns to gold. The porch-chorus rehearses a psalm for the work ahead: *Those who sow in tears shall reap with shouts of joy.* They sing the last line from the threshold and let the lane carry it.

I go to the sacristy and bring out a small bowl. People drift by and place things there that are not money: a nail pulled from a foot, a rock someone almost threw, a cord cut from a wrist, a square of cloth a woman used to stifle anger and now no longer needs. The bowl grows holy by use; this is how altars learn their trade.

When the light reads late, the boy comes with his daily reason. "For Grandmother," he says without drama. "So the valley remembers the word she liked."

"Ring," I tell him.

He pulls. The note moves over hedges and across the water, through houses where grief is folding laundry and over fields where tomorrow has already begun. It says come, and somehow everyone understands it also says go on.

We close nothing. We bank candles; we sweep. I stand at the threshold and look down at the latch. My fingers know its weight, its wish to be useful. I leave it as it should be.

Unlatched.

In the doorway's quiet, I find the four words, not whispered, not declared—simply present, like a table waiting for bread, like a stream that keeps its sentence, like a village that has learned the grammar of carrying.

(Love,) even for you.

The first frost finds the hedges. Breath shows itself and is not ashamed.

Sergeant Alain comes at noon with his cap in his hands and a paper under it. He waits in the nave while I finish mending the wobble in a pew. When I stand, he offers the letter as if it might bruise.

"It is better I bring it," he says. "Doors should know a man who has walked through them both ways."

The seal bears the bishop's name at last—Jerome of Saint-Lys—and the clerk's hand is gone from the script. Fewer barbs. More iron.

To Father Bernard of Saint-Hilaire,

You will present yourself at the fortress within five days for reassignment to Inquisitorial service and review of your pastoral irregularities.

Your zeal is noted. Your obedience is required.

— Jerome, by the mercy of God, Bishop of Saint-Lys.

The stream has thinned to winter talk, but it still says *go on*. I nod once and refold the page.

"Will you read it to them?" Alain asks.

"Yes," I say.

At vespers, I lay the letter on the ambo and do not let it pretend to be larger than the Word. After the Gospel, I lift it with two fingers.

"Our bishop has written," I say. "He notes zeal. He requires obedience. This is good theology when it is pointed toward love. I will answer him from here, because this is where my obedience breathes."

I keep my voice plain.

"I am at my post. I will remain at my post. Those of you who wish to add your names to my answer, add them to the bread and to the burdens you already carry. That is the only list we keep."

I do not incite. I invite. The room takes it in the way a winter field takes light—thin, sufficient.

After the blessing, I leave the ambo as it is, the letter resting where anyone could touch it. No one does. They touch one another instead: shoulder, sleeve, a child's hair.

Master Hervé lingers near the porch, unreadable, as if carrying two drafts of the future and not sure which one to submit. The porch-chorus hums a line low enough to warm feet.

Alain remains in the last pew until the square grows quiet. Then he comes forward—not to the rail, not to the ambo—to the first bench, where a man can sit and be seen.

"I have a… thing," he says, and the word confesses it is not trained for church.

"A burden?" I offer.

"A sentence," he corrects, surprising us both. He looks at his hands. "I am beginning to hate lists."

The nave holds still.

"They taught me to love them," he says. "Order, names, ranks, blame—tools that keep men safe from their worst and from each other. I needed them. I still do. But I am starting to see how a list can make a man smaller than his soul."

He breathes, and the breath sounds like winter air in a good chest. "I do not know how to lead if my men see me doubt what made me. I do not know how not to lead if doubt is the beginning of truth. I do not know how to pray where orders are louder than God."

He stops. Not finished—arrived.

"Come," I say, and we move to a side pew where wood remembers other confessions. No lattice, no booth. Only two men borrowing one honesty.

"What do you ask?" I say.

"To be forgiven for the ease with which I obeyed when obedience spared me thinking," he says. "To be taught how to choose when order is not love."

"For the first: forgiven," I answer, the old words in the new room, exact and enough. "For the second: practice. Start where your hands already know the way."

He nods, a soldier taught to drill.

"Name one thing you will refuse to carry," I say.

"Lists that deliver people to harm more quickly than they deliver them to help," he answers without hunting.

"And one thing you will never set down."

He doesn't hesitate. "The child's cry," he says. "Any child's."

"Then here is your penance," I tell him. "Before you sleep, speak one true sentence to God that is not an order and not an excuse. If it is only a name, let it be a name. If it is only anger, let it be anger. Do not tidy it."

Something unhooks in his face—not collapse, release. "I do not know how to pray where orders are louder than God, but I can do that," he says.

I raise my hand—no drama, no audience—and make the sign that has outlasted better men than me. "God absolves you," I say. "Go in peace."

He sits a breath longer, then rises and bows—not to me, to the room. At the door, he touches the latch the way a man tests a weapon before battle and leaves it as it must be.

Unlatched.

Back at Grandmother's table, with the feather watching and the cracked honey crock holding the place of sweetness, I write.

To my lord Bishop Jerome,

I receive your letter with the respect due your office and with the candor owed by a son.

I remain at Saint-Hilaire. I am obedient to the cure entrusted to me and to the God whose mercy feeds it.

If you would judge my irregularities, come unannounced and sit among us. Watch birth tended, grief borne, bread shared, sins confessed without spectacle, doors left unlatched.

You will find zeal, yes. You will also find prudence and charity already at work.

If you still require my person, send for me—but know I will not carry lists that harm.

— Father Bernard

I sand the ink and seal it with plain wax, then add a line on the outside where any courier can read it and no one will burn for it:

The door here is open to all who hunger.

The bell-boy carries it to the carter with the gravity of a man transporting a relic. At the threshold, he asks, "Shall I ring—for remembering?"

"Once," I say, "for anyone who has learned to hate lists a little."

He pulls. The note finds the hedges silvered with frost and the stream speaking its winter sentence in a smaller voice that is not weaker, only closer to the bone.

I stand in the doorway until the air bites and the blood agrees to be alive. Then I go inside, bank the fire, and lay my palm on the table where a grandmother taught me the most difficult sacrament of all: to decide what I will not carry, and what I will never set down.

Snow comes without boasting. It softens roofs, rounds fence posts, quiets men who prefer clatter. The stream does not stop; it learns a slower grammar.

We practice carrying.

The porch-woman inventories wool the way quartermasters inventory arrows. She assigns shawls by a calculus no man can cheat: "You, because you pretend you don't shiver." The porch becomes a guild of hands teaching other hands to turn clumsy into warm.

Étienne learns to laugh with a cough that doesn't steal him after. His father brings chords from his old lute that he swears he cannot play. At vespers, he plucks one clean note while the porch-chorus hums under it, and no one claims they have started a choir.

The miller and the brother—men who couldn't look at each other without stiffening—meet at the woodpile, each to pay a debt without money. They stack in silence until the stacks are even. The brother says, "Come eat," and the miller says, "I will bring salt," and the sky records the treaty in frost.

Master Hervé returns with a book that smells of wax and ink and winter apples. He sits at Jeanne's table and learns the difference between herbs that help blood remember its path and herbs that ask blood to forget. He notes nothing when she speaks of hands, only watches until his own begin to listen. Once, he reaches for the packet of silver, and she slaps his hand lightly, not unkind. "Buy firewood with it," she orders. "Licenses keep no one warm."

At the well, Sergeant Alain drills fewer formations and more compassion. "When you go door to door," he tells his men, "ask who is hungry before you ask who is absent from Mass." They blink, then practice. Men can be taught to knock differently. Even their knuckles change.

The bell-boy sets himself a winter rule: one ring at dusk "for anyone who thinks being alone is a virtue." He keeps it, even when wind cuts rope-burn into his palm. I see him dip his hands in tallow before pulling. He will make a good priest or a good anything.

I write Cassien a line and no more:

Brother—
The lily passes. We do not keep what we save; we are visited by it.
(Love,) even for you.
— B.

I do not seal it. The rider will come when the road consents. Letters should breathe like bread.

Inside the church, I keep homilies short as breath in cold air.

"God is not stingy," I say when faces tighten around the thought of a lean Lent. "If you have two of something, you are carrying someone else's. If you have none, the table is set for you." The table appears: a jar of beans from a woman who has never trusted priests, a loaf from a man who still doesn't but can bake.

We hold a small reconciliation with no theatrics. I bring the miller and the brother to the first pew and ask them to tell me a sentence they admire about the other. They do, awkwardly, and the wood learns a new sound: men speaking good on a mouth trained for stubborn.

One night, a child is lost between house and barn. The village pours into the fields with lanterns and curses and prayers mixed like sleet. Alain calls the lines; Jeanne instructs us not to shout names, only to sing in a low tone so a frightened thing might come. We do. The child's hand finds a neighbor's sleeve. We count wholeness by head, by breath, by relief, and then by soup.

The bishop's answer does not come. Or it comes as Master Hervé, who learns to bring policy that makes no one bleed.

On the coldest evening, I say mass for six and a cat who will not be reasoned with. The words do not shrink because the room is small; they know their size. After, the porch-chorus sings in the lane for those who never cross the sill. A man opens his shutter two fingers and closes it again after the last line, less afraid of God by the width of two fingers.

At Grandmother's table, I talk to the empty chair the way I once talked to the stream. It answers with the sound of bread cooling. I set a second cup anyway. Absence likes to be acknowledged but not indulged. The feather lies like a sentence that never needed ink.

One morning, the snow glows blue, and the air is the kind you can break your breath on. I walk to the oaks and lay my palm on bark that remembers my cheek. "I am carrying what I said," I tell them. They do not answer. They don't need to. They have wintered longer than my vows.

On my way back, I see Alain at the edge of a field, watching his men carry wood to a house where a proud man lives. He does not order; he lifts his own log. When he catches me seeing him, he pretends to cough and keeps walking. Pride has learned to wear a scarf.

That night, when the bell-boy asks for his ring, I say, "Twice." Once for those who were found, and once for those who are still learning the sound of their name.

He pulls. The notes settle on eaves, on hedges, on a bishop somewhere reading letters in a warmer room. The stream under ice whispers its small version of the same sentence. So do I, not loud, not brave, only faithful:

(Love,) even for you.

Chapter Thirty

THEY CHOOSE A MARKET day to look official.

A narrow man in a fur-lined hood arrives with two clerks and a deacon who carries a book for show. The hooded man introduces himself as Archdeacon Perrot, voice oiled for public weather. Behind him stands Master Hervé, satchel shut, mouth set the way a decent man sets it when he hopes to limit harm.

The charge walks beside them—a young woman from the ridge cottages, belly flat now, eyes that have already done the math of shame. Her husband's name is not the father's name. This is the arithmetic that pleases men who like ledgers.

The square hushes. The porch-woman does not move from her post; she threads her needle as if petitions were hem-lengths.

Perrot stops at the church threshold and gestures as if the nave were a courtroom. "We will examine the matter *here*," he announces, because authority travels better when it borrows the furniture of holiness. He turns to the young woman. "You will stand for inquiry."

Before his next sentence can clothe itself, Sergeant Alain steps forward, not fast, not slow, a man who has practiced deciding. He takes off his cap, faces the woman, and sits her in the first pew— the place of dignity and breath. Then he stands in the aisle like a column learned from oaks.

Perrot blinks, cross that someone has rearranged his stage. "Sergeant, this is ecclesiastical business."

"Which you chose to hold in a church," Alain answers, mild. "She sits where worshippers sit. You may speak where homilies are spoken." He nods toward the ambo. The gentlest redirection is a door.

Master Hervé's eyes say *thank you* without moving his mouth.

The square exhales. The porch-chorus hums one note, low as winter ground, not a song yet—a floor.

I step to the rail without vestments. "Archdeacon," I say, "the door is unlatched. You are welcome. We will listen with you, not for you."

He measures me for defiance and finds only furniture. He ascends the ambo and opens his book to the page that supports him best. "We are gathered to preserve morals," he begins, "and to protect the sacrament of marriage. We seek names, remedies, and assurances that such scandals will not spread."

The word lands like a stone dropped into the basin we are drinking from.

Before his clerk can sharpen a quill, Jeanne steps forward with her basket. She does not face the archdeacon; she faces the ridge woman, hands open. "You birthed bravely," she says, so the first truth named is not a sin. "Your child breathes well. Have you eaten?" The woman nods, almost bows, as if courtesy were the only cover she owns.

Perrot clears his throat. "Woman, you will answer: who is the father?"

Silence tautens. The husband's absence is a fact, not an argument. Shame creeps like frost along the pew.

Alain says, evenly, "Archdeacon, the child is the child." Which is not an answer and is exactly one.

Master Hervé, to his credit, tries the better tool. "We are prepared to offer clemency," he says, "if the household will submit to pastoral correction." His eyes flick to me: Can you make this phrase smell like kitchens instead of courts?

I nod once. "Pastoral correction," I say to the people, "means the church will help carry what cannot be carried alone. It does not mean putting stones in the child's blanket."

Perrot bristles. "It means penance. It means naming transgressions."

A voice rises from the porch—the woman who would not kneel if God Himself asked. "Name mine," she says. Heads turn. "I sang in the lane so I didn't have to step inside, and I judged this girl from the shadow. If there's a list, put me near the top. I will not keep the baby warm by counting."

Something in the room loosens because someone has paid first.

Perrot recovers. "This is not—"

"No," I agree. "This is not sensible if your aim is tidy. But love is not stingy, and winter is here." I turn to the ridge woman. "Do you wish to speak?"

She doesn't. She does. She rises, then sits again—practice. On the second try, she remains standing. "I was lonely before I was a liar," she says. "My husband is a good man who became tired, and a kind man who became far away. The man who is the father is a fool, and I was the kind of fool who believes a kind word is love. My penance is already in my arms." She looks at the first pew where her child is sleeping against a neighbor's shawl. "I ask bread when there is bread and silence when there is gossip."

The porch-chorus finds a second note. It thickens the air.

Perrot opens his mouth for doctrine and finds Alain in the aisle, not blocking, bearing. "Archdeacon," he says in the voice soldiers use to disagree without breaking ranks, "prudence and charity, the notice said."

Perrot flips a page. "Prudence dictates we deter sin."

"Prudence," Master Hervé says quietly, "also dictates we do not make widows by zeal. The bishop's hand was careful."

Perrot frowns; he did not come for mutiny in courteous language. He grasps for something he can grasp. "At least the midwife must be admonished. Herbs and secrecy—"

Jeanne steps closer, not nerve, craft. "I do nothing in secret except keep women's pain from being public. As for herbs, you can smell which ones I use. If you wish to admonish me, do it carrying water. Mouths empty faster when hands are full."

A ripple that is almost laughter—but isn't—runs through the nave. It is a recognition: we are being asked to be adults.

I move a half-step—enough to make it clear we are not trying Perrot; we are trying whether the Church can choose love while it polices. "Archdeacon, we will undertake penance that looks like work: wood hauled to the ridge, milk brought at dawn, a cradle carved, gossip refused at the well. The mother will come for confession when shame weighs less than truth. The man who planted the seed will carry wood twice."

"Named!" someone hisses, hungry for spectacle.

I shake my head. "No lists." I look at the ridge woman. "Do you agree?"

Tears come—the kind that do not want to be looked at. She nods, once. It is a vow stronger than a signature.

Perrot gathers himself to be offended. Alain gathers himself to be useful. "We'll coordinate the wood," he says, to no one and everyone. "No one freezes to prove a theological point."

Hervé, perhaps remembering Jeanne's lesson about leashes, adds, "The bishop's office will provide linen. Quietly." He glances at me: *Say yes before the archdeacon remembers how to say no.* I incline my head. Done.

Perrot, outflanked by untheatrical mercy, tries one last thrust. "And catechesis? Will the priest at least teach the proper form of—"

"—baptism?" I finish. "Already taught. Already done. Already a child who breathes." I touch the rail. "You are welcome to stay and pray vespers, Archdeacon. It works on zeal like water works on fire: it teaches it what to burn."

He hesitates, halfway between dignity and the door. Dignity wins. "We will lodge at the tavern," he says, and goes with what remains of his procession. Hervé lingers one heartbeat longer, then bows the way a pupil bows to a hard lesson and follows.

The square unstiffens. The ridge woman folds onto the pew, and Jeanne's hand finds her shoulder. The porch-chorus slides their tune into an actual psalm. The boy looks at me, rope in his fingers.

"Once," I tell him, "for names we didn't say and for the ones we will learn when they bring wood at dawn."

He pulls. The bell lays its note over hedges and roofs, and a fur-lined hood in a tavern room, and a bishop reading winter letters. It says *come* and *go on* in the same breath.

After vespers, Alain helps place cups on the plank and pretends he was born knowing where cups belong. As the people drift, he stands a moment at the threshold, palm on the latch, thinking his long thoughts.

"You seated her first," I say.

"I only showed her where to sit," he answers.

"That is the first thing a shepherd does," I tell him.

He huffs, which for him is yes. Then: "When the harder day comes—"

"We will carry what we can," I say. "And refuse what is not ours."

He nods and leaves the latch as it must be.

I stand where law tried to enter and found a house instead. The stream under snow keeps saying its winter sentence. Somewhere in a ridge cottage, a child dreams while a mother sleeps without calculating, for one night, the price of bread against the cost of being seen.

On a market morning that smells of wet wool and yeast, a rider comes without heraldry and ties his horse where ordinary men do. He enters the nave, stands in the shadow near the last pew, and prays as if the wood were older than his office.

No one names him. Jerome of Saint-Lys is shorter than his seal suggested, paler than his letters, and more human than either. He watches the table across the two barrels grow itself again—bread, a wedge, a crock, a bowl for coins, and for the things that are not coins. He hears the porch-chorus set a floor under the psalms so the lane can stand on it. He sees Jeanne knot a sling and Master Hervé pass cups with hands that have learned to be citizens. He sees Sergeant Alain seat an old man before a youth and never make a speech about it.

When vespers ends, he leaves as he came, unintroduced, a slip of paper under the cracked honey crock by the sacristy door:

No summons follows.

The thaw begins in the ditch before it admits itself to the stream. Ice loosens by listening.

Spring lays a green line along the hedges. The ridge woman brings her child to the font in a dress borrowed from three houses. Her husband stands on one side, the fool on the other, both looking more like men than math. I pour water that has been winter for months and is glad to be anything else. The porch-woman sings the last line as if it were the first.

Alain drills on the green behind the church—less marching, more lifting, then dismisses his men to carry wood where it's still needed. He stays to mend a fence-post beside a miller and a brother who have learned to stack sentences as carefully as logs.

Hervé leaves his satchel open now; there is more bread in it than parchment. He has started borrowing Jeanne's words without quoting them and finds they still work.

We plant a small garden in the churchyard: onions and thyme and a row of beans the bell-boy swears will grow if he rings "for remembering" when the moon is right. He teaches a smaller child—one of those who lurked at the rope all winter—how to pull once, then wait, then pull again, leaving room for the note to finish being itself.

I keep homilies spare: weather for the work. "Let your prayer this week be something you do with your hands," I say. "If you have two of something, ask your neighbor if they have none." It is not new. It is not meant to be.

A letter comes from the road—Cassien, in a hand that makes space between words as if for breath:

Brother—
Your door reached me without walking. The lily passes as it should.
If we do not meet, it is because flame prefers many homes to one.
(Love,) even for you.
— C.

I hold it for a while, then tuck it under the feather. Some things do not need answering to be answered.

We lay Grandmother's shawl over a bench near the window where the sun remembers how she liked her light. No plaque. The cat prefers it to any throne the church might offer.

One evening, a traveler stops on the road at the sound of the psalm from the porch and asks a man at the well, "What is this place?"

"It's a parish," the man says, as if explaining a simple tool. "The door's unlatched."

The traveler nods, as though doors that open were an idea he'd been trying to recall since childhood. He comes, he eats, he leaves a coin no one asked for, and he goes on less alone.

On a Sunday soft with blossom, the square and the nave braid again. Étienne takes his first staggering steps between his parents' hands while the porch-chorus hums a tune that sounds exactly like a boy walking. Jeanne wipes her eyes and calls it dust. Alain looks away and pretends to check a strap on his glove.

At the homily, I say only, "Thank you." It is enough. After Communion, I place a small bowl on the step. People drop into it what they have finished carrying: a broken nail, a knotted cord, a smooth stone with the heat of anger gone out of it. The bowl learns to be holy by holding.

When the light turns to gold, the bell-boy looks at me, and I don't nod because he already knows. He guides the smaller child's hands —palms on the rope, weight in the heels, pull and breathe, leave space for the valley to answer.

The note lifts and lays itself across hedges and roofs and the road where bishops travel and soldiers change their minds and letters learn to be kind. It says *come*, and it says *go on*, and it does not argue with itself.

At the threshold I rest my hand on the latch, not to close it, only to remember its weight. The stream speaks the same sentence it has always spoken in every season. I add ours to it in my chest, where prayers live when they are not busy being said.

(Love,) even for you.

The door is as it should be.

Unlatched.

A CONFESSOR'S TESTAMENT

(FOUND WITH A FEATHER BENEATH THE CRACKED HONEY CROCK)

I, Bernard of Saint-Hilaire, set these lines down not to make a ledger but to remember what I carried and what I refused.

I carried bread, water, oil, and the names of a few who love asked me not to set down:

- A woman who forgave me in a room that did not deserve it.
- A brother who learned to ring a bell without waking fear.
- A soldier who began to hate lists at the right time.
- A midwife whose hands were wiser than most documents.
- A grandmother who remembered without apology.
- A child whose first cry dismissed an armed argument.
- A village that turned a door into a sacrament.

I refused ledgers that deliver people to harm faster than they deliver help.

If I taught anything, it was only this: leave at the altar what you cannot carry, and take from the table what you must, and let the door be unlatched so strangers do not learn loneliness from us.

If I preached anything, it was that God is not stingy.

If I learned anything, it was that love does not need permission, only room.

When men asked for doctrines, I offered bread first. When they asked for names, I offered my own. When they demanded certainty, I gave them the psalms. When they wanted the future, I pointed to the stream and we listened to its one sentence.

I have been wrong often. I have been afraid as frequently as hungry. I have been forgiven more times than I can write without lying. Still, I testify:

The Church is a house with many doors. Some are watched by fear, some by habit, some by love. Choose your door carefully; then keep it with your life.

If this page is found after I have gone where explanations are unnecessary, let it be used to start your fire or steady a table leg. Good paper should be useful. Keep the door.

And if you need a prayer small enough to carry in your mouth when your hands are full, keep this one. It has steadied me more than my learning:

(Love,) even for you.

Epilogue

The Flame and the Door

I was there when the fire came.
Not in body, perhaps— but in breath, in memory,
in the ache that has followed me across lifetimes.
They called it a crusade. We called it silence.
The hour when truth dimmed, but did not die.
You may believe this is a story of the past. It is not.
It is a remembering, a reweaving of what was torn.
Each page a step home. Each word a vow fulfilled.

Cassien:
I thought I had come to weigh souls
and assign them to tidy shelves.
Instead, a wooden lily lodged in my hand
and would not be put down.
The chant I once sang for duty returned
as breath and made a house of me;
Alais's tenderness taught me how to keep its door unbarred.
I walked out of judgment carrying a music
that chooses mercy first,
and I am still learning its name each time I meet a stranger.

Alais:
I was not a lesson. I was a life alight—
a flame that learned to warm before it learned to warn.
I did not argue with darkness; I gave it nothing to eat.
I loved Cassien without asking him to be other than he was;
I set courage in his palms when my own would not hold it,

and handed him the song I began,
asking him to finish it with his breath.

Clara:
I was not the ash, nor the rope, nor the rumor.
I was the singing that refused to take smoke for an answer.
They named it judgment; I named it mercy
too large for their measures,
the kind that bends iron and leaves the soul unscorched.
I loved the ones who lit the fire
and the ones who tried to look away,
and I learned the four words so fully
that heat forgot how to harm me:
(Love,) even for you.

Bernard:
I kept a door unlatched until the village learned
to keep it so without asking me.
Bread taught me doctrine—how truth tastes when shared;
Midwives taught me courage—how to place hands
where life insists on entering.
I set down lists that hurry harm
and took up names I will not put down.
Four words steadied my hands in winter and in fire alike,
and they remain the only stole I dare to wear: *(Love,) even for you.*

David:
I am the page that remembered before I did,
the hand that came late but not forgotten.
I write because the stream keeps saying *go on*
and the bell agrees—
because the lily passes from palm to palm when no one clutches.

I do not invent; I return—bread to table,
light to window, names to love—
and I sign my work with what the story signed in me: *Love*
a small vow big enough for every door I meet.

All:
What burned did not end us; what opened did.
If you are reading, you are already inside
the house we made of one another.
Leave what you cannot carry here;
take what makes you kinder and pass it on.
Keep the lily moving. Keep the water speaking.
Keep the bell honest.
And when you meet a latch—on a church, a chest, a heart—
remember who you are, and how a door learns to stay open.

(Love,) even for you.

— Cassien, Alais, Clara, Bernard, and David

AND SO IT IS